As Good
as the
First Time

ALSO BY K.M. JACKSON

The Unconventional Brides Series

Insert Groom Here

To Me I Wed

The Betting Vow

Holiday Temptation
(with Donna Hill and Farrah Rochon)

Published by Kensington Publishing Corp.

As Good as the First Time

K.M. JACKSON

Dafina
Books

Kensington Publishing Corp.
http://www.kensingtonbooks.com

DAFINA BOOKS are published by

Kensington Publishing Corp.
119 West 40th Street
New York, NY 10018

All Kensington Titles, Imprints, and Distributed Lines are available at special quantity discounts for bulk purchases for sales promotions, premiums, fund-raising, and educational or institutional use. Special book excerpts or customized printings can also be created to fit specific needs. For details, write or phone the office of the Kensington special sales manager: Kensington Publishing Corp., 119 West 40th Street, New York, NY 10018, attn: Special Sales Department, Phone: 1-800-221-2647.

Dafina and the Dafina logo Reg. U.S. Pat. & TM Off.

ISBN-13: 978-1-4967-1709-2
ISBN-10: 1-4967-1709-0
First Kensington Mass Market Edition: November 2018

eISBN-13: 978-1-4967-1710-8
eISBN-10: 1-4967-1710-4
Kensington Electronic Edition: November 2018

10 9 8 7 6 5 4 3 2 1

Printed in the United States of America

To Will
Each day with you is sweeter than the last.

Acknowledgments

Though writing is a solitary occupation you never really are alone, and as with all my books they are a collaborative effort of perseverance, patience, and prayer.

I have so many people to thank for making this book and series happen. As always, I'd like to thank God for everything and without whom I'd have nothing, and especially for bringing such wonderful people into my life.

I'd like to give thanks to my wonderful agent, Evan Marshall. Thank you so much, Evan, for taking me on. This has been amazing, and I can't wait to see all we do together.

Thank you to my champion editor, Selena James, and the amazing team at Kensington. You all are rock stars, and you make my job a true joy!

To my Destin Divas crew, you ladies are what a sisterhood looks like, and I cherish you.

To Jamie, Synithia, Carla, Kaia, Adrienne, and that blasted dog too, thank you for rooting me on!

I now must give extra special thanks and a crown to my friend Farrah Rochon. Farrah, thank you for carrying me over the finish line with this one. You cheered me through it, and I'll be forever grateful.

And as always and forever to my family, Will, Kayla, and William. You are my reason for everything. But you already know that.

Finally, to Nana, though you are not here with me physically, you are in my heart and your sweet lessons will always live on.

Chapter 1

Hmm, absolutely perfect. Or as close to perfect as one could come up with being that it was an early morning rush job, Olivia Gale thought as she pulled the deep-dish berry swirl pie out of the oven. The homemade crust was golden brown, flaking gently along the edges. Liv couldn't help but smile when she saw how beautifully her hand lettering had come out. It had taken quite a few trials, not to mention the expense of new precision knife blades from the art store, but the results were worth it.

CONGRATS DAD.

The small, baked-in sentiment looked almost magazine photo worthy. She knew her father would love it when she presented it to him later that evening at his retirement dinner.

Careful not to drop any crumbs or—heaven's, no—spill any filling on her cherished cookbook pages, Liv carefully skirted the berry swirl pie around, placing it on the counter with the apple pie and peach cobbler already done. It didn't matter that each of her printed recipes were already saved in a file on her computer and backed up on her cloud drive and that she still had them lovingly protected, each in its own sheet protector; she still took good care of her cookbook. Liv had been collecting her time-tested recipes in that book over the past ten years. She would not let it get ruined.

Oven off and satisfied with her work, she could relax for a moment. Although it was only a small gathering at her parents' apartment that evening—neighbors, old friends, and a few of Dad's best work colleagues—Liv knew that one pie wouldn't have been enough to satisfy the crowd. With that in mind, though it was a workday, she'd decided to make multiple pies to supplement the store-bought cake that her mother was providing. Besides, knowing her mom and her famous open-door policy, you never knew who would show up.

"Absolutely delicious." Damon's voice was a slow, deep drawl as he came into the kitchen and wrapped his strong arms around Liv's waist.

"Are you talking about the way my pies look, or should I take that as a personal compliment?" Liv said, turning to look him in the eyes.

Damon gave her one of his alluring half smiles as his gaze went from her eyes to her lips. But instead of kissing her lips, he bent and kissed her lightly on her neck, she assumed not wanting to get any of her freshly applied lipstick smudged onto him. He hated getting mussed up before work.

"Why can't I be talking about both?" he replied.

Liv shook her head and gave Damon a light nudge against his chest. "You really are a smooth talker. If I didn't know you so well, I'd be a little suspicious."

"Now, there you go with that acute skepticism of

yours. Why can't you just smile and take a compliment, woman?" Damon's half grin went up to include both sides of his mouth. "You know you are delicious. As a matter of fact, everything you are, everything you touch, is delicious. Now, why don't you *be* a peach and share a little bit of that cobbler with me?"

Liv fought back a blush. She'd always found it slightly difficult to take compliments from Damon, not that he was overflowing with them, from him they were rare. Still, she wasn't good at taking them from him, or anyone for that matter, a man especially. Sure, she knew that there was nothing wrong with her, and when she pulled herself together right, she was downright passable in a blending-in type of way. But someone to gush over? Not with her slightly too far apart eyes, and lips that took up too much of her face. Add to that hips and thighs that no amount of squats could seem to slim down, and well, yeah, Liv had a hard time believing Damon and all his extravagant talk. But still, she tried to play it cool. A man like Damon—tall, dark, and, yes, quite handsome—wouldn't find lack of confidence a virtue in a woman. Not many men did. So she'd learned early on to fake what she'd lacked as best as she could.

"No way on the pie, mister," Liv said, making her voice stern, but still playful. "These will all go to my parents for my father's party tonight, as you very well know, since you'll be meeting me there at seven." Liv leaned in to Damon, looking up, giving him her version of her own sly grin as she ran a finger along his smooth, brown cheek. "But no worries. If you're on your best behavior tonight, I have my own sweet treats in mind for you later."

There was the slightest hint of tension that emanated from Damon then, along with the tiniest shift in his eyes. It was so slight that Liv convinced herself that it didn't happen. That she didn't see that small action she'd grown to know was Damon's way of burying something he didn't want to deal with in the moment. And just then she had her own feeling of apprehension. Liv swallowed and made her smile just a little brighter. Nope. It was nothing; she knew she was overreacting. Things were just a little tense, as they were bound to be in any relationship that had reached the nine-month point as theirs had, and the façade of putting on the best face was starting to wear down.

"Fine," he said with a half grin. "None for me means none for you, too. Remember you promised you'd start working out with me anyway. We both don't need the extra calories."

Liv pushed down on her immediate feeling of embarrassment over his comment and let her eyes shift to the old clock above the windowsill. "You better get a move on, Damon. It's starting to get late, and don't you have that early breakfast meeting with new clients?"

Just as she thought, the idea of bringing up business pulled Damon up short and brought him into his usual sharp focus. A marketing analyst for an up-and-coming firm, Liv initially met Damon at one of those usually dull, corporate meet and greets where she was representing her firm as their strategic corporate analyst. One glimpse of Damon, though, and the night instantly brightened up. Sure, she knew he immediately pegged her as a potential business mark, but when he realized he wouldn't be able to sell her on anything his firm had to offer, he switched tactics and went to selling her on himself.

Damon being Damon, he never let anything stand in the way of business. Leaning back, he flipped his wrist, checking the time on his watch that did so much more than just keep time. "Crap, you're right." Damon gave Liv a scowl. "Baby, you knew how important this morning was. Why are you letting me go on so that I'm late? You know how unpredictable the subways can be."

And this is my fault? Liv thought. He was the one who came into her kitchen. Besides, a grown man should be able to tell the time. But Liv kept these thoughts to herself. No need to rock the boat and put him in a bad mood, possibly knocking him off his game when he had important business to take care of. She gave Damon a soft smile. "I guess I just couldn't resist you. I'm sorry that you have to get going. I know you're going to hit it out of the park today, as you always do. I'll see you later tonight."

But Damon was already reaching for his briefcase and heading for the door by the time Liv finished her sentence. All she got was a wave and the click of her apartment door behind him as a response. With a resigned breath, Liv checked the clock once again as she went to cover her pies to ready them for her pickup later in the evening. "I better get a move on myself. Shoot, he's talking about me making him late, what about him making me late?" She gave her head a small shake, whipping off her vintage apron as she headed out of the kitchen. She slipped on her travel flats; grabbed her tote with her ready-for-business, red-bottomed pumps; and made her way for the subway to travel from Harlem, south to her midtown job.

* * *

Fired.

Walking back into her apartment late that afternoon, Liv kicked off the now-useless red-bottomed pumps that, in her haste to get out of the office, she'd forgotten to switch out before getting back on the subway. *Fired.* She'd never been fired before in her life. No, wait a minute, it wasn't fired; she was being restructured, or so they said. As in restructured out of health care; into unemployment, if she was lucky; and into a land of severe anxiety and uncertainty. But no, not fired. Fired was way too explosive a word, nowadays reserved only for hashtags and ex–reality TV stars. Liv let out a wry snort as she stepped into her kitchen with aching bare feet and flung open her refrigerator door. Restructured. Talk about irony. That was so her word. She was the queen of restructuring and upending people's lives in the process. It was she who had restructured Bailey and Wagner onto the Forbes list. Yeah, and in doing so it looks as if she had restructured her smart behind out of their fine mahogany-accented glass doors.

Liv sighed and reached for the fizzy cranberry orange concoction that Damon had picked up the other night. She opened the screw top and drank straight from the bottle. So not her, but in times like this, even reaching for a glass felt like an effort. But, after downing half the bottle, she still wasn't satisfied. In that moment, all she wanted to do was open a bottle of wine—no, better yet, a pint of ice cream—crawl into her bed, and drown her sorrows in a little Rocky Road. Unfortunately, though, Liv looked over toward the top of her stove. There would be no relaxing, ice cream, wallowing, or any such thing—at least not for the next few hours—since she still had pies to pack up and her father's retirement dinner to attend.

It's so odd, she thought as she packed up her pies.

She still hadn't heard back from Damon. He hadn't returned any of her calls that afternoon. She assumed his day must be pretty busy, because if he'd had any clue what she was going through he'd surely have gotten back to her. She'd been trying to reach him ever since she'd heard the dismal news, but it seems he was all tied up. She knew he'd be just as surprised as she was. *No matter,* Liv thought when telling Damon came to her mind. Damon was smart, and he knew so many people in the business that she was sure with him guiding her in the right direction she'd find a new position in no time. Who knew, maybe she wouldn't even have to tell her parents about being restructured at all. No use worrying them, not when they were so happy about finally being able to take their long-awaited retirement dream vacation.

Feeling slightly more bolstered, at least enough to get through the evening, Liv suddenly couldn't wait to take off her gray, corporate linen skirt and silk blouse. *Once I get out of my "restructured" suit and more party ready, I'll be fine,* Liv told herself as she hit her bedroom door, then froze.

First fired and now robbed? Freaking crap on toast, could this day get any worse?

Turning a quick circle in her bedroom, Liv fought to calm the rapid thumping of her heart. The closet was flung wide open, and hangers were haphazardly strewn on the floor. Some drawers were opened and emptied, and her brand-new television was gone from on top of her dresser. An intense feeling of fear grabbed her as Liv wondered if the culprit could possibly still be in her apartment. She froze completely and listened for any sort of sound. Looking over at her bedroom window, Liv saw that it was still shut tight and didn't look as if it had been disturbed.

She didn't remember seeing anything out of place in the living room. As she started quickly backtracking with a tight grip on her bag, grateful she hadn't left it in the living room, she reached inside for her cell.

But before completely backing out, her mind couldn't help its analysis. She glanced at the closet again. It looked as if all her clothes, from what she could see, were still there. But where were Damon's shirts? The five white shirts he left at her apartment along with the two pairs of pants—one gray, one black—and the navy suit that she'd just picked up from the cleaners were gone. Shifting, her eyes went to the drawers; there were two open. The bottom two on the left. The ones that held the T-shirts and boxers that she had just folded the night before. And the bottom one that held Damon's running outfits. Shifting again, her eyes went to the now-empty corner where Damon usually kept his favorite pair of running shoes. Dropping her bag, Liv let out a moan.

Today. Why today of all days would he decide to pull this?

She thought they were fine. At least he said they were fine. Liv groaned again. And he was supposed to meet her at her parents tonight. So now what was she supposed to tell them? The silence of her apartment suddenly felt suffocating, and all Liv wanted to do was fill it. On instinct, she got up and reached over to the night table for the remote control before remembering, as her eyes shifted to the large, empty space where the TV should have been.

Going for her bag, she pulled out her cell and hit Damon's number once again. This time he had the nerve to pick up.

"Really?" she said, fighting to keep any sense of her true frustration out of her voice. "I can understand you taking your own things, who cares about that? But what makes you think I'm going to let you get away with running off with my flat-screen TV?"

Damon's voice was just as smooth as it had been that morning as it came across the air and reached Liv's ears. But what should have been a caress to the senses now sounded akin to a dentist's drill. "Your TV?" His attempt at feigning shock almost made Liv laugh. "If I recall, that television was a gift to me, so technically it's mine. And I really didn't consider you the type, Liv, who would renege on a gift."

Liv pulled back and stared at the phone in her hand as if it had just turned into a pogo stick and she couldn't understand the odd sounds coming out of it. This day seemed to come at her all at once, and she was well and truly, for the moment, dumbfounded. Shaking her head, she clicked off the phone without another word. She couldn't deal with it. With him. Not now. Not when there was a calm, perfect daughter mask she had to put on. Tonight was supposed to be a night for celebrating. She wasn't going to ruin it. Besides, her parents already had two other screwed-up adult children to worry about. They didn't need to add their oldest to the list.

After a short cab ride, farther uptown with her pies, Liv used her old key and made her way into her parents' modest, but now quite valuable, three-bedroom Harlem apartment. Using her foot to balance the door, she picked up her shopping bag, took a deep breath and made her way in.

"Hello. Ma, Daddy, it's me," she called out, half hoping she wouldn't get an answer and this whole shindig was some other night so she wouldn't have to deal with people and her jumble of emotions all at the same time. But she knew that was ridiculous. Of course it was tonight. The date had been firm for months, and she could smell the aroma of her mother's collard greens practically before the elevator doors opened on their floor.

"I'm in the kitchen!" Her mother's voice sounded light and bouncy, though Liv could detect the slight undertone of pre-party anxiety below the surface.

After closing the door and locking it behind herself, Liv made her way down the short foyer, passing the living room with its new matching suite of couch, love seat, and coffee table, not to mention the showstopper: the fabulous new recliner with the flip-out cup holders that was her father's pride and joy. A joint retirement gift from Liv and her siblings, though to date both her brother and her sister still owed her most of their share for the chair. She shook her head and let out a sigh. What did it matter? Daddy was happy, and that was most important.

Turning a short corner, she looked into the long galley kitchen just in time to see her mother pulling a baked ham out of the oven. Really, a ham? She could have sworn there was some sort of rule about ham after Easter and before Fall. Glancing around, she could see that the counters were already full of food, not to mention every burner on the stovetop looked occupied. "Geez, Mom, think you've cooked enough food, or will we have to order out for reinforcements?" Liv said, teasingly.

Her mother, Anne Gale, gave her deep chestnut curls a shake as she slipped the pot holders off her hands and walked over to her daughter, leaning up to kiss her on her cheek. "Not today Miss Smarty-Pants. There is way too much to be done for me to listen to you trying to be cute. I still need the buffet table put out, the bar set up, and all the food arranged and laid out." She let out a long exhale and looked around as if searching for something. "And Lord knows where my good tablecloth is. I could've sworn it was in the front hall closet, but then again it's been lent out to Lynn so often . . . she may still have it." She leveled Liv with a conspiratorial stare. "You and I both know she's not the best when it comes to returning things."

Liv walked deeper into the kitchen and went to place her pies out on a small breakfast table near the window. "You're way too nice, Ma. I don't know why you continue to lend her all your things when you know she's not good at giving them back."

"I know, honey, but she's still my friend and my neighbor, so you know how that goes."

Liv had no answer for that. Her mother was her mother, and she just couldn't help being the giving type. All her life she had done for others, be it for Liv or her two younger siblings, Alexandrea and Elijah, or in her capacity as a teacher for the past thirty years. And though she was now retired, she still volunteered as an after-school literacy specialist three times a week. Just then, she could feel her mom coming up behind her and knew she was checking out the pies. "If you're finished assessing, care to share your thoughts?" Liv asked as her mother lifted the tops off the plastic pie covers.

Her mother gave her shoulders a warm squeeze. "Oh, sweetie, all these pies look delicious. You've outdone yourself. They will be absolutely perfect. I know everyone is going to go crazy for them. The cake I ordered is really just a cute extra. I hope your father gets a kick out of the photo I put on it."

Liv raised a brow. "Oh, Mom, why did you do that?

I hope you didn't go too far with the photo cake. You know how Daddy is. He's not one for surprises."

Her mother got a wicked twinkle in her eye, and it did nothing to soothe Liv's nerves. "Oh, I know, but this is all in good fun. And besides, he's retired now. It's time to shake things up a bit. It will be good for him to laugh and step out of his comfort zone."

Liv shrugged. "If you say so, lady. That's your husband. You'll be the one dealing with the consequences." She teased her mom, then looked around once more. "Speaking of, where is the retirement boy of the hour? As a matter of fact, where is everyone else? I know the guests won't arrive for another forty-five minutes, but what about Drea and Elijah? Shouldn't they be here helping out?"

To that her mother shook her head once again, and her eyes went toward the ceiling. "Oh, honey, please, there you go starting things. Your father will be back shortly. He was getting a little antsy about the party, you know how he is—not really one for fanfare, so he was bugging me by getting too underfoot—so I sent him out to the grocery store for some extra supplies. And as for your sister and brother"—she let out a breath— "Alexandrea should be here after she finishes a quick shift at the restaurant. Her boss called her in and asked her to cover for just a few hours because someone called out sick. And Elijah, well, he'll get here when he gets here. You know how your brother is, always more intent on his studies than anything else."

It took all she had for Liv to keep her comments behind her teeth. Yeah sure, Drea got called in for a quick shift. *And just how quick would that shift be,* she wondered. Was it long enough for her married boss to try to put the moves on her way-too-gullible younger sister? The thought of Drea being used by her jerk of a boss always sent Liv's blood boiling. Though Drea steadily denied anything was going on, and that she was tough enough to handle her handsy boss, Liv didn't believe it. All it took was one visit to the trendy Soho eatery and a moment's look at Drea's boss in action, and she knew. The guy was up to no good.

And as for her perpetual college student younger brother, Elijah, well, he always conveniently found himself deep in his studies when it was time for any sort of hands-on work to be done. The day their very own Peter Pan finally grew up and took a little responsibility would be a great day indeed.

It was with that thought that not quite Peter Pan actually walked in. Tall and lanky with a surprisingly disarming smile, Elijah knew how to play to a room. It was with that smile that he sailed in and took their mother into a tight hug. "I thought you said there was a party going on here tonight, Ma? You think you made enough food? I can polish off this ham myself," he said as he stepped away from their mother and reached for one of her sweet potato biscuits.

"Now, Elijah, you know that food is for the guests. Don't you go spoiling your appetite," their mother said without any real censure to back it up.

Elijah paused mid-chew and gave his mother a grin. "As if one little biscuit could put me off my appetite for more of your food." He looked around, his eyes finally landing on Liv for the first time as he waved his half-eaten biscuit in front of her face. "Hey, big sis, did you taste one of these? Mom really put her foot in it this time."

Liv gave him a tight smile. "No, I'll get mine with dinner. There is too much to be done right now for me to get into eating. And for you too," she added.

Elijah gave her only an eye roll by way of a reply,

which had Liv shaking her head while her mother let out a frustrated breath. "Okay, kids, don't you two start in now. Yes, there is plenty to be done. Elijah, you go on in there and set up that buffet table for me. We don't have a lot of time before the guests get here. Olivia, look in the hall closet and see if you can find the good tablecloth. Maybe I missed it. And if you don't see it, go on ahead and use the backup one. It'll just have to do."

"Do you want me to run over to Ms. Lynn's apartment and ask if she's got it? I will if you don't want to call."

Her mother just shook her head. "No need. I don't want to put her out. Besides, I'm pretty sure she does have it, and when she sees I'm using my backup cloth, hopefully that'll spur her conscience on to give me back my own."

It was no use. Her mother was way too easy on people, but she wasn't going to bug her with speeches about getting tough and standing up now. Not today—well, not any day. Her mother's kindness was what everyone loved about her.

"Is that my Livy girl I hear in there?" Liv couldn't help but smile, despite her father calling her by the long-standing childhood endearment "Livy." No matter how often throughout middle and high school she tried to get them to call her what she considered the more adult sounding, Liv. It never quite stuck. They did what they wanted. Olivia, Livy, Girl Child Number One, it was a free-for-all. Guess they figured they made her, they'd name her.

"Yes, it is, Daddy." Sure, she may technically be too old to be calling her father Daddy, but hey, if he was still in with Livy, then so what? She'd revel in it and stay his little girl.

She listened as her father came down the hall toward

the kitchen, imagining him in his usual well-worn pants and soft, rubber-bottomed boots as he made his way to her. When he appeared in the kitchen, he was as she envisioned, only slightly older and a little more weathered than the little girl's image she'd kept in her head. Tall, wide-shouldered, and still handsome for his age, with a big craggy smile, Mitch Gale greeted them by waving the plastic grocery bag in his hand. He then walked fully into the kitchen and placed it on the last available spot on the table, giving her mother a knowing look. "Don't think I don't know what you did there Anne, sending me on that fool's errand. If you wanted me out of the way, you should have just said so. Looking around here, it sure doesn't seem like you needed anything."

Not put out in the least by his words, her mother gave him a light admonishment. "Oh please, Mitch, you know you were driving me crazy. Honestly, you should have stayed out for another good half an hour longer, at least." She waved a hand. "But no matter, why don't you go on in the living room and help your son set up the buffet table and then you can arrange the bar area. After that, go on in the bedroom and you'll see I've laid out some clothes for you."

Liv's father chuckled as he turned toward her. "See, just like I said—busywork." He took Liv into a warm hug, then pulling back he gave her a soft smile and looked her deep in her eyes, as he always did. Only this time Liv had to fight to keep her gaze steady and bright so as not to give a hint of any of the turmoil that she'd been through earlier in the day.

For all her putting on, her father was quick to see through her façade, and his smile quickly faded, casting down into a frown as he peered at her more intently. "You all right there, Livy?" he asked.

Liv smiled brighter, but in a rookie move she shifted her gaze away from her dad a bit too quickly, gesturing to show him the table as she shrugged. "I'm fine, Dad. You know there's no need to worry about me, so stop trying to deflect from you not wanting to have this party tonight." She waved a hand across the table, indicating her pies. "It's gonna be quite the gathering. And look, I made your favorite."

At the indication of Liv's handiwork, thankfully her father looked over at the table and grinned. "These look delicious, sweetheart. Once again, you've outdone yourself." He turned toward Liv's mom. "See what she's made here, Anne? Not only is our daughter smart as a whip, but she's a whiz in the kitchen. I tell you, this one here will be quite a catch for some man."

Both Liv and her mother groaned at the same time, and her father looked back and forth between them slightly bewildered, as if he didn't know what he said. "What?" he asked.

"Daddy, you know that's not very PC," Liv said. "My skills in the kitchen shouldn't have anything to do with my ability to catch a man."

Her father gave her a put-upon look. "I swear, you millennials are so sensitive. Did I not talk about how smart you were first? I'm just pointing out that you have other qualities besides your brains. It wasn't like I was attaching a gender to it. Though your mother's pretty good at cooking, and I've been known to throw down in the kitchen myself."

Liv's mom wrinkled her nose.

"Hold it now," her dad said. "Don't you go sleeping on my skills or trying to call me some sort of chauvinist. I'm trying to do right here. I'm just saying that I'd hope that whoever you settle down with appreciates both your brains and your other talents and, more than that, I hope he has more than one or two to bring to the table himself. Speaking of your attributes and appreciating them"—Liv noticed her father's expression turned decidedly less jovial—"I suppose we will be graced with the presence of that Damien of yours tonight? He doesn't strike me as one to turn down a free meal."

"His name is Damon, Dad, not Damien, and you know it," Liv said. She also knew her father couldn't care less what Damon's name was. Never could from the first moment he'd met him. Score one for dear old perceptive dad. Why Liv hadn't taken her father's overzealous nature to heart and been a bit more perceptive herself, she didn't know. She did know that she now regretted ignoring his dislike for her ex-boyfriend. But Liv definitely wasn't in the mood to get into it tonight, and she scrambled to get away from any Damon talk without too much explanation. "Well, I don't know." She fought to keep lightness in her tone. "Damon says he'll try to make it, and he wishes you all the best. But he is working on a big client acquisition right now, so he may not be able to get here in time for the party."

Her father shrugged, as if he was saying "Good riddance." Just as her brother had done before him, he grabbed a sweet potato biscuit before heading out toward the living room. "Oh well, it'll be his loss, not ours," he said before taking a big bite.

"Don't worry about it, sweetheart," her mother said. "I've got plenty of plasticware, so you can always bring him a take-home plate.

This pulled her father up short just as he was hitting the hallway. "Take home to where? Doesn't he have his own place? And if he really wanted something to eat, he should've shown up himself." Liv's father gave her a quick glance and then turned away once again, mumbling. "Shoot, you're not taking any of my good plasticware out of this house for some smooth-talking no-show. At the most, he gets a Dixie plate."

Liv couldn't help chuckling and shook her head at her father's reaction as she went to work helping her mother prepare everything for the buffet table. But just as she was pulling one of the good serving platters down, her mother stopped her short. "So Damon is doing pretty good at work, you say?"

Seriously? Were they really going to stay on the subject? There was a party to get ready for. No need to fill the dead air with talk about her suddenly non-existent love life. But of course, she couldn't tell her mother that, so instead Liv just continued pulling the platter down and made as if slicing the roast beef were the most interesting task she'd ever encountered. "I didn't say," she mumbled, "but yes, he is." She purposely tried to keep her voice as nonchalant as she could. Stay light and move on.

"That's wonderful, sweetheart," her mother said. "Though you'd think for an important family function such as this one he would be here. I mean, it's not like you two have been seeing each other for a short time—what is it going on a year now?"

Liv squashed back a huff. *So we're not just letting this talk lie. All righty, then.* "Not quite a year mom, only nine months. And as I said, he's pretty busy."

"If you say so."

Ugh. *If you say so?* Liv mimicked the words in her head. Liv knew her mother just as well as her mother knew her, and that "if you say so" meant so much more than a light agreement. It meant that the subject was definitely not closed and would surely be continued at a later date. *Thank you, Damon, for taking what was merely a devastating day and tilting it into the horrific column.*

Chapter 2

Liv couldn't help but smile; for the moment, all thoughts of the lack of a job and a surprise dumpation by a boyfriend were erased from her mind as the last guests left the retirement party, and she glimpsed her father taking her mother into a sweet embrace and whispering in her ear over by the kitchen pass-through. Seeing them both so happy was what this was all about. Despite her father saying he didn't want the attention, he'd practically preened as many of his old coworkers and friends came by to wish him the best in his new life of leisure.

Not that leisure was exactly how her parents had mapped out spending their retirement years. Her mother had come up with a pretty elaborate travel plan for the next three months. They were taking a long-dreamed-of cruise to Europe. Well, the European trip was more her mother's dream as opposed to her father's. But he'd do anything to make her mother happy, and Liv knew her mother's travel dreams had been derailed by the reality of children, tight finances, life, and all that came with being an adult and trying to just make it day to day. But that was done now, and after they returned to the States, the plan was for the two of them to do something that was more in line with her father's wishes. They were going to rent an RV and drive across the country, hitting all the best fishing holes and barbecue spots along the way.

To Liv, as far as dreams went, it might not be everyone's cup of tea, but it was what they wanted and the least of what they deserved after spending so many years essentially living for their three children.

Liv found herself suddenly blinking back tears thinking of family, children, and dreams deferred, which only made her angry at herself for even going there on such a good night, when she felt her shoulder nudged forcefully.

"What's with you, Livy? Don't go and tell me the ice queen is thawing," her sister said at her side. She waved her wineglass toward their parents. "Ugh, those two are sickeningly sweet at times. Don't let their magical picture of forever get you to thinking that it's something for mere mortals. You keep grounded in the real world. That type of stuff ends with their generation."

Liv let out a slow breath through her nose. Leave it to Drea to pretty much be the wet blanket nobody ever needed. She gave her sister a side-eye glance. "There's nothing wrong with me. And everything about Mom and Dad *is* pretty much perfect. They should be admired."

Drea shrugged. "Well, if you call struggling for over thirty years perfect, then sure, they've got it all going on."

"You know for a fact that's not what I'm talking about. I'm talking about their relationship. How they get along together. That's what's perfect. Or as close to perfect in this day and age as you can get. Why must you be so jaded?"

Drea gave Liv a stare that was just long enough to be intrusive. "And I suppose you being Little Miss Perfect, that's exactly what you have going on with Damon?"

Liv stared back at her sister, the corners of her own eyes tightening when she caught the fight in Drea's. She was clearly egging her on. "Whatever," Liv said, raising her shoulders and then lowering them again in a dismissive gesture. She wouldn't give Drea the time or energy for the confrontation she was clearly itching for. Besides, she wasn't going to let her sister bait her into spilling the beans on the demise of her and Damon's relationship. It wasn't as if she could expect any sort of sympathy from her sister on the subject; they didn't have a relationship like that.

"Whatever do you mean by whatever?" Drea asked, immediately latching on to the dangling thread. "And where is Mr. Right tonight anyway? Aren't you two always joined at the hip? I expected him to be here all suited down and overdressed. Shouldn't he be about ready to make some sort of grand proposal by now anyway?" Drea's words came out harsh and slightly warbled.

Liv wasn't playing this game. Not now. Not tonight. Liv started to walk toward the kitchen, but her sister grabbed her by the arm and pulled her up short. "Well?"

Liv jerked her arm out of Drea's grasp, annoyance and a hint of nervousness licking at the back of her neck. "Why are you so concerned about my relationship? What's going on? Don't tell me, Mr. Married Boss once again putting on the moves, or is it that his wife got wind? Either way, Drea, you can't deflect by taking your problems out on me, and you sure enough can't flirt your way cutely around the issue forever. That job is never going to lead to you becoming a star no matter what sort of so-called connections that boss of yours says he has."

With that Drea's pretty brown eyes quickly lit up with a spark of fire. "Flirting? I'm not flirting with anything!" She shook her head. "Look at you. Once again Ms. Judgy Gale coming down with her verdicts and no facts to be had. I knew you couldn't last the night."

Liv moved in closer toward her sister, getting inches from her face, making her voice a hiss of a whisper. "And I knew you couldn't last the night without trying to bait me and making yourself the center of attention. What is it? Is your life not complete unless you're all up in mine? This is supposed to be Dad's night. This little brat act won't play cute for much longer."

Drea looked as if she was about ready to stomp her foot. "Cute! Look at you! As if you'd know cute if it bit you on your—"

Liv opened her mouth to reply before Drea got out her final word, but was stopped by the sound of her mother's voice. "Seriously, you two." Her mother spoke slow and steady, but the underlying edge of anger was all too real. It immediately silenced both her and her sister and took them right back to preteens and weeklong groundings. "Tonight *is* your father's night, and I won't have you two arguing and ruining it for him."

Her father came up behind her mother and wrapped his arms around her waist. His smile said he was feeling no pains on this night and his daughters arguing would not be getting to him in the least. Still, when he looked at Liv and Drea, Liv didn't miss the hint of disappointment. "Oh, Anne, don't pay these girls no never mind. As if I'd let their usual going at each other ruin this night." He took Liv's mother's hand and gave her a twirl. "Besides, I get to stay up as late as I want and dance with my sweetheart. No work for me tomorrow, or ever if I want. This guy is chilling out, living off a fixed income pension now."

Liv couldn't help but laugh at that and let her annoying sister's words roll off her back. No, her parents wouldn't be living off their retirement money in the lap of luxury, and even with tight budgeting, things would probably be a bit tough. But both her mother and father seemed happy, and in good enough health to enjoy these latter years together. So she could totally understand her father's exuberance tonight, and she felt bad about letting a squabble with Drea potentially ruin it.

It was then that the familiar sound of the house's landline rang out. Although usually to Liv the sound was comforting, since she only ever heard it at her parents' house, being that she and most of her friends who had their own places now relied solely on their cell phones, the fact that it came at such a late hour startled all of them.

"Who could that be calling at this hour?" her mother said as she went toward the kitchen to pick up the phone.

"It's probably Mrs. Jenkins calling to complain about the noise from the party," her father said.

Her mother shrugged. "Well, she's got no reason to complain. She should've come up and that way she wouldn't have had a problem with any noise. It wasn't like she wasn't invited."

Her father waved a frustrated hand. "Blah, as if that crab apple would have come out of her cave to give a kind word. Please. You know she's one of those

Sunday-only kind of Christians. By Monday her religion is long forgotten till the next Saturday after midnight." It must have been the Christian talk that brought his gaze back over to Liv and Drea, and he gave his head another shake before walking back toward the sideboard. "Nope, I'm not even going to talk about Crab Apple Jenkins tonight. Tonight is my night." Their dad picked up the CD player remote and turned the volume up a bit before turning back to Liv and her sister and taking both of their hands, this time swinging them, doing his version of a little shimmy dance to a '90s groove track.

"Get it now, Daddy," Drea said, snapping her fingers and dancing around him. "Mom had better watch out. You still got plenty of moves left in you."

But Liv let her own hand slip away from her father's as she moved closer to her mother when she caught the hint of urgency in her voice.

"What is that, Joyce? Oh my Lord!" her mother said, bringing her hand to her chest and causing Liv's own heart to skip a beat.

What was Aunt Joyce doing calling with news that would cause her mother to figuratively clutch her pearls? Liv gave her mom a concerned look and mouthed the words, "Is everything okay?"

Her mother just shook her head, and Liv couldn't tell if that meant things were fine or if she was giving Liv the brush-off. Either way she knew she had to wait to get the news. After listening in on a few non-sensical sentences that ended with, "Are you sure?" ". . . surgery," and "What about Katherine?" Liv could only surmise that somebody was having surgery and it had something to do with her aunt Katherine. After a few short nods, her mother hung up the phone with a promise to call her sister back.

By then Liv's dad, having realized something was wrong, had turned down the music and was waiting for news of what happened with concern in his eyes. So was Drea, a fresh glass of wine in hand, and this time Elijah was by her side, obviously ready for round three with the food, Liv guessed, since it seemed nothing else would coax him back out of his ham and biscuit stupor at this hour.

"Well, what is it?" Liv's father asked. "What was Joyce calling for at this time of night?"

Her mother let out a sigh, then looked up at her father with worried eyes. "Well, unfortunately Joyce, being Joyce, a little too headstrong, decided that she could clean her own gutters and took a tumble off a ladder and broke her hip."

"Oh boy. That sounds just like Joyce," her father said with a knowing tone.

"Yeah, well, the break was pretty major, and Joyce, not being as young as she thinks she is, is shocked that it will take as long as it will for it to fully heal." Her mother's frown deepened as she thought of something. "I honestly can't believe Kath didn't call me as soon as this happened. I may just wring her neck for this. Joyce said she told her not to call, but since when does Kath do what she's told?"

"You said a mouthful there," their father agreed.

Their mother nodded. "Well, at least now Joyce is calling. She's out of the hospital and, with the shop back open, having trouble keeping it running as it should on her own."

"But what about Kath and her kids?" her father asked. "Doesn't she have one of Kath's girls working in the shop now?"

Her mother shook her head. "No, she's got one of Clint's children, Rena, working there. As Joyce said,

Kath's kids are a bit too sadity and wouldn't dare get their hands dirty by messing around in flour and dough."

"Okay, so she's got Rena working there," their father said. "What's the problem? Just call in some extra help."

Her mother gave her father a "come on and get real" look. "You know how Joyce is, complaining that Rena is only half there and more worried about her babies' father than about what she has to do in the shop. Not to mention she's convinced she can't get decent help in town, at least not someone who is up to her standards. You know what a control freak she is."

"And whose fault is that?" her father asked, and Liv could see that her mother was immediately torn as she looked for an answer to the question. Liv knew as well as her mother that her father was absolutely right. Though a real firecracker and Liv's absolute favorite, it was true, Aunt Joyce was a total control freak. She ran the family's pie shop, passed down from their mother and their grandmother before— Goode 'N Sweet—with love; care; and total, exacting control. Although it was Aunt Joyce who ran the shop and did all the baking, Liv's mother and Aunt Kath were still part owners, but really in name only. Goode 'N Sweet was Aunt Joyce's baby. She'd often said there was a reason that she'd never gone on to marry or have any children of her own. That taking care of the business was just about as much nurturing as she was able to dole out.

And she doled out plenty in that old shop. Liv's mind went to her summers down at Sugar Lake. In the shop's kitchen with Aunt Joyce were some of her happiest times. Although she was a tough cookie, all her warmth came out when she was sharing her love of baking and the Goode family tradition of nurturing through good food and fellowship. Liv had only fond memories of her aunt and could attribute all she knew about making desserts to her.

"Well," her mother said, "her being controlling is neither here nor there. Joyce must be in dire straits for her to swallow her pride, pick up the phone, and call to ask for help. I have a feeling it's not just about hiring extra help. It may be a money issue too. With hospital bills and all. Maybe she can't afford it. Mitch, you know that calling like this is not like her. It must be serious."

Liv's father's expression changed to grievous, which in turn sent a feeling of dread to the pit of Liv's stomach. "You do have a point there. But what can we do? We leave on our vacation soon. Everything is all booked. How can plans be changed now?"

"I don't know," her mother said. "Maybe if I call the travel agent we can make some sort of change and not have any heavy penalties."

"Oh, Anne. There you go. Always putting others first. This has been your dream for so long. There has to be another way."

Liv could see the pain on her mother's face and the joy of the wonderful night fade as it slipped from her father's expression. Why was it that things must always go wrong at the exact worst possible time? There had to be a solution that didn't involve her parents putting their dreams on hold, yet once again for someone else.

"Uncle Cole has other kids," Drea chimed up from by the bar. "Why can't one of them just step in?"

"Because they all have jobs that they can't just walk away from," their mother said.

Drea nodded. "Yeah, well I know how that is."

"Do you?" The words were out of Liv's mouth

before she could shore her brain up fast enough to stop them.

"Seriously?" Drea said, quickly turning toward her sister. "You use this moment to jump on me and put me down about my job."

"I'm not jumping on you, Drea. I'm just saying it's not like your job is one that you can't, well, take a leave from. That is, if your boss can do without you for a while."

"Don't start," Drea said by way of warning. "It's not like I see your man here worried about what you're doing."

"What you mean by her man?" Liv's mother asked, speedy with the perceptive pickup. "Your boss is your boss and nothing more. Right, Drea? So why would you even equate him with Livy's boyfriend?"

Drea looked at her mother seemingly at a loss for words and then turned to Liv with a look that both said she'd like to kill Liv while it asked how she could put her in such a position. Crap. Liv felt horrible for even bringing the subject up and putting her little sister out there like that. She didn't think there was anything going on with Drea and her boss, but that tongue slip was really a bit too much. Even if she annoyed her to no end, she didn't want her sister put in a compromising position and be ratted out in front of their parents tonight. Not without talking to her privately first. "I can go help out with Aunt Joyce," Liv said in a rush.

Everyone turned toward her with confused looks on their faces, but it was her mother who spoke up first. "What do you mean you can go and help out Aunt Joyce? You're just as busy as everyone else. Sure, you may be able to take a couple of days off of work, but it's not like you can just walk away from your job,

Livy. Joyce seems like she will need help for a few weeks at least, maybe more." She waved a hand indicating her frustration. "No, it's not an option. Your dad and I will figure something out. I'm sure we can make adjustments with the travel agency."

"You'll do no such thing," Liv said firmly. "You will take your trip and you will have a wonderful time. In the meantime, I'll go and help Aunt Joyce. It'll all be fine, you'll see."

"Of course it will. Why, it's so like you to jump in and save the day, big sister," Drea said from over her shoulder. "Would you care to tell us how you're actually going to do that with your job and everything?"

It was Liv's turn now to give her sister a look. Her eyes let her know that she'd indeed pushed the right button this time.

Liv sucked in a much-needed breath and let it out before she began her next sentence. "As of today, I don't have a job." The air around her chilled, and she couldn't tell if it was her body reacting to her admission or that her mother and father had just sucked all the air out of the room at the very same time.

"Don't worry, don't worry, I'll be fine," Liv quickly added. "The company used words like *downsized* and *restructured* to make it all very PC, so I got a decent-enough severance package to keep me going for a while." She could do this. "Though I will admit it still sucks to be fired. That's never happened to me before."

"Well, welcome to Club Screw Up, Miss Perfect. We're happy to have you here," Drea said, and their mother thankfully told her to hush it up before Liv rounded on her.

"I'm so sorry, honey," her father said. "These corporations have no loyalty. And for them to do something like that to a star like you, they obviously have no sense either. That's okay, you'll find something in no time. But are you sure you want to take on going to Sugar Lake? You know as well as I do that Aunt Joyce can be a handful and Georgia is just starting to heat up this time of year."

Her father's words pulled her up short. He was probably right. Well for one, Georgia was getting hot, but with the job, Damon and all, Liv was feeling like she could use the change of climate. And two, Aunt Joyce was a lot to handle, so Liv knew a trip to Sugar Lake probably was setting herself up for trouble in more ways than one. Sugar Lake held more than a few memories, some sweet and a few bitter. But it didn't take away from the fact that Aunt Joyce was family. And her mom and dad needed her right now, and well, that trumped any apprehension she had.

"Yes, your father is right, and what about Damon?" her mother asked. "How's he going to react to you going away for a couple of weeks to Sugar Lake? It may even be a month or two. You can't really judge what Aunt Joyce needs until you get there. I don't know about this, dear."

"Well," Liv said as she prepared herself for more judgment, "I'm sure Damon won't care, since he and I broke up today."

"Today!" Drea shouted from over her shoulder. "Isn't his timing stellar? Was it before or after he'd heard you'd gotten fired?"

Liv rounded on her sister with a sharp look. "Not that it matters, but my getting fired had nothing to do with it."

"Yeah, sure," Drea said.

Liv let out a long breath. She would not let Drea pull her in. This was not about her and Damon right now. And besides, she didn't get to tell him about getting fired before he'd had a chance to move his crap and her TV out of her place, so one had nothing to do with the other, she guessed.

"Drea, don't start," her mother said by way of warning.

"I'm just saying, the dude picks today of all days to break up with her. That's classic bum behavior." She turned toward Liv and gave her a sharp look. "But hey, now I get why you are being so altruistic and running off to Sugar Lake. It will be a perfect place to make your escape and to lick your wounds."

Liv's jaw dropped. "You've got a lot of freaking nerve talking to me about escaping and running off!" She'd gone too far now. "You've been running and escaping life ever since you finished college. Fluttering from job to job and man to man looking for your so-called big break. How about you get real? You're not going to get any big breaks from some walk-in asking for a corner table by the window. When are you going to take your life into your own hands, and when are you going to take a little responsibility and help your family out? At least I'm standing up and doing what needs to be done so Mom and Dad can still go on their trip. Live out their dreams. What are you going to do to help them along, to help the family? Continue to take your acting and singing lessons while never going on auditions, while you live under their roof, eat their food, spend their money? Either grow up or shut up once and for all!"

Drea's eyes narrowed to slits. "Oh, I'll show you growing up, all right," Drea said as she took a step toward Liv.

"Enough!" their father yelled, silencing them.

"Finally," Elijah sighed from the kitchen entryway,

plate in hand. When he slipped away to make it, who knew? Their father whirled on him with a look, one that told Elijah that stuffing his mouth full of sweet potato pie would be his next best step.

Their dad then turned back to Liv. "Sweetheart, what you're looking to do is wonderful, and if it's really in your heart to do it and you're sure you're ready to take such a big step for the next couple weeks, at least until we get back from our European trip, we will be greatly appreciative."

"But Mitch," their mother started, but their father put up his hand, stopping her, and continued his speech, this time turning toward Drea.

"And as for you, young lady, you and your sister need to cut all this fighting. I don't know what's going on with your work situation, but whatever it is, you need to get it straightened out. Or do I need to take a trip downtown to talk to this boss of yours myself?"

Drea quickly shook her head. "No, sir."

Their father nodded. "Good. Though not eloquently said, your sister is right. It's time to live up to who you are. Who I know you are great enough to be. You're a talented young woman. Time to show it."

Drea looked at her father, and for a moment it seemed as if she was going to say something, but instead she swallowed and her gaze swept the floor.

Their father clapped his hands together loudly, turned around, and picked up the stereo's remote control once again, turning the music up. "Good. I'm glad that's all settled. Anne, let's get in a couple more dances before my night is over. And then tomorrow you can call that loony roof-climbing sister of yours and let her know that reinforcements are on the way." He gave Liv a wink before he took their mother into his arms, twirled her twice, and kissed her soundly enough to bring a deep crimson blush to her mahogany cheeks.

"Come on with that!" Elijah said from his spot by the kitchen doorway. "Some of us are trying to eat over here."

With that Liv just shook her head and enjoyed the moment as she tried to squelch down the budding feelings of nervousness over the decision she'd just made.

Chapter 3

"You have got to be kidding me!" Liv shouted just a few short days later as she came down to load her luggage into her father's old sedan only to find Drea leaning against it, large duffel bag in hand. "What are you doing here?" Liv asked. "And please tell me that bag is chockablock full of food that mom prepared for me for my trip."

Drea gave a sly grin. "No such luck, big sis. After all your talk about family and sacrifice and getting my act together, well, it got me thinking that maybe I could help out a little bit. So I decided to take this trip with you."

Liv groaned. "Please tell me you're joking," she said, looking her sister in the eye for some sign of gameplay but, sadly, finding none.

"Nope. No joke here. I'm as serious as they come. You're looking at a brand-new me. I'm all about getting myself together once and for all."

Liv walked over toward the car and put her luggage inside. She started to close the trunk, but Drea stopped her, giving her sister a look. "Not so fast. The way you are acting makes me think you don't want the extra help. We both know Aunt Joyce can probably use it. Two hands are better than one and all that," she stated as she tossed her duffel bag in the trunk and slammed it shut.

Liv then made her way over to the driver's side and opened the door, looking at her sister from across the roof of the car. "Don't be such a smarty. Of course Aunt Joyce can use the help, that is, if you are really going to be a help. I'm not going there for a vacation. I'm going there to actually work for our aunt, who's fallen and broken her hip, mind you. She may be in need of medical care, and from the way it sounds, that shop needs running. Which means baking, cleaning, and tidying up. Come on, we both know that none of those things hit high on your radar as fun."

Drea gave Liv an exasperated look. "And like I said, you're looking at the new me. I can be open to getting my hands dirty. And I do have customer service experience from working at the restaurant."

To that, Liv gave Drea a raised brow.

"Don't start," Drea said, pointing a well-manicured nail. "It's too early in the morning for it."

Liv felt her lip curl as she gave her sister a quick up and down. Young, beautiful, with a flawless chestnut complexion; almond shaped, deep set bedroom eyes, accented by just the perfect amounts of liner and mascara; full, deep brick red lips made extra pouty by one of those expensive lip glosses that she loved so much. Her hair, this week, was a thick mass of twisted braids that were swept to one side and worn long past her delicate shoulders in an inviting, haphazard bohemian way. It didn't go unnoticed that during their five-minute exchange, no fewer than five guys couldn't help but pause and stare at her sister. She was only three years younger than Liv, and although they had similar features, if not body type, they were night and day when it came to style and appearance. No, there wasn't much stopping or staring when it came to Liv's no-nonsense manner. "Yeah, I still see the same old you," Liv quipped back. "Getting those perfectly manicured nails dirty? I doubt that will ever happen."

Drea gave her a shrug before getting into the car. "You just watch me. Now, are you happy taking the first shift driving, or shall I? I mean, I would like to get there before next week. We all know you drive like an old lady."

Liv growled as she got into the car and caught her own reflection in the rearview mirror. Her sister made her want to pull her own shoulder-length, blown-straight hair out of the confines of its low ponytail. But she resisted and instead started up the car and gave Drea's hand a light slap as she went to reach for the radio. "Don't you dare. I've already preset the stations and I have my CDs loaded. When I'm driving, it's my choice."

Drea moaned. "Oh God, is it going to be smooth jazz and news radio all the time, or will I have to listen to call-in shows?"

Liv shrugged. "Like I said, when I'm driving it's my choice."

In answer to that, Drea reclined her seat and closed her eyes. "Well, wake me when it's my turn. I'll show you what real driving music is."

Liv shook her head, eased out of her coveted parking spot, and said a silent prayer and good-bye to her apartment, which she had sublet astoundingly quickly to a Barnard College student looking for temporary housing until something in the dorms became available. The fact that she didn't have to worry about making rent on her apartment was a relief, but what she had gotten herself into with agreeing to help Aunt Joyce and dealing with the idea of heading back to Sugar Lake and all the memories that that entailed was now at the forefront of her mind and ramping up her anxieties. To top it off, she now had Drea along for the ride. The two of them together were nothing but a recipe for disaster.

"We're here."

"Where?" Drea said as she groggily came awake and looked over at her sister.

"I thought we'd stop, get a little dinner, and maybe check into a hotel to stay the night. Then we can get back on the road early in the morning."

Drea frowned. "There is no need for us to check into a hotel tonight," she said. "You've driven enough, so I can take over driving the rest of the way and then we'll be there not long after midnight, by two or three a.m., the latest."

Liv looked at her sister with frustration. "No, that's not necessary. I've mapped it out with just me driving myself and timed it that way with stops to rest and refuel. Besides, why would we want to get into town and bother Aunt Joyce in the middle of the night? She won't be expecting me until tomorrow."

"Us," Drea corrected. "It may be a surprise to you, but I did call Aunt Joyce to let her know that I would be joining you."

This bit of news, which should have given Liv a sense of relief, only filled her with more anger. She hated surprises, and even more than that she hated being the last to know. "Nevertheless, you're tired and I'm beat, so we might as well check in here. I've already made the reservation for a room and for dinner."

It was then that Drea pushed herself up a bit more and finally looked around to check out their surroundings. She turned and gave her sister a shocked expression. "Come on. Why do we have to stay in a place like this? This level of pomp and froufrou looks like it'll set us back at least four hundred bucks a night. Not to mention it looks stuffy as all get-out."

Liv looked over at the Beaumont Inn, where they had pulled up. She took in the regal colonial columns, the freshly painted black doors, yellow shutters, and pretty window boxes overflowing with flowers, and shook her head. "Don't worry about it. It's not like I'm asking you to contribute anything."

She watched as her sister tried to hold on to what looked like her last thread of calm. "See, there you go with your assumptions and high-handedness. Must you make all the decisions on everything? And do you really always have to assume that you're better than someone else, better than me? Who says I can't contribute my fair share? I just would've liked to have been included in the decision-making process. Not for nothing, but staying in a place like this for nothing more than glorified sleep is a waste of time and money, if you ask me."

Liv let out a meditative breath then and made a mental note to add her part of the hotel room to Drea's mounting tab as the attendant came over to open her door. Goodness, did her sister have to go all in and read so much into every little thing she did and said? Still a twinge of guilt over her choice of words niggled at Liv's spine. "Well, I didn't ask you because this trip was planned out before I knew you'd be tagging along. You can contribute whatever you want to or not since I made this choice without you. But like I said, I'm beat and I want to stretch my legs and have a decent meal."

Drea got out of the car behind Liv, acquiescing though still not quite able to let the argument go. "And how do you know you'll get a decent meal here? What's the matter with fast food along the way? It's what people do on road trips. They loosen up."

Loosen up. Sure. Tell that to her supertight shoulders, Liv thought as she walked past her sister toward the lobby. "Their online ratings said their restaurant is top notch. Besides, some of us have higher standards than a quickie at the drive-through."

Drea came up to her just as she was hitting the reception desk. "Well, Ms. High Standards, we will see how far those get you when it comes time to pay the bill. And as you good and well know, it always comes time to pay the bill."

Darn, Drea and her premonitions. Over dinner that night in the hotel's highly rated restaurant, Liv could only admit silently to herself how underwhelming the meal was, since she refused to state her thoughts out loud and give her sister the satisfaction of knowing she was right. As a matter of fact, Drea couldn't have been more right. They could've stayed at a roadside motel and gotten a friendlier welcome than the one they'd received from the overteased middle-aged blonde with the clearly antiquated, bordering on offensive ways at reception. As for this meal, once again Drea was right there too. Liv's chicken was barely done and her rice was overdone, and she tasted better green beans out of a can from the grocery store.

But looking over at Drea's way-too-smug expression

as she picked at her lobster macaroni and cheese made with a crab substitute in place of the advertised lobster let Liv know that even in her silence she wasn't fooling her sister one bit.

"Nice dinner, huh?" Drea finally said, after she took another long pull from her glass of wine.

Liv let her fork drop with a loud clang and looked at her sister straight on. "You know it's not, so you might as well get your gloating out of the way now so I can give this plate back and order some ice cream. Hopefully they can't mess that up."

Drea shook her head while her lips took a soft upward turn. "Nah, no need to do that. Just knowing that you know that you were wrong, at least in this one thing, is enough." Liv looked on as Drea signaled toward their waiter for him to come over. She asked for the restaurant's manager, and soon a tall, thin middle-aged man appeared at their table. He was smiling weakly with eyes that had no true sincerity and showed that he had an inkling of what was to come.

"Good evening, ladies. I'm Mr. Bradley, the manager, and I hear you are not happy with your meals this evening?"

"No, we are not," Drea said, her tone soft as room temperature butter, but eyes way more firm. "I have to say we were extremely disappointed. My sister and I are coming from New York, and she stopped here because your place had gotten very good reviews. It's sad to see that you're not living up to them. It does make one wonder about the authenticity of such reviews."

Liv watched as the man's forced smile dropped and anger flickered around the edges of his eyes. "Ma'am, if you are implying that our reviews are anything but authentic, I will have to take offense at that."

Drea's voice still came out sweet, but louder than it was before. "I am not implying anything, sir. All I'm saying is that your meals are not coming out of your kitchen as advertised. Do you deny that it was not real lobster in my macaroni and cheese?"

Liv looked around, noticing that there was a bit more of a hush in the dining room now, and in their immediate vicinity all eyes were turned toward their table. She fought hard to brush off feelings of mortification over being the center of attention and not embarrassed by the scene her sister was pulling. But then she noticed Mr. Bradley's smile come back into place as he noticed the attention they were getting also. "No, ma'am. I'm sorry to say I do not deny that today we had an unfortunate problem with shipping from our usual seafood vendor, and we had to do a substitution. I am very sorry for the inconvenience, and you can rest assured that we will remedy that on your bill."

Drea gave him an affronted look. "Just that? How will you make up for my sister's horrible meal?"

Mr. Bradley looked at Drea as if he would be ever so happy if the floor opened up and swallowed her. Despite his look, she didn't falter and gave him the most serene smile. Which, even in her mortification, kind of made Liv want to stand up and cheer. Then the man leaned in closer to the table so that only the both of them could hear. "Of course, I do apologize if the service this evening was unsatisfactory. We pride ourselves on our dishes and making the customer happy. Your meal this evening is of course complementary. And to make up for it, please let me have dessert brought out to you."

Liv couldn't believe that Drea had done it. Sent the meal back, gotten them a freebie, and scored them a dessert on top of everything else. But then her sister went further and opened her mouth again. "That will not be necessary," she said, just about sending Liv into a silent fit of rage. What was she going on about now? Get out while the getting was good girl. She wanted her ice cream! "We thank you for the complimentary meal, but the dessert is entirely unnecessary."

Drea picked up her glass of wine and took a final sip before reaching into her purse and pulling out two twenty-dollar bills. She placed them on the table. "But this is for Charlie. His service was impeccable. Please be sure to relay our thanks. Maybe he could help train your shoddy front desk greeters in hospitality and making folks feel welcome."

Mr. Bradley, seemingly unable to form any words, just gave them both a nod as he backed away from the table.

"Really, after all that talk and complaining, you couldn't at least accept the dessert? You knew I wanted some ice cream to clear my palate from that horrible meal," Liv whispered to her sister as they gathered their things and got up from the table.

Drea paused midstand. "Would a 'thank you' kill you?"

Liv stared at her. "For what? Causing a scene or the free meal," she hissed "If the meal, then thank you. If the scene, then no thanks. I kind of like to keep a low profile. I don't like to go around causing scenes and making fusses."

Drea's brows pulled together as she stared at Liv. "And how's that been going for you so far?"

Liv stood still for a moment, then grinned before Drea's cheeks spread and she broke into a grin too. "Now, come on, don't get so serious. This is just a fun road trip. Besides, after all that, why would you accept even a scoop of ice cream from them and trust that it will come out of the kitchen untainted. I'm sure we've annoyed both the manager and the chef to no end." She grabbed Liv's hand, pulling her toward the hotel's doors as they made their way into the lobby. "Wasn't there a convenience store just a few doors down? We can go there and grab some ice cream and even a hot dog, which is what we should have done in the first place. The night will be complete. Let's make this quick. Best to be on the road first thing in the morning, and don't forget, I'm driving so I choose the playlist."

Liv sucked in a long breath of air . . . as well as the exhaust of a passing 18-wheeler. "Don't remind me."

SUGAR LAKE 126 MILES. Upon seeing the sign, Liv couldn't ignore the quickening beat of her heart. She and Drea had been silent for the past hour and a half, Drea seemingly focused on belting out her new age rap/bohemian music while Liv was, for the moment, content with leaving her to it while she tried to come to grips with the jumble of thoughts that were churning through her own mind.

It seemed that the more miles they ate up, and the closer they got to Sugar Lake, the more she couldn't quite wrap her head around her making such an impulsive decision to come to the small town. Yeah, sure, she'd spouted all that to Drea about stepping up, and helping out, and putting family first. And for the most part, yes, she believed it, but still a part of her knew there was something else, something that she needed to face, needed to deal with, and maybe that something could be found in Sugar Lake. But why leave New York? Was Drea right? Was she running away from something or toward something? For the first time in her life, with no set school classes or job to rush off to at a specific date, Liv was slightly panicked. She was also a little excited. Yes, she'd be going to help out Aunt Joyce, but she was now also open to something new. When had she'd ever had that opportunity? The last time she remembered dreaming seemed so long ago—heck, it had to be when she was back in high school. Back in Sugar Lake.

Liv squeezed her arms tight and squelched down the sigh that was tempted to escape.

Sugar Lake. It was such a big part of her, but she had to make sure that, though she was going back, she kept her feelings where they were. In her past. This was about helping out and getting her mind sorted to think about her future. The rug being pulled out from under her so abruptly with her job and with Damon had reminded her she'd become complacent. She'd failed to look ahead and plan properly. She should have seen it coming with both the job and Damon. As for her job, she'd restructured the department, so she definitely should have seen her position being eliminated. And as for Damon, he was just another in the line of men who had claimed to have loved her, but disappeared right when she thought they would step up and be there.

And now she was about to head back to where it all began. Sugar Lake. Liv did sigh this time as she shook her head. If you weren't inclined to get the message, God, the universe, whatever, was going to keep pounding it at you until you good and well did. She looked up and out the window at the sky and the fast-passing treetops. *I'm starting to hear now*, she thought. *Message received. Loud and clear.*

She closed her eyes and let a vision come to her. Young love. Kissing by a moonlit lake. She hoped coming back wouldn't stir up the heartache she'd left by the lake, long ago. But Aunt Joyce did need the help, and it was time she faced her past. See where it all began so she could once and for all let the past go. Leave it at the lake, where it should be.

Besides, that young love had moved on. Out of Sugar Lake to live his happy life, with his happy wife, and she assumed happy kid. That's how it was done, wasn't it? Liv needed to get out of the past and do the same. What she'd been doing so far was a poor act at pretending to do so. She smiled to herself. It would be good to go back.

Just then, a motorcycle roared by them on the passenger side, and Liv got another flashback of the carefree young girl she used to be. When trust was still a word that she wholeheartedly believed in. And hope was something she clung to strongly. She closed her eyes for a moment and breathed in deep as she remembered the feeling of the wind whipping around their bodies, the intense exhilaration mixed with a tingle of excitement and anticipation as the world whizzed by and they sped up to outrun it. Moving fast toward their dreams of the future. The innocent thrill of hope and trust as she wrapped her arm around his trim waist and rested her head on his wide, strong back. He'd made the younger her feel so sure and so secure that she would have gladly ridden off with him into forever. Liv couldn't help but wonder now, all these years later, if she'd ever feel that free again.

"Woman, where were you?"

Liv snapped back to reality as her sister's voice hit sharply against her eardrums.

"Huh? What are you talking about? I'm right here," she said.

"Uh, no, you weren't. Because if you were, you would've heard me calling your name three times and asking if you thought the next exit was a good one for me to take to go and pee. There's no way I can hold it for the next couple of hours until we get to Sugar Lake. Besides, I can use a Coke and something carby to keep me going. That breakfast sandwich I had has long worn off."

Liv shrugged. "You're a grown woman, Drea. No need to ask me. If you've got to go, choose a place and stop. Besides, you're driving."

Drea gave an arched brow. "No need to get testy. I was just being polite. I know how you are about rest stops. You like your places all fancy. Besides, I didn't want to waver from your planned agenda."

"Don't start. This has been a long-enough ride."

Her sister smiled at her. Big and beaming and dang it, Liv was pulled in. "Don't you just love it, all this sisterly bonding?" She winked.

"So now you've got jokes. Great," Liv said. Her expression was deadpan, but inside she silently chuckled.

Having switched over the driving at the last rest stop, Liv stopped short from humming her favorite show tune and turned the radio down low, causing Drea to sit up in the passenger seat and become alert. "What is it? Why'd you turn the music down? Are there cops on our tail?"

Liv shook her head. "No, we're just about to come into town. And I really wanted to take it in. It's been so long and all."

Liv was grateful for her sister's quiet as they eased

off the highway service road. They took a few rights and then a left down a long road past the now-faded Pepsi sign on Turner's old mill and then there they were. Suddenly it was as if the sky got brighter, and wider, and the air was more fragrant, though Liv knew it was her imagination as she looked to the left and saw the green-and-white sign that said, WELCOME TO SUGAR LAKE WHERE THE AIR IS SWEET BUT THE PEOPLE ARE SWEETER.

"Holy moly, this place has really changed," Drea said from Liv's side.

Liv couldn't help but nod her agreement. The main street was not all that much to talk about when they were kids. It had a few shops: The post office, general store, and the ice-cream shop were the biggest attractions. The street in front of them was now bustling with cars, stopping every few feet to get in where they could when a metered parking spot became available. Liv couldn't get over the fact that there were now multiple restaurants, at least three small office buildings that she could see, not to mention a full lineup of boutiques along Main Street and its outskirts. And check that fancy looking new chain Roasters coffee place. "What happened to the quaint, off-the-map Sugar Lake where I spent all my lazy childhood summers?"

"Well, this sure ain't it," Drea said.

"No, it sure isn't," Liv said. "Ma and Dad said it had been built up a little, but this is definitely not what I expected. No wonder Aunt Joyce needs help in the shop. With all these tourists milling about, how can she be expected to keep up with business?"

"Well, we'll see about that shortly, I guess," Drea said as they were nearing the bakeshop. "Or maybe not," she added at the same time they both saw the heavy backup of traffic and the fire trucks up ahead.

"Looks like they've got some kind of situation up there, close to the shop. Hope no one's hurt," Liv said.

Drea leaned forward. "Yeah, that is kind of close. I know I was young the last time we were here, but wasn't Aunt Joyce's shop right across the street from the general store?"

And with that, Liv's eyes shifted back and forth from the general store up ahead to where the fire trucks were parked. "Oh no, don't tell me it's the shop," she said, her heart plummeting to her stomach with fear.

Chapter 4

Liv quickly whipped into the first open space she saw, and she and her sister went running up ahead to Goode 'N Sweet, their family's bakeshop.

Making their way through the small crowd of on-lookers, Liv and Drea entered the shop, wide-eyed and anxious. It all looked so much the same. Only smaller. Funny how time does that to places, Liv thought. And thankfully this one was not in the midst of a raging fire. No, all Liv caught from a whiff of the air was the old familiar smell of warm butter, vanilla, and peaches. She frowned. It was a bit tinged by the smell of burnt crust. A slight shiver waved through Liv as the overwhelming feeling of somehow stepping into a snapshot of a moment from a time long past came over her. She quickly blinked to dislodge herself from the odd sensation and take a quick inventory.

There were the same old square wooden tables with what looked to be the same mismatched table-cloths thrown over them. The only further decora-tions were the little dime store vases that held plastic flowers she was sure hadn't been updated in years. At the back of the shop was the counter, illuminated and filled to the brim with her aunt's pastries, though it was clear its better days had long past. Even squinting, Liv could barely make out the rose blush of her aunt Joyce's cherry pie through the now slightly cloudy glass.

Wow, Aunt Joyce really could use some help, Liv thought as she took in the obvious toll that the years had taken on the old bakeshop. Glancing around, she could see that the curtains that were once so bright and cheery, now held a sad reminder of a faded glory of time gone by.

But just then, quickly pulling her out of her bordering-on-sad musings, a sharp voice could be heard over her temporary melancholy. "You've got a lot of nerve coming in here telling me what I should be doing, young man. Don't you know to respect your elders? Why, if I wasn't a God-fearing woman I'd show you just how much mobility I have left in this old hip of mine by sending my foot clear up your—"

Liv looked toward Drea. "Ouch! Well, if she's giving someone a good dressing down, that must mean she's not that bad off. And despite the fire trucks it doesn't look as if there's any real damage to this place."

Drea looked around, then shook her head. "No real damage? Did you get a good look at the place? By the looks of things around here, I'd say there is plenty of damage. A fire wouldn't be the worst thing. Maybe insurance money would do this run-down place good."

Liv's eyes went wide, and she grabbed at her sister's forearm. "Hush. You can't go saying something like that out loud. Especially within earshot of Aunt Joyce. Of course, I noticed the shop is a little run-down," she whispered close to Drea's ear, "but that's not for us to critique, and you know Aunt Joyce would be highly offended if we brought it up. So you're going to keep those opinions to yourself. That is, if you don't want to be kicked out on your rear before you're even let in the place and have gotten a piece of pie."

Drea pulled her arm sharply away from her sister. "What, do you think I'm stupid or something? Of course I won't say anything to Aunt Joyce." Drea turned away and looked around. "At least not yet."

Liv slid her a side-eye.

"Don't start," Drea said. "I'm just kidding. Stop being so paranoid and, once again, stop thinking the worst of me. I wish you'd give me just a little credit once in a while."

Drea was right. Of course she wouldn't say anything to Aunt Joyce. Liv was sure that deep down she cared about their aunt's feelings just as much as Liv did. She may be impulsive, but her sister wasn't malicious.

Just then Aunt Joyce's voice came at them loudly, once again from the back kitchen area. "Now, if you'll excuse me I've got more work to do, and as you can see plenty of cleaning up after you all traipsed in here like a band of wild buffaloes."

Liv looked at her sister. "Well, whoever it is she's getting on, I guess we should go back there and save them. Maybe we can be a distraction."

Drea nodded in agreement, following her sister though, Liv could tell, barely focusing as she eyed the cute firefighters that were exiting the kitchen area with their equipment. Liv almost couldn't blame her sister for her lack of focus. But still, their aunt was waiting.

"Really, girl?" Liv said. "We are on assignment here. Think you can focus?"

"Oh, I can focus all right," Drea said from behind

her sister. "But what's the harm in a little multitasking?" she added, while giving a particularly saucy grin to quite the handsome cutie built like a pro wrestler with deep eyes and a boy-next-door smile that signaled nothing but trouble. Whew! Oh boy. Sugar Lake truly had changed. Did they even grow guys like this back when they used to visit? Liv gave her head a shake as she let out a breath and continued to make her way toward her aunt's voice.

"We're here!" Liv said brightly, hoping to distract her aunt from the reprimand she was giving and the chaos in the back kitchen. But when it came to distractions, chaos, and surprises, the joke was fully on Liv, as her aunt and the firefighter with her turned and looked at them in unison.

"So now who's losing focus?" It was Drea's voice. Or at least Liv thought it was Drea. The voice came at her faint and hollow like from a faraway tunnel, and it took all Liv had to concentrate on the words as she took in what, no who, she was seeing standing in front of her in her aunt's kitchen. She knew she should be focused on the older woman whom she was there for. The one with the bottle-dyed auburn curls, cat eye glasses with the "now where did I put those?" neck string, and put-upon expression. But she couldn't. No, all her focus was on the tall, broad-shouldered fireman in front of Aunt Joyce, the one who Liv was sure Aunt Joyce had moments ago threatened to give a swift kick in the rear. The very same one who, all those years ago, Liv herself would have very much liked to have given a swift kick. He was the last person she expected or wanted to see while she was back in Sugar Lake. Clayton "I'll love you forever," though *forever* turned out to be only for *whenever*, Morris.

It was as if all the air was sucked from her lungs as

everything around Liv seemed to whirl around, then stand still, then zoom in until it reached a tiny pinpoint. She could hear her own breath become a low, quiet hum as she blinked. Her Clayton Morris. Or at least a version of her Clayton Morris was here. The Clayton Morris she remembered from twelve years ago had clearly been the boy version of the man before her now. This person, this firefighter, had more height and muscle and, she could tell even from the space across the expanse of the kitchen floor, somehow more intensity. But clearly this Clayton Morris was just as surprised as this Olivia Gale at the blast-from-the-past visitor. In his intense, deep brown stare she saw mirrors of her own shock glimmering back at her. But she saw something more when he blinked and recognition dawned like the first glistening sparkles on Sugar Lake. It flipped her mind in on itself, and it made her feel as if she were seeing him for the first time all over again. As if summer break never ended.

God, how very like Clayton. To turn every moment into a first. He was her first crush; her first love; her first kiss. Her first, well, everything. Yeah, he was the one who started it all. Including the first to break her heart. When it came to Liv's pattern of failed relationships, Clayton Morris was subject zero.

Liv sucked in a deep and much-needed breath as she struggled to gain her equilibrium. *What is he doing here?* According to the auntie-to-mom newsline, Clayton Morris was no longer a resident of Sugar Lake and hadn't been since he'd left all those years before to marry the girl he'd dated after Liv. Well, technically, there wasn't so much dating involved. More like a quickie marriage after a surprise pregnancy, after leaving Liv brokenhearted by reneging on his promises and running off to the military. But no, she wasn't bitter at all, thank you very much. Liv quickly plastered on her brightest smile.

"Livy! Drea! You two made it!" Aunt Joyce said, her voice booming with happiness and exuberance, the argument they had walked in on seemingly forgotten as she hobbled their way, leaning on her cane with one open arm.

Both sisters stepped forward at the same time to meet her more than halfway. Liv reached her first and leaned down only slightly to wrap herself in her aunt's warm and immediately familiar embrace. Momentarily pushing annoying thoughts of Clayton Morris away, she let herself enjoy the moment as she took in the smell of sugar and maple mixed with a hint of gardenia that always reminded her of the woman she loved and admired so much. Liv swallowed as she blinked back tears that she didn't expect to well in her eyes. Why did she stay away so long, and why did time fly by so darned fast?

"Stop hogging the hugs and let me get some of that!" Drea's voice came from over her shoulder, pulling her out of her musings and causing her to reluctantly tear herself away from her aunt's embrace.

The chuckle from Aunt Joyce made her smile. "Now, girls, don't go to fighting over me already. Listening to talk like that could give an old lady a swelled head, and everybody knows we don't need my ego to get any bigger." She gave a little nudge with her head toward Drea. "Now, get on over here, girl, and let me greet you properly. Look at you, just as pretty as you want to be. And not big as a minute. I hear you trying to be a model or get into acting up there in New York? You sure got the looks for it. You know they got all them movie studios over in Atlanta, or so I hear. Either way, I bet you breaking all the boys' hearts."

"If only it were so easy, Aunt Joyce," Drea said as she stepped into Aunt Joyce's arms.

Aunt Joyce hugged her, then pulled back and took them both by the hands, grinning wide and looking them over. "Oh yes, both you girls are looking mighty fine. And you, Little Miss Livy, I see you still got that gorgeous smile and that clear skin, and with those curves, yes, seems like everything went and hit you in all the right places too, just as I knew they would."

Aunt Joyce's frank appraisal of Liv's looks brought heat to her cheeks, made worse by the fact that she could feel Clayton Morris actively taking in the exchange. What could he possibly be thinking after so many years of not seeing her? Not to mention she hardly looked her best after spending a good portion of the day on the road.

"I wouldn't go that far, Aunt Joyce. But thanks for being so kind," Liv said.

"Oh hush. You know at my age I don't go in for wasted words just to be kind. Just accept the truth when you hear it."

With that, Aunt Joyce seemed to remember all the goings-on in the shop and people surrounding them as she turned back to the man who was the source of her annoyance when they walked in. "Don't they look fine, Clayton? I know you remember both my nieces. Especially Livy here."

Liv had to stop her eyes from bolting out of her head at her aunt's slightly loaded statement.

Clayton looked at her straight on and gave a nod.

Breathe. Just breathe. You remember how to do that. It's supposed to be automatic. Suck in air and then you blow it out. It's not so hard to do, you've done it more times than you can count. She started to feel light-headed. *This should not be so hard. Look at his hand. Remember he's married. Remember the past.* Liv looked down. *Where the heck was his ring? Ugh. She hated married men who didn't wear their rings. They were so darned confusing.* She let her focus go back to those liquid eyes of his, and he smiled. Liv clenched her fists at her sides so as not to fan herself at the sight of his gorgeous dimples popping into view. Lord, she'd nearly forgotten about those.

Dang it!

"Yes, ma'am. I will say that they definitely do. It's good to see you again, Livia."

Livia? Why all the nerve. To act all familiar and call her Livia as if he'd just seen her last holiday or something. As if they were still old friends. As if he'd just told her he loved her. Said he'd wait for her only to have her return to Sugar Lake to find him gone and moved on to a whole new life without an explanation or a word.

"Well, there you have it. In that at least we can agree on something today." Aunt Joyce was happily directing her remarks to Clayton and thankfully giving Liv something else to focus on besides drifting to a twelve-year-old past best forgotten. "And as for the rest, you can see with my nieces here I have more than enough help in the shop, so you don't have to go giving me unsolicited advice about working or not working in my so-called condition, not that I particularly have a condition."

It was Aunt Joyce mentioning her not quite condition that caused Liv to pull her attention away from Clayton's eyes and disarming dimples and bring her firmly to the problem at hand, and the situation they were supposedly there to remedy. "Speaking of," she said, "what is going on here, Aunt Joyce? What's with the fire trucks and all the uproar?"

Aunt Joyce waved an impatient hand in front of her face. "Oh, it's nothing, honey. Just a little fire in the kitchen." She cast a sharp eye Clayton's way. "Nothing to get in a twist about, even though our fire chief here seems to be getting quite knotted up about it."

"Now, Miss Joyce, you know any fire is a potentially serious situation. And I wouldn't be doing my job properly if I didn't look out for your safety."

Aunt Joyce rolled her eyes skyward. "Well, you just get on and keep doing that, Chief Morris. You do your mama and us taxpayers a good service taking everything so very seriously." It wasn't lost on Liv how mocking Aunt Joyce's tone was, and it brought to mind past minor feuds between Aunt Joyce and Clayton's mom, Mrs. Morris. It also wasn't lost on Liv the extra rich bass that had deepened the tone of Clayton's voice over the years or the immediate charge that it brought to the air around her.

But thankfully, or not, Aunt Joyce continued. "Like I said, this is all a little bit of nothing. I will have the oven checked out thoroughly and see what's going on with the temperature controls. I know what I set that oven to, and there was no way that thing should've gotten out of whack like it did. You know me, I've never had any sort of incident like that in my kitchen, and I make that same batch of pies often, so something must've just gone faulty. No worries, I will get it straight. I'll have Errol come by and give it a good looking at."

"Well, just be sure that you do," Clayton said, his voice stern, and Liv noted his eyes full of concern as he looked at Aunt Joyce.

But her aunt was having none of it. "Now, if you

don't mind, can you just move on and get all these overgrown boys and equipment out of my place? It is definitely not good for business. You will have folks thinking I really have a problem. And you know I don't need that with tourist season just starting to heat up. Heck, people nowadays practically live on the Internet and that Yelp."

Liv watched the corner of Clayton's lip quirk up. "Yes, ma'am. We'll be out of your way in no time," Clayton said.

He turned back toward her and Drea. "It really is good to see the both of you."

"Oh really, is that so? The both of us?" Drea chimed in coyly.

Seriously? The itch to reach out and give Drea a good pinch as if they were middle schoolers was coming on strong and hard.

Clayton seemed amused by this, and once again his dimples came into view as he nodded his head. "Yes, both of you," but he turned toward Liv. "Though I am especially happy to see an old friend back in town."

Do not blush. Do not blush. Put it on repeat and keep it there, Liv.

She forced her expression to stay neutral as she tried to keep her voice in the neutral zone too. "I won't be around too long. Just helping out Aunt Joyce in the shop for a bit, then it's back to the city for me. But it was nice seeing you today too." *See, that wasn't so hard.* She could do this. She could play it cool. She was an adult now, doing adultlike things. First hurdle, the most unexpected, and probably the hardest, was done. The rest of her time in Sugar Lake would be a piece a cake. Besides, she'd probably never even run into him after today. With any luck, he'd live on the other side of town and not visit his mother all that often. He was grown and no doubt a busy man, with a kid and a wife. Sugar Lake was clearly a growing and bustling town. Being the fire chief had to keep him hopping. There was no reason to get her knickers in a twist over running into Clayton Morris. A one-off was a one-off.

"Oh Clayton, before you go, just so you don't think I'm the worst grouch in town, you take a few pies for you and the boys back to the station. And I'll be seeing you tomorrow with my usual honey order, right?"

Tomorrow? Usual order? What was happening?

Clayton turned Aunt Joyce's way and gave her a nod. "Yes, ma'am. Tomorrow it is. Unless you want me to bring any by after my shift tonight."

"No need," Aunt Joyce replied. "Rena has done all the shopping, and you put in a long-enough day. I have enough to get me through the morning's baking. You give Hope and your mama my regards tonight. I'll see you tomorrow."

And with that Liv's mind did catapults and a few summersaults as Clayton's guys quickly packed up and made their way out of the shop. Then after one last sweep of the shop, Clayton left with a wave and a smile and, not to mention, an arm full of pies.

Liv bit back a groan. Yeah, so much for not running into him. From the way Aunt Joyce was talking, it seemed as if she'd be practically living next door to Clayton Morris.

Wait. Would she really be living next door to Clayton Morris? Again. There was no way a grown man like him was back in town and back to living with his mama. Was there? Why, he was a fireman. And a good-looking, strapping one at that. Of course he'd have his own place. Goodness. She wasn't thrilled about the thought of his wife, but she wouldn't wish having to live with his mama on the poor woman. Saying Mrs. Morris could be a tinge prickly was putting it mildly. She must be thinking crazy. There was no way Clayton was back living next door with his mom, and that was final.

Chapter 5

"So I see you New York girls still bringing the heat!" The Gale sisters turned toward the booming sound of their cousin Rena Goode's voice. "The big city comes to town and our place practically burns to the ground!"

"Hey, don't blame that on us, cousin," Liv said as she wagged a finger and gave Rena a grin. She would have given her cousin a hug, but this time it was Drea who beat her in the race toward their family member's open arms.

"Look at you, all grown up and everything," Rena said to Drea as she gave her a quick assessment. "Looking good, girl. I like what you got going on with your hair. Those twists are banging."

"Thanks, cousin, you're looking good yourself," Drea said, and she wasn't lying. Rena did look good and still so very Rena. Never one for downplay. She was wearing tight, ankle-skimming jeans and a white shirt tied in a knot to accentuate her small waist and amply curved hips. There were quite a few buttons undone on her top to show off the red lace camisole that she was wearing underneath, which matched her red plastic hoops perfectly, but clashed with her bright purple lips. Her hair was piled high in tousled, wild curls on top her head. The only bit of comfort Rena seemed to allow herself were the high-top retro-style sneakers on her feet.

Rena turned her gaze from Drea to Liv. She raised a brow, which made Liv feel immediately self-conscious and wonder what she was thinking. In true Goode woman blunt form, she didn't have to wait long to find out. "And look at you, Miss Fancy. Check you out."

Liv frowned. She didn't think that was quite a compliment the way Rena said it. Even with the smile. "And how am I supposed to take that?" Liv asked.

"Take it well, cousin," Rena said. "Girl, you are looking great. Like a stack of new money. Like you could take over a corporation at any moment. But I always knew you would do good for yourself. There was never any doubt about that. You were always a smart one." She grinned wide and waggled her brows. "And don't think I didn't notice Clayton Morris bringing up the rear of the departing firemen. Arms full of pies and smile as wide as Sugar Lake. I bet that's due to you, Miz Livy."

Liv pulled back sharply and gave Rena a frown. "What would Clayton's smile have to do with me? I'd think he'd be saving any smiles for his wife."

Rena gave a smirk, and Aunt Joyce started to laugh as she came forward with two bowls of bread pudding and ice cream handing them to Liv and Drea. It had been ages since Liv had bread pudding and she was already salivating but Rena pulled her attention away with her next comment.

"What wife?" Rena said. "You mean the one that off and ran out on him and his daughter to find herself? Whatever in the world that means."

Liv blinked, pudding spoon poised by her open mouth.

Rena nodded.

"From what I hear it had been over for quite a while," Aunt Joyce said, picking up the story. "According to his mama, his wife just up and was gone one day. Said she wasn't cut out for marriage. I don't think Delia is any bit torn up about it. Though that poor child of his was devastated. And when Clayton's dad passed away and his mama fell ill last year, Clayton made the decision to head back home and help her out over leaving her with that house to tend on her own. It wasn't like his brother was being all that much of a help. Poor thing he just hasn't been himself since he's returned home from serving. Still he don't have to put his mama to worrying like he does." She let out a weary sigh then as if the whole sordid mess exhausted her to tell it.

Liv was stunned. Her mother filled her in on practically all the happenings in Sugar Lake. How could she leave out a juicy story like this one?

But once again, Rena picked up the story getting right to the bottom line. "So you see, the Clayton Morris field is all clear. That is, if you have any interest."

Liv got her wits about her and gave her cousin a sharp look. "Now, why would I have any interest in that direction?"

Rena tilted her head and curled her lip in response. "You did say you looked at him and your eyes are working, right?" She put her hand to Liv's chest. "Are you breathing? Are you dead? Why would anybody not have any interest? The man is fine with an O and not an I, is all I'm saying."

Liv shook her head. "Well, say all you want. That

ship has long sailed. I'm here to see family and help Aunt Joyce. Clayton Morris is a nonfactor in my plans."

"That's her story and she's sticking to it," Drea said, hardly able to keep the giggle out of her voice.

"Oh, shut up, you," Liv said as Rena joined in on the giggles.

Suddenly Rena sobered and looked from her cousins to Aunt Joyce. "Wait, help Aunt Joyce? She's got me." She turned to Aunt Joyce then. "Did you call them? Do you really need more help?"

Oh goodness. Would she and Drea's being here insult Rena? She didn't want to put her cousin out or put Aunt Joyce in an awkward situation with their presence.

"Rena, you know we can use some extra hands here in the shop," Aunt Joyce chimed in. "You're as busy as a one-armed paperhanger chasing after those children of yours. I do appreciate all your help and you know it, but your focus can't be in a million places all at once, and with me being slowed down because of this bum hip and tourist season picking up, we just need a little bit more help in the shop."

Rena's smooth smile instantly slid into a frown, causing Aunt Joyce to continue. "Now, don't go getting your lips twisted, gal. You know we need the help, and I can't rely on strangers to do it. It's no disrespect to you."

"Oh, it definitely isn't," Liv chimed in. She looked down and then back up at her cousin. "And besides, I was kind of looking for a bit of a break from the city for a while. Not to mention I get to spend time with you guys."

Rena looked skeptical for a moment, but thankfully her cell rang, diverting her attention. Reaching into her back pocket, she let out a growl after glancing at the screen. "That blang it Troy. He's been blowing up my phone nonstop after having the nerve to hang out with his boys at those clubs out on 77 till well past three a.m. the other night. Like I don't know ain't nothing but wild women with wrecked weaves out at that hour." She shook her head, and Liv and Drea glanced at each other, then over to Aunt Joyce, who just gave Rena a pot meet kettle once-over that said her point was proven.

Rena shrugged. "Well, he's just going to have to suffer a little longer. He needs to know that our money is not for flossing at the club, but for shining bright over at the gas and light company." She smiled wide. "If he don't learn easy, I'll make him learn hard. Shoot, I got my cousins in town from New York now!"

"Oh, he definitely is," Drea chimed, in agreement.

Liv's eyes went wide as she started to shake her head.

"Oh, don't start with your fuddy-duddy ways even before the party has begun, sister dear," Drea said. "Our cousin here is in need of a pick-me-up, and we are just the people to give it to her. Looks like we've come just in time."

"If you recall, we're here to help Aunt Joyce with the shop, not help Rena get back at her man," Liv corrected.

"Hey, don't let me stop you young folks from getting into some good old mess," Aunt Joyce said, chiming in. "Just so long as you remember to get to work on time, I have no problem with it. Rena, get on in there and see if we can't set things straight for the day. I'd like to go and get the girls settled in at the house, if you don't mind."

"Yes, ma'am," Rena said.

"We don't mind pitching in now if you need some help setting up," Liv said.

But Rena shooed them off. "There will be plenty of time for that. You two go on and get settled." She glanced at Aunt Joyce. "And maybe get her off her feet for a bit too. I'll be seeing you later. I'm sure the whole family will be stopping by at some point to welcome you."

It was then that Aunt Joyce started to laugh. "Oh yes. Come on and let's get you girls settled at the house. I can't wait to call Kath and tell her that you're in town. She's gonna be just about bursting with jealousy when she hears you're staying with me."

"Now, don't go in on Aunt Kath. No need to get her riled for nothing."

Aunt Joyce snorted. "When have I ever been the riling type?"

They started off slowly, Liv offering to bring the car up, but Aunt Joyce insisting that the short walk up the street to the car would do her good and make her doctor happy. Liv now took the more leisurely moment out on Main Street to take a look at just how much things had changed in the sleepy town. It would seem Sugar Lake was definitely starting to wake up. There was now a large CVS on the corner where Baker's dress shop used to be. Next to that, she could see there was a trendy-looking art gallery. But Liv was happy to see there was still a hardware store, though it didn't look to still be run by the Millers and had been converted to one of the bigger chain franchises.

"Hey, at least the old ice-cream shop is still here. That's good to see," Liv said, pointing toward the bakeshop's near neighbor and friendly rivals in sweet treats. She, her siblings, and their cousins would go to get a fifty-cent scoop as a rare treat when their uncle Clint was feeling splurgy. Also when he was feeling brave enough to sneak them over since it was a half unwritten rule that pies and cobblers ruled in the Goode family.

Suddenly, Liv's mind drifted to the memory of sharing a cool cone on a hot day with Clayton Morris. She was coming out of the shop with her ice cream, and he was walking beside her, asking if he could have a taste. Lord, those words alone, coming from his lips, just about had her teen self melting right there on the pavement faster than the ice cream. Liv shook her head to clear it. Did she ever really stand a chance when it came to him?

"Yep, it's still there," Aunt Joyce said. "The Clemenses were ready to sell and move to Miami when their daughter up and married a rich"—she snapped her fingers in the air—"what do they call them with the man buns?"

"Hipster?" Drea said, and Aunt Joyce nodded.

"Yes, that's it. Hipster type who for some reason thought living out his life scooping ice cream would be the best thing since sliced bread." Aunt Joyce let out a bit of a huff then. "A bit too friendly for me though. All that smiling, and I'm all for helpfulness but, I don't know. There's something about that hairdo of his I just don't trust."

Drea laughed at that. "Man buns can be cute on the right guy, Aunt Joyce."

Aunt Joyce snorted. "Says you. And I suppose I'd look good in a Mohawk."

"Wait a minute," Liv cut in on what she suspected was about to turn into a heated debate on male versus female acceptable grooming between Drea and Aunt

Joyce. "You mean Deidre Clemens, that rough gal you and Aunt Kath used to go on about, the one who used to chase Brent around. She took over the ice-cream shop?" Liv asked.

Aunt Joyce shook her head no, but responded with the opposite. "Yep, that's the one. She ran off, disappeared for a good two years, leaving both her parents wondering where in the world she got to. We all were sure she'd joined up with a cult or some such thing. But no. She came back with a husband who seemed pretty much just as flighty as she was. But shock to us and her long-suffering parents, the flighty husband was loaded. He is an ex-Internet guy who'd cashed in. So she, the husband, and their baby moved in with Rick and Lucy Clemens. They darn near drove Rick and Lucy out of their minds in that little bungalow of theirs." Aunt Joyce got wistful. "I do miss Lucy, though. Miami is so far and we shared so many laughs over coffee during the quiet times. She loved coming and sitting a spell with me, and vice versa. I could always count on her and Rick when the chips were down. Rick was like a second brother the way he watched over me. They'd even watch the shop when I'd be in a pinch. Yeah, you don't come across friends like that every day."

It was then that two older women walked out of Cartland's Cart-Away grocery next door to the ice-cream shop. "Hey there, Joyce, looks like you're getting around real good," one of them said to Aunt Joyce, though her eyes were clearly trying to figure out who Liv and Drea were, while the other woman was much less circumspect in her perusal. She didn't even go in with pleasantries.

"Who's this you got here with you, Joyce?" the other

woman asked, getting right to the point of identifying the strangers in town.

Aunt Joyce quickly pulled herself up to her full height, barely putting any weight on her cane as she gave the women a regal smile. "Lottie, Liz, you both must remember my nieces from New York, Anne's girls, Olivia and Alexandrea. Why, when they heard that I was not feeling well, can you believe the both of them got in the car right away and just hightailed it down here to see about me? Silly girls. Both takin' time out of their busy schedules, and away from their jobs, to come and see their aunt. I told them it was unnecessary, but there was no hearing it. Now, how lucky am I?"

The women looked at each other skeptically in that covert southern way, but covered it with polite smiles. "Oh, bless their hearts. You sure are a lucky woman," the first woman said. "I can barely get my kids to visit now that they've moved to Atlanta."

"A shame," Aunt Joyce said, her voice full of sympathy.

"And mine are always underfoot, but around doesn't necessarily mean they are of any help," the other woman chimed in.

"Don't I know it," Aunt Joyce agreed. "Well, we have to be off. So much catching up to do." She smiled wide. "But I'll be seeing you girls, that is, when I have the time."

The ladies gave Aunt Joyce tight smiles and then smiled at Liv and Drea, the both of them expressing pleasantries and good-byes.

"You know, you really were laying it on a bit thick there, Aunt Joyce," Drea said as she got into the car.

Aunt Joyce shrugged. "Eh, it's expected. Besides, I

have to listen to them go on day in and day out about their kids, their husbands, their bunions. At the least this way, with you all in town, they will be a little bit jealous and steer clear of me for a while. It'll be nice to not have to hear them yapping." Aunt Joyce grinned wider. "See, you girls are already doing me a huge favor."

Liv shook her head and started up the ignition. "We aim to please."

Clayton Morris was all riled up. Normally a trip to Goode 'N Sweet was a nice and calming experience, one that left him with a sense of the community he loved and a sweet treat on top of it. But today with the fire and then running into Olivia Gale . . . calm was the furthest thing from his mind. Sure, Joyce Goode could be, at times, what some would describe as prickly, but Clayton knew that once you looked beyond her quills, she was essentially soft and sweet with a gooey interior. Much like her delicious sticky cream puffs. Though try as he might, he couldn't even be distracted by a sticky cream puff today. His mind was in a whirl because any fire, even a small one and no matter how minor, or how much Miss Joyce tried to dismiss it, should give them pause. She *was* getting older, but still, it was unlike her to make a mistake. For as long as he'd known her, which was pretty much most of his life, she'd never made any type of mistake. Especially not when it came to her ovens, not in her kitchen. Miss Joyce was a master of baking precision, and she had the blue ribbons from all over the state to prove it. So he guessed he should be happy to see that she had reinforcements coming in.

But Clayton was anything but happy. No, he was distracted, was what he was. And agitated and a complete tangle of rambling incomplete emotions. Sure, he'd put on a good face, or at least he hoped he had back at the shop, but come on, how could he be happy coming face-to-face with Olivia Gale after all these years? For so long he'd thought of how he'd react if he ran into her again. The chances had been highly unlikely when he lived in California and she in New York. Gosh, distance was wonderful. And in all his mental scenarios he'd play it cool and would hide his regret behind an easygoing smile while she'd be happy in her new life. Moved on well past him with a successful corporate type dude on her arm. He would smile and be happy for her. Or at least pretend to be. It would all be cordial and brief, they'd part with a peaceful closure, and never to see each other again. As the years went by, Clayton stopped playing that scene over in his head and let the image fade.

Not once, for some stupid reason, had he imagined anything like today happening, and the possibility of her being back here in Sugar Lake. So close that he could reach out and touch her. And with a gaze so piercing and direct, he could tell immediately that, though time and distance had kept them apart all these years, time had done nothing to cause Livy to forget or forgive the fact that he wasn't there that summer she returned to Sugar Lake, expecting to see him and expecting him to make good on the promises he'd made to her the summer before.

"Hey, Chief, you gettin' out of your truck, or you going to sit in there all day?"

The sound of Braxton Lewis's voice, his second-in-command, pulled Clayton out of his melancholy reverie and back into the present day. Embarrassed at being caught daydreaming, he quickly picked up his cell, pretending to be engrossed in sending a text. He nodded, fiddling with his phone for a moment more before getting out of his truck.

Finally, Clayton hopped out of the cab trying his best to force the image of Olivia Gale to a recessed corner in the back of his mind as he reached for the stack of pies from Miss Joyce.

"So, the lady gave you something sweet for this morning's trouble?" Braxton said, stepping toward him from the side of the smaller fire truck, which was not yet fully back into its loading dock.

"What?" Clayton asked, at first not fully catching Lewis's meaning. "Oh, yeah. That she did."

Lewis took the pies from his hand, leaving him free to gather the rest of his gear.

"Yep, seems, fair," Lewis mumbled from over Clay's shoulder. "By the way, did you happen to catch the beauties who came in to see her?"

Clay couldn't help his sudden pause. He swallowed, then tried to seamlessly and smoothly pick up his duffle as he turned back to Lewis, suddenly taking in the younger man's smooth skin and broad shoulders. His slightly annoying and too cocky grin.

"I did."

That grin went wider, and Lewis's brows waggled as Clay squelched down on the irrational need to snatch the pies back out of his hands. "They didn't look like tourists. Seemed like they knew old Miss Goode. You too. Are they kin to her?"

Clay had to remind himself to stay neutral. He was Lewis's superior and, though Lewis was a bit cocky, he was essentially harmless and one of his best men. Besides, what did it matter what he thought of either of Miss Joyce's nieces? "No, they aren't tourists, and yes, they are kin to Miss Joyce. Her nieces. They're here to help her out for a bit. And yes, I do know them." He probably didn't need to add that last bit, but for some reason it just came out. Which caused him to wonder if his response sounded as stern as it sounded in his own head. The answer came to him by the way Lewis quickly sobered and his grin disappeared.

He coughed. "Oh, ah. Knew them? I get it, Chief." Lewis frowned. "Which one?" Lewis looked down, then back up. Catching Clay's glare. "You're right, that doesn't matter."

Wait, did I answer out loud? Clay thought. He guessed he didn't have to.

Clay shook his head. "You going to take those pies to the back, or just stand here all day holding them?"

Lewis looked down, as if just then remembering he had his hands full. The smile was back. "Yeah, sure. Sorry about that. On it, boss." The gleam that had jumped back into Lewis's eyes, not to mention the fact that Clay caught no fewer than two other guys eyeing the boxes too, let Clayton know the pies would barely make it to the back pantry with their wrappings intact.

"You think those might make it till after lunch?" Clay yelled over Lewis's shoulder.

"Can't promise you that, boss."

Clayton held back a replying grunt as he made his way to his office at the opposite corner of the building. Shutting his door as quickly as he could, he was relieved by the solitude of his small office, and he let out a long breath as the muffled sounds of laughter, jibes, and the general camaraderie of the crew on the other side of the door made it faintly to his ears. Going around to his desk to take his seat, he first gave a glance out his window, which looked mostly onto the crew's parking area. But when he angled himself just right, he could also catch a glimpse of the passersby along Main Street and even see the old Redheart Theater, which now mostly ran only third-run movies and the occasional art-house pieces. It had long given up on the first-run features to the big multiplex out by the mall. Seeing the theater, his mind now of course immediately went to the times he'd been there on so-called dates with Liv. Frustrated, he told himself not to go there. Why waste the wandering energy? But the waste was in the fighting, as he leaned into it and for a brief moment smiled.

Never quite formal dates, they were always group things, but Clayton knew them for what they were, and suspected so did Liv by the way they always ended up seated together shoulders touching, fingers grazing over the large popcorn he'd bought with extra butter because he knew she loved it so much. He laughed to himself then. God, he'd always hated all that extra butter. Wasn't the biggest fan of popcorn either, but the off chance of his fingers meeting hers was worth the greasy mess of it all. Clayton focused his gaze as he craned his neck and could just make out the brown-and-pink awning of Goode 'N Sweet.

What was she doing back here, and why now? Yes, he knew the reasoning, and sure, it made total sense. Her aunt needed help, but Miss Joyce had Rena, and there were plenty of other Goodes in the area. Why her? Didn't she have a high-powered job that should be keeping her up in New York? Not to mention, what about a high-powered man who should be keeping her there too?

Clayton ran a hand over his close-shaved head. There was no use thinking about any of this right now. Nor was it any of his concern. Nothing besides this morning's fire and the pile of paperwork on his desk should be preoccupying him right now. He had files and budgets to go over and no time to worry about the Goodes or their problems. Now that Liv and her sister were in town, he was encouraged that there would be no more mistakes like the one Miss Joyce had made this morning. Anything else to do with Livia, well, that was in the past and long—or so he hoped—forgotten. His jaw clenched as once again the image of Liv and her sharp, way-too-direct gaze came to his mind's eye.

Was it really in the past though? And forgotten? That hope seemed now highly unlikely, he thought as he leaned back in his chair.

There was no denying the immediate effect seeing her had on him. The way his heart seemed to stop for a moment and then quickly pick up pace, thumping out of control. Or the way, for the first time in a long time, he felt the strangest stirrings of excitement and a silly, irrational desire to smile.

Clayton shook his head, hoping for some sort of clarity. Why should he smile over seeing her? It made no sense when every thought of her over the years only brought him intense feelings of regret and longing. She was the woman whom he'd always consider the one who got away. No, scratch that, the one he stupidly ran away from. Clayton knew that, deep down, he'd hoped he'd never see her again and have to face that fact. Despite all that, still today something in him bubbled up, filling him with inexpressible joy. He shook his head, trying to figure out a way to rally against his feelings.

Once again, he had no time and no place for them. He was a single father with a daughter on the edge of puberty who was this close to trying his last nerve. No, there was no room in his life for personal angst or joy or the thought of second chances. That was the stuff of boyish dreams. And he was a full-grown man; he turned into one the day he made the dumb decision to leave Sugar Lake and enlist in the army, supposedly to pick up where his brother left off. That decision to leave Sugar Lake and the dreams he and Livia made were the foundation of where he was now. It was best that he took it for what it was and stood true in it.

Chapter 6

Taking that left and going over the old Wee Dee Bridge and passing into what was considered the "old town" side of Sugar Lake made it officially feel like coming home for Liv. Where there were signs of modernization along Main Street and in town, once they went over the railroad tracks and crossed the bridge, that's when the first real view of the massive beauty of the lake came into focus and the true magic of the town took over. There was both a distinct buzz of excitement and a quiet stillness.

Sure, Liv had pointedly chosen to ignore the massive cell tower she passed along the way and the not-so-inconspicuous cable company building. It was just a part of modern living now, she supposed. But no matter. Right now it was all about the beauty of the lake. The sheer size of it, the fact that she could see a few fishing boats bobbing lazily, even at this late hour in the day. How amazing it seemed that people could be doing that while back in the city the mere thought of such a thing would be chuckled at over a conference room table, then secretly dreamed about.

As she drove, Liv remembered how she'd first

learned to swim off a dock out in those very waters, then the image, unbidden, immediately came to mind of her jumping off those same docks, hand in hand, with Clayton Morris. The chilly shock of the cool water was not even able to bring down the temperature of her overheated young heart. God, she was so trusting in those days. And yet here she was so ridiculously stupid to think that coming back wouldn't stir up better forgotten memories. How could she not have anticipated it? How could she not have anticipated him?

Driving as if by rote, Liv let the car go where it seemed to want to go, GPS not even necessary as her body tuned in to the changes of the terrain underneath the wheels. Things got wilder and a bit rockier as they went along the lake's winding roads, but that was parallel to life out here. Though it looked calm and serene, you never knew exactly what was going on underneath the ripples of the water or behind the picturesque homes and cabins that dotted the woods surrounding the lake.

Liv pulled up and around to the front of the house, which was oddly situated on its side to afford a view of both the lake and the oncoming road. This was a kind of genius on the great-grands' part since in their days the area was so heavily wooded, and times being what they were—heck, time still being what it is—you'd want to see whoever was coming onto your property well before they got there.

Getting out of the car, Liv smiled as she looked up at the large front porch, happy to see that the old swing was still there where her grandmother used to sit for hours while she rocked and shelled peas or shucked corn.

Their side of the lake was filled mostly with the originals, as they liked to call themselves. Early settlers of

Sugar Lake, Olivia's great-grands acquired the property back when no one saw the value of trudging through the rambling woods and rocky terrain in order to build their home. But now with new business coming to town that meant the potential for new residents. And looking out on the other side of the lake and the newly built McMansions, with their docks large enough to fit two or three boats at a time, they had to be running out of space quickly. Coming from New York where real estate envy was all too common she could just bet the view over to their side was starting to look mighty fine.

Built in the late 1800s, the Goode home was a mix of both farm and lake style with hints of Victorian in its wraparound porch. It had a prime lake location—more prime now, Liv was sure, since so many tourists were recently finding out about Sugar Lake. Being that the house itself backed up to the lake with a beautiful, level yard going down to the old dock and a couple of acres going out the other way, well, it was something to behold.

Liv hurried around the car to take Aunt Joyce's arm to lead her up the few stairs to the porch while Drea pulled out some of their bags. "How in the world have you been handling the stairs every day?" she asked while her aunt gripped the old wooden railing tightly.

Aunt Joyce shook her head. "It's not so bad, honey. I only have to do it twice a day. Besides, exercise is on my prescription list from the doctor, so it's good for me to do this. Not to mention physical therapy. Which I'd like to know when I have time for while running the shop?"

Liv didn't think of this. "Well, we're here now, so you'll be able to make time for it."

Aunt Joyce pulled a face as well as pulled her arm

away. "Now, don't go getting too far ahead of yourself, missy."

Liv laughed and regripped Aunt Joyce's arm. "Oh, don't start, Aunty. We're here to help, so you might as well accept it."

Aunt Joyce gave a begrudging grunt, but there was a hint of a smile at the corners of her mouth as she did so.

They made it up to the porch, and Aunt Joyce let out a long, slightly winded breath before she went to open the door. She stepped inside, letting the sisters follow. Taking in the sight and smell of the old, familiar living room, Liv let it envelop her senses in its familiarity. There was the matching love seat and sofa set astonishingly now sans plastic, from Bradford's Family Furniture, a store long since shuttered, but popular down here back in the day. She could still recall how happy her grandmother was to get these new pieces and how proud she was to show them off to her friends and neighbors who came to view them as if it was an event. And yes, there was still the heavy oak coffee table and side tables, made by her great-grandfather, just because he could, and lamps from when she was in elementary school. Liv was glad to see, though, that the old, ditzy wallpaper had been taken down and replaced by fresh-looking creamy-white paint and that the heavy drapes that used to block out so much of the sun had been changed into light-as-air, barely there sheers that would let in the breeze from the lake. She inhaled deeply, taking in the smell of the lake mixed with the house, the smell of coffee, and the scent of Aunt Joyce's honey biscuits, which always seemed to linger in the air.

How Aunt Joyce ended up with the family house was pretty much, as most of these things seem to go, by default. But unlike some families it hadn't caused too much animosity between the siblings. Their uncle Clint, he moved out to Sweet Bluff, not far, but in its day considered a better area for starting a family. And their Aunt Kath went on with her husband, and they live on the ritzy—well, ritzy at the time—Cocoa Estates on the other side of the lake. Her house was visible through the attic window. Then there was their mom. She broke everyone's hearts when she went and married their father and moved to the scary, wild north to follow their father's work. So, with Aunt Joyce being the last sibling standing, so to speak, and living in the house after the grandparents passed on, it just sort of fell into her hands.

She'd never married, though it's been said that she'd dodged quite a few offers. And she stated that she was happy to tend to the house and the shop to keep it safe for future generations. Liv for one was grateful to her for it. At times, she wondered if it was a sacrifice that Aunt Joyce felt was truly worth it. Especially now that she'd had to call all the way to New York to get help in her time of need. Suddenly Liv got an odd pang of both understanding and fear. Would this be her not so many short years from now? Possibly calling to Drea or Elijah for help from her apartment in New York? The mental picture it brought to mind didn't give her a view half as happy as the one she was seeing reflected in the eyes of Aunt Joyce right now.

"Well, you girls are home now," Aunt Joyce said, pulling Liv out of her thoughts. "And while you're here, I want you to truly consider this your home. I have extra sets of keys for each of you, so you can come and go as you please. You know I'm not big on formalities around here. And I know you both are grown, so I won't be checking up on you." She turned and gave Liv a pointed look. "Not too close."

Liv pulled back. "What's that about? Why are you looking at me?"

"Yeah, why are you looking at her?" Drea chimed in from over her shoulder.

Liv should have felt partially relieved at that comment, but it was in no way a compliment and she knew it.

Aunt Joyce feigned a shocked expression. "Who says I'm looking at you? Why should I be? I'm not saying my memory is long. But it sure ain't short is all I'm saying too."

Liv let out a groan. "How about we just focus on that hip of yours and the future and keep memories where they belong, in the past? Cool?"

Aunt Joyce chuckled as she swatted a hand in the air. "Cool? If you say so, sweetie. Oh, how I'm going to love having you young people around for a while."

It was Liv who was laughing and head shaking again a few minutes later as she stepped into the upstairs bedroom she used to share with Drea when they would visit as kids. Once again, the lack of change took her on a quick mental trip back in time. The large-print floral wallpaper was the same, just a little bit more faded, and the same twin brass beds they'd slept on as kids, separated by the small wooden nightstand, still sat opposite the white dresser. The only change was that now it was not missing only one knob, but three or four.

As she made an attempt to stay grounded in the here and now, Liv made a mental note to stop in the hardware store and pick up dresser knobs. She could at least do that. She reached out and ran a hand across the dresser. It came back spotless. Wow. Missing knobs or not, her aunt had done her best to clean and prepare this room for them, even with her bad hip. She let out a frustrated sigh. Aunt Joyce shouldn't have done that. Not in her condition. She hoped she'd gotten someone to help her with the cleaning and hadn't risked injuring herself by doing it on her own. But as quickly as Liv thought it, she knew Aunt Joyce hadn't arranged any help. The woman was a powerhouse and stubborn as all get-out. Of course she'd done her own cleaning, risk of injury or not.

Liv turned from the dresser and looked up as a soft breeze hit her face, and she got a glimpse of the light curtains as they fluttered. As if by instinct, on slow, quiet feet she walked over to the window, pushed aside the ruffled fringed curtains, and looked out. There it was, not close enough to touch, but definitely close enough for a short walk over. Clayton Morris's house. Well, his mom's house, and now apparently the house where he was living again too. Glancing across and slightly to the left, taking in the closed, nondescript cream curtains, she wondered if he still used that room. Back in their day the curtains had never been closed, and oh, how many days and nights did she spend sitting on this little padded ledge just waiting for the moment when he would appear? Liv blinked, suddenly wanting to break away from her useless, frustrating thoughts. She stepped back from the window, desperate for distance.

Goodness, if she could not get a grip on even being near his house, how would she deal with seeing him in town? *Get over yourself, woman.*

But the words rang hollow in her mind as they melded with images of growing through the years. All her growth spurts happened over the summers here at Sugar Lake, with the warm southern sun seeming to coax her limbs along their journey. From child to girl to young woman. As she'd run barefoot through the grass, an unheard-of luxury back in New York. Bare feet? That was so unlike her. Now that she thought of it, it was only something she'd wanted to do when she was here. But along the way, during those summers that her mother would come down to spend some time to visit with her family, and Daddy would follow later, there was always Clayton. The little boy who'd lived next door. By sheer proximity he was enlisted with the task of entertaining the city kids come to the country for a visit every year. His older brother was there too, but Clayton being closer in age, only one year older than Liv, he was the lucky—or perhaps, unlucky—one constantly pressed into service.

When they were little it was just thrown-together backyard games of tag, kick the can, and hide-and-seek, but as they got older she didn't quite remember when she started to anticipate those summer visits. And more important, seeing Clayton Morris again. It must have been when the games changed, and it was no longer hide-and-go-seek, but catch me if you can.

Liv let out a frustrated snort. Is this what happens when closure never happens, or worse, you carry a ridiculous adolescent torch for way too long? Jeeze, she was so too old for this. And besides, she was five minutes past broken up with Damon, and she didn't even have her TV or the money for it back yet. She frowned, not sure if she should laugh over what this line of thought said about the state of that relationship or the time spent in it.

"So you're going to sleep in this room?" Drea's voice pulled her up short and had her spinning her head around and away from the Morris house.

"Where else am I sleeping? Why? Where are you sleeping?"

Drea gave her a grin and a shrug. "Hey, you have at it. If you don't mind sleeping in one of these skinny little twin beds. But if you haven't noticed it's just you and me now, and only Aunt Joyce here. Finally, we're here without Mom, Dad, or Elijah. The other bedrooms are free and clear. I'm going to sleep in the bedroom where Mom and Dad usually sleep. I'm stretching out."

Liv started to object, but in that moment she decided she didn't have the strength to put her back into it. The day had already been long enough. She glanced toward the window once again and looked over at the big, white rambling lake house across from theirs. She should fight with her sister and move to the other bedroom. At least that way she wouldn't be haunted by this view of the past. She'd have enough thoughts of Clayton as she traveled back and forth through town; she didn't need this daily wake-up reminder. Liv turned back to Drea and opened her mouth when something stopped the intended words in her throat. "You know what, you have at it. Live it up, girl. But don't come running to me when you're missing me. I'll be good here. Besides, I can use the other bed to spread out my clothes and things."

Drea grinned and then frowned as if a case of conscience was trying to catch hold. "Are you sure? I know you think I'm selfish, so we can flip a coin or thumb wrestle for the other room if you want."

Liv shook her head at the sweet gesture. "That's not necessary. You take it, it's fine."

Just then, Aunt Joyce's voice came from downstairs at the same time they heard the sound of a car pulling up in the driveway. Drea went to the window and angled her neck to get a better view of who was coming. "You girls come on and get down here. Seems the word is gotten out and here comes ol' Kath. I knew it wouldn't take her but a hot minute to get on over here when she heard the news," Aunt Joyce said. "And you might want to put on a sweater because I'm sure she's bringing a storm."

Liv and Drea looked at each other with skeptical expressions. "Did those two ever get along?" Drea asked.

Liv sighed. "I don't think so. At least not that I can remember. Come on, let's go. Might as well see what we've gotten ourselves into." She hooked her arm through Drea's, clearly surprising her sister with her wide-eyed expression. "How about we show them a united front and let them see how the northern sisters do it."

Drea pulled a face. "If you say so. But you think we can pull it off?"

Liv tugged at her arm. "Just come on. You're the one who's supposed to be the actor in the family."

"Hey, Aunt Kath," Liv said as she and Drea came down the stairs by way of greeting, but she momentarily froze midflight when she caught sight of her aunt and the other folks she had with her. Not only was Aunt Katherine, formally Goode, now Howell, looking up at them with her clearly assessing gaze, but so was her husband, Uncle Cole, and their cousin Pearl, formally Howell now Gleason, and Pearl's two little girls. Oh well, the gang was all there.

The air practically crackled around them as everyone was silent for a moment while the little troupe eyed the familial delegates from New York. Aunt Kath's gaze was cold and unreadable. Her countenance was very much a mirror image of their own mother's, except Aunt Katherine's complexion was lighter, sort of a buttery yellow with the smattering of freckles that she sported on her otherwise unblemished skin, where their mother's was more of a soft cocoa brown. Liv watched as her aunt's eyes roved over Liv from her head to her toes, then they went over to Drea, down to her feet and then back up to Drea's head. No doubt Aunt Kath had just made her own quick judgments about where the two had been, what they had been doing over the past ten to twelve years, and how they had faired during that time. All of this, she was sure, would be relayed as a direct reflection on how their mom and dad had done with raising them. The phone lines would soon be burning up between here and New York and the rest of the county as she spouted her opinions.

Finally, a flicker of light flashed in her eyes. "What's with the 'Hey, Aunt Kath'? Y'all acting like you ain't been away way too long to be respectable. What you doing standing all the way back there? Get up in here close and let me have a look at you. Give me a proper hug! It's a shame how long it's been since you've been home. I could shake your mama." She said the biting words with a smile firmly in place. Her coral-colored lipstick barely budged, but Liv still couldn't help but bristle at the obvious dig at her mother.

"You're right, it sure is. And it's a shame you all have never made it up to New York to see us. I know my mom would have loved for you to accept one of her many invitations. We particularly missed you at our graduations." She knew she'd probably pay for it later, but Liv couldn't help giving a little push back. She was her mother's daughter, and like her father always said, "It wasn't like the road only worked one way," although at times it seemed like it.

Aunt Kath blinked, obviously surprised by Liv's comeback. "Oh, we are sorry we missed them, but all that congestion in the city is just no good for my delicate respiratory system. I know your mother understands."

Liv frowned, but nodded and decided to let Aunt Kath off the hook. "Well it would seem, delicate or not, you're no worse for the wear. How is it that time has stood still for you? You haven't changed a bit or aged a day. I have to spend a little time learning your secrets so I can work on stopping the clock now too."

Her words had the desired effect, and Aunt Kath gave her first genuine smile as she giggled. "Oh, stop, Livy. Flattering your old aunt won't get you anywhere. I'm still going to be angry over finding out about you two being in town from the local gossips." She turned toward Aunt Joyce with a hard glare. "I suppose you thought you were doing something smart by keeping the secret from me, Joyce. Well, you weren't." She gave a curt head nod, then turned back toward Liv and Drea, reaching her arms up and making a gesture for them to come closer. "Oh well, no matter, you all are here now and we're going to make the best of it. Joyce had her little moment, and now that's done. We will get to welcoming you in a proper Goode family way."

She didn't know whether it was a groan, but Liv suspected it was and that it came from over where Aunt Joyce was by the kitchen.

"Come on, now, don't overwhelm the gals, Katherine," their uncle Cole said from Aunt Kath's side. "I'm sure they want to get settled. We don't want to make too much fanfare out of things."

"Yes, Uncle Cole," Liv said. "We really are happy to see you all, but please don't make a big deal out of our

being here. We just want to help out in the shop a bit
and have a little visit with the family. It's no big deal."

"I'd say it's not," came the voice from by the entrance
to the living room.

"And it's good to see you too, Pearl," Liv said, turning her gaze to her cousin, Aunt Kath and Uncle
Cole's oldest daughter. Pearl was older than Liv by a
mere ten months, and Rena was only a year and a half
older than that. They were always compared to stair
steps when they were kids. A fact that Pearl hated
because she never liked being wedged in the middle
of anyone. Period.

Being Aunt Kath's oldest and most entitled child,
Pearl seemed to think the sun rose and set with the
fluttering open and closing of her eyes every morning
and night. Or at least that was a running joke within
the family. It would also seem, from her comment,
that nothing in her sunny demeanor had changed.
Still in true Pearl form, she put on her best, local
beauty queen fake smile and laughed. "Oh, cousin,
you know I'm just playing with you. Bless your heart,"
she said, and held out both her arms as she walked
forward toward Liv and Drea, taking them both in her
ample arms and giving them a tight squeeze.

Pearl's skin was like her mother's, a beautiful and
unblemished light buttercream hue, and her eyes
were a pale hazel passed on from her father's side of
the family. She still seemed to carry on with her home-
coming beauty queen airs, though now she was hitting
the thirty mark, married, and a mother of two. And
by the looks of the swollen belly she was showing off
in her minidress, number three would be making an
appearance in a few months.

"Oh, I know you're just playing," Liv said. "It's good

to see you, Pearl. And looking so wonderful. When are you due?"

Pearl rolled her eyes skyward. "Can you believe I still have three and a half more months to go? This one here is gonna be the linebacker that Terrence has been hoping for. He's a big one and has me constantly on the go. But like I told Terrence, after this I am done. It's tubes tied up in a tidy bow for me. I've got my little angels, Tiffany and Taylor. And with this little one, my Tegan, coming on, my set will be complete."

Liv heard a groan from over her shoulder. This time she knew it was Drea. She tried as inconspicuously as she could to give her sister a small poke in the ribs, but she missed the mark when Drea anticipated her and slipped out of the way. "Three Ts, huh? Like Tony! Toni! Toné! You trying to start a singing group?" Drea said with a straight face, but Liv could see the laughter in her eyes.

Pearl totally missed the joke and gave Drea a look that was serious. "Oh, no, I wouldn't have my kids going into anything as trite as entertainment, at least not that form of entertainment. Not this little man here." She rubbed her belly. "He will be All-State just like his father, and then hopefully he'll go to the pros. Heaven knows his father could've done it if not for his injuries. And as for my girls, who knows, the world is open for them. There's Miss Georgia, Miss America, Miss USA, and then Miss Universe. The sky is the limit." With that comment, the littlest of Pearl's mini-me's looked up at her with sparkling, blue-shadowed eyes.

"I'm gonna be Miss Georgia like you, Mama?" little Tiffany said. She was looking a might bit grubby around the edges of her mouth, as if she'd just wrestled with a blue Popsicle and the Popsicle had won. However, Liv knew by the annual holiday recap letter and card she got from Pearl that when done up, little Miss Tiff was an all-out *Toddlers and Tiaras* wannabe . . . when she put her heart in it.

"Now, baby, Mama wasn't Miss Georgia, but you sure will be if I have any say so in it." She looked back at Liv with a wide grin. "Like I said, the sky's the limit."

"As long as you're looking toward the sky." Liv forced out a smile, one coming more easily when she looked down at little Tiffany. Tiffany looked like a happy and well-adjusted child. She didn't have any right to judge how her cousin raised her.

It was then that the front door opened. "Hey now! Ain't that just like New Yorkers to try to slip into town undercover. Y'all think you're slick?"

Liv swallowed down on a groan.

"Hey, Brent, it's good to see you," Liv said as Brent walked forward, then gave her a hug. His cologne clung to her nostrils a moment after he pulled back.

"It's good to see you. Been way too long."

She nodded as she looked at Aunt Kath's and Uncle Cole's youngest. Sure, Liv knew she should not go in for judging her cousin Brent Howell when she hadn't seen him in years, but even as a kid he was a bit of a slippery one. Running with the bad boys and getting into all sorts of scrapes, but just quick-tongued enough to always skirt out of trouble. When the other kids would end up punished, no, not Brent. No matter whether he was the ring leader or not. And from what Liv had heard from her mom through the grapevine over the years, little had changed. Not that you could tell from the looks of him. Gone were the oversized T-shirts and low-slung baggy jeans he used to wear as a teen. Today he wore a well-tailored suit paired with an open-collar shirt. His high-top fade thankfully had been cut low and cropped close, and his face was clean shaven except for a well-trimmed, thin mustache that Liv decided rode a fine line between dastardly and suave. Either way it suited him, so it was cool. But still, just like in the old days, something about her cousin gave off that air of selling you overpriced insurance or hitting you up for twenty bucks that you'd never see again.

Liv almost snorted out loud when it was Drea who, as if reading her thoughts, beat her to the punch. "Hey there, Brent," she said. "You are looking like new money in that suit. What, you hit the lotto or something? Let me hold twenty bucks."

Brent was momentarily stunned by Drea's boldness and totally taken off guard. She grinned then, letting him know it was a joke, but the intent was clear. Game knew game, and I had to respect her move.

"Wowza, little cuz," he finally said. "What they feeding you up in New York that got you looking so good? You need to be modeling or something. Listen, if you're not, I know a guy who's opening up an agency in Atlanta. We've been talking about getting into business. I could hook you up."

Well, that took all of 1.5 seconds. Yep. Some people never change no matter what the exterior looks like.

"Oh, Brent, cut it out with all that and leave that girl alone," Aunt Kath said. "I don't want to hear no talk about Atlanta coming from you. You just got in good with the real estate agency and you need to focus like we talked about. As if you know a thing about Atlanta or modeling."

Brent pulled a face and gave a slight pout, and in that instant all the signs of the petulant child they remembered were back. "Mama, I didn't say I knew about it. I said I knew a guy," he whined.

Aunt Kath let out a huff and waved her hand. "Like you don't always know a guy. All the guys you know could fill a stadium. You and your pie-in-the-sky dreams. You could come to earth and spend a little while on the straight and narrow for once, boy." She leveled him with a hard stare then. "And I'll hear no more about it."

Brent's eyes went wide as the house went silent, all eyes taking in the little five-second drama, looking for hidden clues between the silent moments. Finally, properly chastised in front of the New York cousins, Brent relented. "Yes, Mama."

Aunt Kath nodded then and cracked a satisfied smile before turning toward Aunt Joyce. "Now, what is this I hear, Joyce, about a fire this morning?" She shook her head. "What is going on? There is no reason for you to be up so early messing with those ovens. I thought Rena was supposed to be there to help you with those things? Especially with the condition you're in now with your hip and all. Am I right, Cole?"

Uncle Cole looked up, surprised to be included and then clearly uncomfortable about being asked. "Well, uh, yes, sure, dear. You're right." But then he glanced over at Aunt Joyce, who gave him a leg-quivering death stare, and he started to stammer. "Though, um, I'm sure Joyce knows what she's about and has everything under control."

Aunt Kath let out a sigh and shook her head. "Oh, I just can't with you. Brent, what about him?"

Brent blinked and looked over from where he'd meandered toward the front room window as if the view were suddenly the most interesting thing. "Ma'am?" he said.

"What about him?" Aunt Joyce asked with a frown.

"Well, do you need him to at least stop by in the morning to check on you before he goes in to work?

Make sure you're on your feet and started all right before Rena gets there?"

Aunt Joyce frowned. "I'll need no such thing. I've had enough of Brent and his ideas about the shop."

"Now, Aunt Joyce, you made it clear. I was just letting you know the value of your prime real estate."

Aunt Joyce huffed. "Well, Mister Real Estate Man, you worry about the value of those new developments out on the other side of the lake and keep your nose away from the shop."

Brent shook his head. "Yes, ma'am."

Aunt Kath chimed in then. "I'm sure he was only trying to help Joyce. Just like he'd only come to help you in the mornings. He could at least do that, maybe on his way to the gym?"

Aunt Joyce shook her head and waved a hand in front of her face as she turned toward the kitchen. "Enough of this. No need to start in on me today, Kath. It was no big deal. Something went wrong and faulty with the ovens; I'm going have them checked out. I thank you all for the concern, but as you can see, with the girls in town I have more than enough help. As a matter of fact, I'll be practically tripping over it."

Aunt Kath followed her toward the kitchen, with Liv and Drea coming up behind them. "Well, I'm just saying if it's getting to be too much for you . . ." Aunt Kath started.

Aunt Joyce quickly turned around from where she was pulling out what looked like seasoned chicken from the fridge. She gave Aunt Kath a look of death. "I'm warning you, Katherine, I'm in a pretty good mood, don't ruin it. Now, ain't a bit of nothing getting to be too much for me. You have not been worried about the bakeshop all this time, and you sure don't need to start worrying about it now."

Aunt Kath looked as if she was about to say something. She opened her mouth and the sounds almost came out, but with one last look at Aunt Joyce's rigid back it seemed as if better reason took over and she shut her mouth once again. Instead, she walked over to one of the other cabinets, leaned down and pulled out the big cast-iron skillet for Aunt Joyce, and put it onto the top of the stove. "You going to fry that chicken?" she asked.

Aunt Joyce gave her an incredulous look. "No, I'm going to crochet with it. What you think I'm going to do with it, Kath?"

"I'm just asking, Joyce. Don't be so dang blang mean. What are you having with it?"

"I don't know. I got some potato salad up in there, and some greens from Sunday, a little cobbler. I think there may be some leftover macaroni and cheese." She shrugged. "Just a little something that I can put out for us to nibble on for lunch."

"Well, come on," Aunt Kath said. "Let me do some quick red rice to go with, and we'll sit down and have it. . . . That is, if you'll take the help," she added in an exaggerated tone and gave a poke to Aunt Joyce's side.

Aunt Joyce shook her head. "I swear, Kath, just because you're now an old broad, don't think I won't wallop you one. Remember I used to get you but good when we were kids. I'm still your older sister. Don't you forget it."

Aunt Kath let out a long breath. "How could I ever, Joyce?" She then smiled toward Drea and Liv, who had been silent during the entire exchange. Liv had been taking in the tense back and forth between the sisters and the seemingly odd, but natural, way they resolved it over the decision to make the family lunch. "You girls go in and talk with Brent and Pearl. Get yourselves reacquainted. Lunch won't be but a minute," Aunt Kath said. "And come the weekend, we'll have ourselves a right good cookout out here on the water to welcome you back properly."

Liv silently took in her two aunts, feeling as if she were somehow glimpsing her own future, and she thought, *As if this isn't welcome enough.*

Chapter 7

Why in the world did I let Rena talk me into coming to Jolie's tonight? Liv thought as the four of them stepped into the old country bar and, just like out of some bad movie, it seemed like everything stopped. Just perfect. Liv didn't appreciate the eyes immediately turning their way or the self-conscious feeling it gave her that had her wanting to turn tail and head back to the comfort of Aunt Joyce's place to hang with her in the den with the big TV.

But she couldn't say the same for the rest of her crew. Drea, as usual, seemed to be blossoming under the attention of admiring male eyes, and Rena was born without a shy bone in her body, not to mention the fact that Pearl thought the sun rose and set on her, so she was fine with the attention even though she did a poor job of pretending to be put out over the fact of having to come to Jolie's to eat and not the fine dining of the country club's restaurant.

Squaring her shoulders, Liv pasted on what she hoped was a confidant smile and went along with her sister and cousins following the hostess to their table. This was clearly Rena's spot. She strutted, smiled, and waved as if on the catwalk—first at the bartender, whom Liv immediately recognized as Caleb Morris, Clayton's brother. He was so close to Clayton in looks, it was almost impossible for her not to recognize him, despite the fact that he was covering up his handsome face with an unruly full beard. Still, she could pick out the Morris eyes anywhere. Caleb gave Rena a warm, slow smile and a nod, and Liv was surprised when she saw the look of recognition dawn in his eyes when he saw her. He gave her a nod and a wave, and she watched as his eyes immediately went to an area at his right. She followed his gaze, and her eyes landed on none other than his brother, Clayton.

Liv clamped down on a groan as she fought to keep her walk steady. Just as she thought. She should have good and well stayed in at Aunt Joyce's tonight. This town was too darned small. With things turning out to be the way they were, she should seriously think about reassessing her plan. Make it a lot more focused on just the mission at hand. Aunt Joyce's, the bakeshop, and maybe a venture to see other family, but as for traipsing around the rest of the town, she could already tell, with Clayton Morris here, it was best not to. She clearly was still a little too muddled in her thinking to stay on track when it came to him.

But just as quick as that thought came to her, anger bubbled up too. So what, Clayton Morris was in town at the same time she was? It was her life, and his living there was just something she had to deal with for a short time. She was a grown woman, and he, very obviously by the looks of things, was a grown man. They were no longer kids, and she'd have to just get her mind right and deal with that fact. Just like they coexisted all those years ago, they could surely coexist now without there being any animosity or issues whatsoever. Couldn't there?

Purposely not ignoring Clayton's gaze as she went by, Liv gave him a smile and made a point to acknowledge the rest of his table, some of whom she'd recognized from the incident at the shop earlier. Hey, she might as well; they were all gawking hard enough. *Just keep smiling and just keep walking,* she told herself as she fought hard to ignore the insistent and erratic flipping of her heart; she tried her best to not acknowledge the strange spark she thought she saw in Clayton's eyes or the way his own grin seemed just as forced as hers.

"Well done with the fakery, sister," Drea whispered in her ear.

"I don't know what you're talking about," Liv said as she slipped into the booth, purposefully next to Pearl, on the opposite side of her sister.

Rena, not missing a beat, took the seat next to Drea, but looked straight ahead at Liv. "Oh, don't try to ignore it, cousin. I saw you eyeing Clayton. And better than that, I saw him eyeing you right back. Hot jam! That didn't take long." She picked up the plastic placemat that also served as Jolie's menu and waved it in front of her face. "Talk about a spark of magic. That man has been a dormant explosive for the longest time and suddenly you step into town and it feels like he can blow at any moment. It's like watching a volcano. A person should hold on to their weave in the same room as you two."

Hot jam? Liv would have laughed at Rena's choice of words if they weren't directed at her.

"I don't know what you two are talking about. Leave the poor woman alone. Can't you see you're embarrassing her?" Pearl coming to Liv's defense was a surprise.

"Besides, Clayton Morris is nothing to get all in a tizzy over. Livy, being a woman of the world, has got way more sense than that. So what? They may or may not have had a thing back when. I'm sure that ship has sailed, and anyway, he's got enough on his plate with that half-wild child of a daughter that he's got." She turned toward Liv. "You mark my words, just stay away from Clayton Morris. No matter what people say about him being all sweet and scoutlike with his kind fire-fighter ways, he's not as sweet as he seems." She shook her head and then slid a slightly disdainful look toward the table where Clayton was seated with his crew.

For the first time, Liv noticed a particularly pretty woman with wide eyes and a wider smile who was laughing at something Clayton was saying while she had her hand draped casually across his forearm. What was Pearl going on about again? Liv pulled her cousin back into focus.

"I tell you he's more than likely nothing but trouble," Pearl said.

"Really, Pearl, you only say that because Clayton's been nothing but trouble for you. Or a lack thereof," Rena replied.

What had been going on all these years that she'd been away? Had Clayton and Pearl had a thing? For as long as she knew, Pearl only had eyes for her very own football star husband.

Rena continued, "Talk about holding a grudge. You're still mad over the fact that Clayton Morris never gave you the time of day and neither did his brother. Not when you thought you were the hottest thing in a cheerleader skirt back in high school, nor when you won Miss Sugar Lake. And not even when you and Mr. Perfect were on the rocks and you went out to his fishing cabin crying on his shoulder and he carted your drunk behind back home."

At that, Pearl put her hand on her chest and pulled a shocked expression. "Why, I never. You know I don't go around getting drunk."

"Ahh," Rena said. "But you're saying nothing about going to men's fishing cabins." She nodded.

Pearl shook her head. "You are the worst. As usual you don't know what you're talking about, and your overactive imagination is running away with you."

"Okay, Miss Pageant, you play it like you want to," Rena said. "But just know that some of us understand that everything that glitters really ain't gold."

Just then their waitress came over to the table. She was a pretty, brown-skinned young woman with an easy, open smile. Liv found it funny how, despite her protests over supposedly not being a frequent patron of Jolie's place, Pearl didn't have to glance at the little placemat menu once, but instead quickly placed her order for a combo of the barbecue ribs and chicken with slaw, mac and cheese, and greens on the side. Liv, Rena, and Drea exchanged pointed looks as they went around the table with a round of, "I'll have what she's having," but instead of going for the sweet iced tea that Pearl had ordered, since she was indeed eating for two, the trio opted for the locally famous Jolie's Joy juice, a rum punch that packed quite a kick with its first sip.

As the cousins prodded on with the chitchat, Liv tried her best to join, but she couldn't quite let go of the little bombshell that Rena had placed when they first sat down. She shouldn't be surprised to hear about Pearl's feelings for Clayton. Just about everybody had a crush for Clayton back in the day. But the fact that there was or could be some recent lingering, and the fact that he had to take a drunk Pearl home, now that really gave her pause. Did he actually take her home? And did anything ever happen between them before he did? Was there more to this than even Rena's deep wells of Sugar Lake history knew about?

There was no time for Liv to get into that. The food was up, and so was the music and the mood. Liv let out a long breath and decided then and there to let herself have fun and enjoy the barbecue in front of her. She picked up a rib and took her first bite, savoring the sweet and spicy flavor as it exploded on her tongue, suddenly finding herself seat-shimmying in time to the bar's soul livening music. "This is absolutely delicious," she said to the table in general, then turned to Rena. "I'm so glad you thought of it. Now I'm actually feeling like a real Sugar Laker."

"Make yourself right at home, cousin," Rena said. She picked up the pitcher of Joy juice and topped off Liv's glass. "Wait, when did it become half full?" Liv grinned as she took another sip of the sweet concoction. Pretty slick of Jolie; making those ribs so deceptively spicy on the back of a person's tongue. She suspected half her profits were due to people replenishing their drink pitchers.

"Hurry up and finish that. I want to get in a game of pool because I'm a little low on funds, but still feeling lucky," Rena said. She turned Liv's way again. "Do you still play? You used to have a real mean game back when we used to play in Uncle Clint's basement."

Liv practically choked on her drink and shook her head quickly. "Oh, no, I haven't played in such a long time." She let her mind flip back, and she remembered that the last time she shot pool was a particularly disastrous online date two guys before Damon.

She'd won the game, which totally put the jerk off. Her winning closed the door on any options for a second date. He could barely look her in the eye after she won, let alone text her back. Insecurity was a terrible look on a man. Still, she refused Rena. "I don't think you should count on me. I'm too rusty. What about Drea or Pearl?"

Drea held up her hands. "Not with these nails. Sorry. I'd be useless."

Pearl held up a rib and shook her head. "Sorry, with this belly my balance would be too off. You're on your own."

Rena turned back to Liv and gave her feigned sad eyes. "Come on, Livy, for old times' sake. I promise I won't be mad if we lose, though I know we're gonna win!"

Liv hung her head in defeat, and Rena clapped her hands. She turned toward Drea. "Don't worry, I still have a job for you. You work the perimeter with the beauty queen over here. Just keep the competition off balance. I got both the lights and the gas due. Heck, 'past due' is practically my middle name right now. We've got to make this work."

"I swear, Rena, you will never change. Can't you show just a little bit of class for once in your life? I don't know why you deal with that no-good man in the first place. And now here you go hatching up a scheme to swindle folks out of their hard-earned money. Why, it's enough to bring shame to the family name," Pearl said as she daintily scraped up the last of her collard greens and put them in her mouth.

"Well, if it offends you so much it's a good thing you're married and don't have to use the family name, Miss Hyphenation-dash-Trophy-Wife."

Liv and Drea looked at each other wide-eyed. Lord,

these two cousins were just as bad as the two of them, if not worse. Their argument took on the same biting edge as Aunt Kath and Aunt Joyce. Liv thought briefly about intervening when Rena spoke before she got her mouth open. "How about this? If my actions offend you so much, just leave your cash on the table for your dinner and head home. You don't have to stay and watch. I know I drove you out here, but I'm sure you can call that husband of yours. He should be over right quick. That is, unless he's busy tonight, working late or something?"

At that Pearl seemed to stiffen, then she cleared her throat and waved a hand. Astonishingly she chuckled at Rena's comments. "Stop being such a pill. I'll stay. You know Terrence is happy for me to get out and have a little fun every once in a while. It's not like he keeps a tight leash on me."

"Or you on him," Rena mumbled.

But Pearl ignored her. "Besides, someone has to be here to make sure you don't get in any big trouble. Lord knows I don't want our dear cousins from up north to get the wrong impression about us."

Rena's lips twisted while she gave a slow and steady side-eye to Pearl. "Uh-hmm," she said by way of an answer. She then took a long pull of her drink and went to get up. She turned to them all as she wiped her mouth and stood, shimmying her hips a little and adjusting her top to show off her curves to their best advantage. She gave Liv and Drea a big smile before looking over toward Clayton's group and then back at them. "Come on, girls, it's time for the real fun of the night to begin. Let's go crack some balls."

Along the way she couldn't help but steer past Caleb Morris. Liv's instinct was to just give him a quick wave and keep on moving, but for some reason it didn't feel like enough. Not for an old neighbor and not for someone who inadvertently had such an impact on her life. Letting out a breath she veered off from her group and headed toward the bar.

"Hey there, Caleb. It's great to see you. You're looking fantastic," Liv said, her possibly too bright, bordering on cracking, smile in place as Caleb leaned over the bar and gave her a surprisingly warm hug.

She was surprised because though he was Clayton's older brother by a little over three years, back in the day Caleb was the true star of the family and a little untouchable to her. There was nothing sadder, if you let the townsfolk tell it, than the rise and then sad military fall of poor Caleb Morris.

Liv remembered how much Clayton always looked up to his all-star older brother and wanted to follow in his footsteps. She also knew how tough it was for him constantly feeling as if he fell just a little short. Not making varsity, not getting the top grades. But everyone was shocked when Caleb ended up taking an ROTC scholarship in order to pay for college when his sports scholarship fell through. And then when he enlisted after that, well it almost pained her to think of how drastically the tables ended up turning for the two brothers. The last she'd heard of Caleb, he'd just started his army tour and was only in a combat zone less than two months before he was back in a military hospital, down a limb.

Liv pulled back from his embrace, not wanting to, but how could she not notice the marked difference between the feel of his left and right sides despite how well he seemed to maneuver his prosthetic arm. She purposely didn't look down at the prosthesis, though she marveled at the amazing dexterity he showed handling bottles and serving drinks without any hindrance.

He rubbed at his bushy beard. "Naw. I know you're being kind, and I'll take it. You, on the other hand, are looking great," Caleb said. His smile was easy and relaxed, though Liv could see there was more than a little bit of weather behind his expressive brown eyes. "I'm glad to see life has treated you so well all these years."

Liv fought against the surprising knot of pain his lighthearted comment brought her. As if by rote, Liv smiled brighter. "Yeah, thanks. I guess you could say that." She paused. That probably wasn't the best response, but it was all her stupid mind could string together, and she immediately felt like an idiot. "Well, I'd better head on over to the pool tables. My cousin is waiting. This promises to be interesting."

Caleb chuckled at that. "Things usually are when it comes to Rena. Here, hold on a second." He pulled a pitcher of beer from the draft and gave it to her, along with four plastic cups. "Take these over for me. Consider it a welcome gift. Just watch out for your cousin, there. Make sure she doesn't hurt them too bad. That woman is pretty mean with a stick."

Something in his tone gave Liv pause. Doing that automatic thing that some girls do, she couldn't help but look at Caleb's hands. No ring, though it was his lower left arm that was left back on the battleground, so Caleb could be married and just not wear a ring on his left finger. Thinking that somehow made Liv feel guilty. Why should she be all up in Caleb's personal business, worried about whether he wore a wedding ring on his prosthetic hand? Also, why should she be mentally pairing him with Rena when Rena already had one baby daddy too many and enough drama to fill a daytime television show? Liv gave herself a mental head slap as she took the pitcher of beer and nodded at Caleb. "I'll be sure to try. Thanks."

She made her way over to where Rena had already staked her claim at one of the tables and was getting the balls racked while Drea and Pearl were doing their thing staking out the corners. The balls were racked, and it seemed for the moment they weren't going to get any additional action when a voice from the past hit Liv's ears from over her left shoulder and stopped her cold. "Care to make this game more interesting, ladies?"

Liv felt her grip tighten around her cue as she whipped around, not quite judging how near he was and nearly hitting him with her pool cue, coming close to taking off the tip of his nose. But thankfully, or not, he quickly leaned back and ducked out of the way.

"Whoa, there! I'm just coming by for a friendly game. I didn't know you were brandishing that thing as a weapon," Clayton yelped, with more than a bit of uneasy skepticism in his eyes.

Liv eyed him right back for one beat, then another, and though seconds went by without saying a word, she hoped her eyes told him where he could take his friendly game. But then the sounds of the bar, the laughter, the music, and the general merriment caught up with her, and her eyes shifted as she noticed the gazes of the people around them suddenly trained their way. There was Rena looking as if she were just about to burst, and Liv could tell her overzealous imagination was going into hyperdrive with possibilities. There were also some of Clayton's crew gawking. The folks she'd noticed at his table were now standing around, and she could tell they were clearly curious about the out-of-towner who was currently taking up their chief's attention. Most notably the tall beauty who was seated next to him at their table. Though she was currently chatting happily with a couple of the other guys, still her eyes kept shifting toward the two of them. Liv couldn't quite make out whether she was more than just a friend. She immediately told herself that it didn't matter. It was none of her business.

Liv coughed, regaining her composure. "Sorry about that, but you were a little too close," she said to Clayton in what she hoped was a light voice. She was sure it didn't quite come off that way, but hey, A for effort.

Clayton held up his hand and took a half step back. "You don't have to tell me twice, Miss Gale. I get what you're saying. But I do come in peace, as a friend and neighbor to welcome you properly back to town."

Liv felt her eyes narrow. "Better late than never, huh?" Just as the words escaped her lips she wanted so desperately to pull them back.

Darn it! What happened to cool?

She watched Clayton's expression change. His dark eyes went from soft and brown to so deep and dark they were almost black, and his brows drew straighter as his jaw clenched. She didn't mean to do it. Well, she did, but on her life she didn't want to show him how much he'd gotten to her. Not then, not like that. Liv laughed. Big drawn out and way too exaggerated. "Come on, lighten up. It's been a long time. You want to play or not?" She turned away from Clayton's too intense eyes and looked over at Rena. "Are we doing this or what?"

Liv could see Rena mentally calculating. She hoped it was on a potential game bet and not on anything to do with her and Clayton. Her gut told her it was the latter, and she shot her cousin a "shut it down" glare.

"I'm game," Rena said in response, going in her pocket to pull out some crisp bills. She looked past Liv and gave Clayton a challenging look. "It's all on you, Chief."

Liv steeled herself, then turned back his way, meeting his eyes once more. "Yep," she said brightly. "It's on you."

"Come on, Chief, don't be a stick-in-the-mud. Like a lady said, the night is still young, and don't we all have to get up early for work? Let's play," the young woman who'd been sitting next to Clayton earlier chimed in as she moved away from the guy she was talking to and went to grab a cue of her own. Just great. She'd be playing too? "You know we've got your back. Sugar Lake's finest can't be beat."

Rena turned to the young woman and gave her a smile and a hip check. "That's why I like you, Avery Duke. You're a fighter. I can respect that. Now, that doesn't mean you're going to win, but I still can respect that. Put your twenty down and let's cut the chatter and get to playing."

Liv and Clayton looked at each other for a moment longer, then he grinned. His lips spreading, his eyes softening, and for just that moment a calm settled over Liv. It felt as if she were seeing him for the first time, but also being hit with a bout of déjà vu. She was bobbing lazily on that beat-up old canoe on the lake. Supposedly fishing, but not catching anything but heat. She was on one end of the boat and Clayton was on the other. Just floating to wherever the current would take them. It was so perfect how they used to be able to just sit together in peace and quiet and not feel the need to fill the air. The sun was at his back, and she could barely make out anything but his silhouette. That was, until the boat shifted and he came into full view again; he looked at her and smiled.

Clayton shrugged his shoulder, bringing Liv out of the past and into the present as if he were saying, "Hey, better to know when we're beat." He turned to the woman she now knew to be Avery. "Okay. I'm in. But remember you are the one who asked for this."

Clayton tried his best to hold on to any semblance of cool as he picked out a pool cue. Not an easy task when walking suddenly seemed difficult. What was he thinking coming up to her with that line about a friendly game between friends? Who did he think they were? One, they were long past friendly, and two, nothing when it came to Olivia Gale was just a game. It never had been. Not for him, and not when it came to her. But here he found himself, across a pool table getting his behind royally clocked by both Livia and her cousin because he was totally and completely preoccupied by the nearness, the presence, the very idea of breathing the same air as Livia again. The whole thing infuriated him to no end and, from the look of Avery and the rest of his crew, was entertaining as all get-out for everyone else.

Focus, man, Clayton told himself. *There is no way you can go out like this. At least have some dignity.* He looked over just as Livia leaned to take a shot. She met his gaze, and he felt sweat break out on the back of his neck. Clayton reached for his beer as Liv shot him a look that was so cool and smooth it told him that, yes, she had indeed changed from the sweet, innocent girl he'd known all those years ago. It was as if she were reaching into his chest and physically crushing his heart with her fist. Well, maybe not his heart. He couldn't be that dramatic in the pool area of Jolie's, but he could admit to a stunning blow to his ego. How did she manage it? Acting so cool, as if he didn't affect her at all. The woman was knocking balls off the table with a vengeance.

Clayton stilled, then stared deeper.

Something in this woman was different. He swallowed, needing an immediate cooldown. Something, or someone, had hardened her in a way he couldn't say wasn't altogether an improvement on the naïveté she used to have. That sort of innocence could end up getting a person played one time too many. But he still couldn't help missing that sweet sparkle in her eyes. And he could admit to himself that he didn't like being the one on the receiving end of her calculating gaze.

For a moment, he imagined all the men in New York who may have gotten that exact same look, and anger threatened to bubble over. It steeled his spine. And for that, Clayton gave Livia a wink just as she was going forward with her shot. She went wide, veering left, and ended up sinking the eight ball, conceding the game to them.

"That was no fair, you distracted me!" Livia said from over the table while giving him a look that could kill.

"What are you talking about? I did no such thing," Clayton said, trying his best to put on an innocent voice. For an answer, Livia just let out a low breath and a groan of frustration, which brought her full lips close together, giving them a certain pouty look that only tortured him more and at the same time made him practically itch with wanting to charge over the table and kiss her until every ounce of frustration had melted from her lips. If this was what losing looked like on her, he'd pay to see what winning was.

The spell was broken though when she turned to Rena. "Sorry. It was my fault. I'll pay you back."

"No worries, cuz," Rena said. "It's just money. And if you really want a chance to pay me back, the night is still young. Follow me over to the bull."

Clayton watched Liv's pretty lips go wide in shock, and Avery laughed. "It's not like you guys are really losers anyway. You already beat us the first two games. And I for one would love to see some of you city slickers on the bull. That is, if you can handle it."

Clayton glared at Avery. Enough was enough. What was she playing at? "Listen, it's getting late," he said by way of warning.

But she shook her head. "We're not on the clock yet, Chief." She linked arms with both Livia and Rena. "Come on, let's head over before the boss takes all the fun out of the night."

Livia looked back at him and gave him a challenging glare. "As if we'd let him."

Clayton couldn't ignore the immediate rush of excitement he got or the heat that flowed through him over Livia's challenge. His eyes followed her while she made her way with the rest toward the bull pit, and he frowned. Did he always used to have this sort of reaction when she walked away when he was eighteen and she was in beat-up sneakers and cutoffs? He was sure he didn't. It had to be something about the years apart and those darned heels. He scratched at his head and gave it a shake before looking back up and meeting the eyes of his brother.

Wonderful. Caleb was eyeing him just as he was eyeing Livia, and now the heat he felt was akin to embarrassment, because Caleb was looking way too smug for his own good. Clayton suddenly wanted to punch something. If anyone should look embarrassed it should be Caleb. Their mother was up in arms worried sick over not seeing him in over a month.

Clayton shored himself as he picked up his beer and headed over to the bar. He took a seat at one of the only open barstools and waited for Caleb to finish a pour for a customer. Sure, the curt nod may have seemed a little cold for two brothers as close as they once were, but their current state could at best be categorized as complicated.

Since Clayton had returned to Sugar Lake after things fell apart with Hope's mother, he'd hoped that at least the upside would be that he and Caleb could grow closer and that his return would help bring Caleb back to his normal self after his injury. But no. He was disappointed to see that instead of further coming out of the fort Caleb had been building, with Clayton's arrival Caleb only made his walls stronger, fortified them, and built them higher, blocking out not only Clayton, but their mother too. He made himself scarce at family gatherings, church, and any other social activity; he was pretty much the town recluse, all except tending bar at Jolie's.

When Clayton and Hope came to town, Caleb moved out of the family house and got himself a trailer on the west side of the lake, where communication was conveniently spotty, or so he'd said, and for the most part lived off the land. Though his skills as an engineer and weapons specialist went far beyond what it took to be a bartender at Jolie's, here he was. Working here most nights, sporting a beard that would do Grizzly Adams proud. Out of the two things combined, Clayton didn't know which drove their mother madder.

"Hey, lil bro. I can't say I'm surprised to see you here. According to the calendar and my cell blowing up, it would seem about the time Ma would send you around checking up on me." Caleb took Clayton's half-empty beer and topped it off, then handed it back to him. "Though I don't suppose it's a coincidence you're here on the same night that Olivia Gale walks in from the great beyond." He snorted. "Never pegged you to be such a skirt chaser, but then again, she was the skirt that got away, or was it the one you ran away from?"

Clayton took a deep breath and started counting. He got to three before he gave up on that plan. There was no counting to control his feelings when it came to Caleb. His brother was an expert when it came to pushing his buttons. He'd been doing it longer than anyone, therefore he knew how to do it better than anyone. Luckily, Clayton had almost as much experience at pushing Caleb's, so he'd give back as good as he got. He gave his brother a steely look to let him know that he wasn't in the mood.

"Don't start," Clayton said. "If you are so good at noticing things you'd also notice I got here before she did, so it's a coincidence and—" He suddenly clamped down on the absurdity of explaining this to his big brother. "Why do I have to explain myself to you? I'm not here to talk about Olivia Gale. It's just like you said. If your calendar, not to mention your cell phone, are so on point, why is it that Ma should have to send me over here? You're supposed to be the older brother, not to mention a caring son, so shouldn't you be going over to check up on her?" Clayton chose to keep things focused on Caleb and his responsibilities and not even give any play toward his stupid comment about Livia. He wouldn't let him rile him.

"Why would she need me to check up on her when she's got you?" Caleb said, his words a question that

Clayton knew he didn't really want answered. "You, my dear younger brother, are all the son our mother needs. Perfect fire chief with the lovely daughter. Always making it to dinner on time."

Caleb watched Clayton, but then just for the briefest moment Caleb's eyes shifted toward his prosthetic lower limb. "Yes, she's got everything she needs in a son when it comes to you."

Clayton felt his eyes go skyward, and he let out a wry laugh. "Cut the pitiful, jealous act. You're not talented enough to pull it off. You know that I know that you're just hiding out from Ma because you are having too much fun sulking out in the woods, playing at being the recluse. You're well past pitying yourself after all this time. For all I know, all this mystery crap could be just to pick up women."

Caleb shrugged, though there was a hint of melancholy in his eyes. "Hey, don't hate the game."

Clayton got serious and lowered his tone. "And don't think I don't know you're also afraid that the more time you spend around Ma, the more she may guilt you into coming down off your mountain and remembering who it is you really are."

It was Caleb's turn to roll his eyes now, and he was just about to say something when his eye was caught by another patron. A pretty blonde waving for attention with a couple of her excited friends. They had tourist written all over them. Caleb flashed them what couldn't quite pass for a smile, but still had a bit of a smolder. Clayton knew his brother was putting on his mountain man act full force.

Clayton let out a groan. "Laying it on a little thick there?"

"Hey, they look like big tippers," Caleb said. "Listen, I've gotta work." He nodded his head toward the group by the bull pit. "Now, why don't you head over that way and continue not chasing after that city girl. From the looks of things, she has no intention of giving you the time of day, and with the crowd she's drawing, you'd better do your best if you plan to take a shot."

Clayton felt like a fool when he immediately swiveled his head toward the bull pit seeking out Livia and noticed the men clearly in her vicinity not by happenstance.

Caleb laughed. It was a bit rusty sounding and kind of craggy, and Clayton would've enjoyed it if it wasn't at his own expense.

Once again, the urge to count popped into Clayton's head. He gave his brother a hard look. "Who says I'm chasing after anybody? How about you worry about your own business and do what you need to do by giving your mama a call?" With that Clayton picked up his beer and, against his better judgment and worse yet with the sound of his brother's chuckle echoing in his ears, he headed off to the rest of his crew, which was unfortunately in the same direction as the bull pit and Olivia Gale.

Chapter 8

Liv woke with a sore behind and even sorer head. How in the world was it that four-thirty came so darned quick? And how was it she thought she could handle getting up at four-thirty without any problem? The sound of the old tin alarm clock buzzing did an incredible job at magnifying her pain, and it had the added bonus of quickly bringing her mortification of the night before sharply into focus. Trying her best to block it all out, Liv threw a pillow over her head and groaned.

"No need for all that groaning, Missy."

Liv lifted her pillow and peeked a bleary eye out toward her aunt Joyce. Her aunt was looking at her with what she was sure was supposed to be sternness, but she couldn't miss the distinct look of mirth in her eyes. She was clearly enjoying this. "That's what you gals get for hanging out with Rena till the wee hours while knowing that you have to get up in the morning."

"You call this morning?" Liv moaned.

"Hey, it's morning around here. At least it's what a baker calls morning; now have at it." She clapped her hands together loudly. "Come on. You're young, this is what you signed up for. Let's get to going. We need to be out of the house in thirty minutes. Now you look like you've got a little spunk in you. Get up. I need to get back to see if your sister is moving. I've already tried rousing her once, and she didn't budge. I'm afraid I may have to go back in there and pull out my water pistol."

"No need for that, lady. You can holster that squirt gun idea. I'm up," Drea said from behind Aunt Joyce.

What? How in the world was Drea up before she was? She was kicking it back pretty hard last night. Whooping and hollering on that mechanical bull as if she was made for the thing. Meanwhile Liv, with barely a couple of the Joy Juices in her, had a head that was spinning like mad.

Not to mention she didn't even want to think about her one trial on that ridiculous mechanical bull or the mortification it led to. She'd never forgive Rena for talking her into getting on that thing in the first place.

"All you've got to do is last for a second," she had said. "Come on, it'll be easy, and such a good time. This'll make you real local for sure. Besides, don't you want to show you-know-who you're not afraid of no bull?" That last one. That was the one that did it. Like a silly kid bowing down to peer pressure, she took one look at Clayton over on the sidelines and took in how he was eyeing her with a challenge in his eyes—like he didn't think she had the heart to take on the bull—and she was in. Liv inwardly groaned. What an idiot she was. An idiot who landed on her behind, hard. Looking like a fool in front of the entire bar, not to mention in front of Clayton Morris.

"I'm glad to see I don't have to resort to my commando measures," Aunt Joyce said, and Liv was happy for the mind shift. "Now, you girls get a move on. I want you both dressed in the next twenty minutes. I've already got breakfast ready downstairs. Nothing big, just some honey biscuits, hot grits, and slab bacon. A little something to get in your stomach so you're ready for the work to come. Now let's hop to it. I like to have my ovens warmed up by five-thirty and my first pies in by five forty-five. If I don't have my first batches of biscuits and mini pies out by store's opening, I could have a revolt." She paused. "Well, at least a revolt from Old Carl Perkins. And I wouldn't want that." She gave a chuckle and headed off, Liv supposed downstairs, which left her wondering about how well she navigated them.

Liv threw back her pillow and eased up, giving a bleary look to her sister, who gave her head a shake. Liv gave her a perplexed look right back. "I can't believe you're up! How can you possibly be standing upright?"

Drea shrugged her shoulders. "I can't believe it either. Must be the country air. I slept like a log for the few hours that I did sleep. I don't understand it. The bird started chirping, and my first instinct was to throw a shoe out the window, but then I thought, What good would that do? They would only be back tomorrow. And besides, don't you smell that bacon?" She shrugged again.

Drea turned, then headed toward her own room to dress and, Liv was sure, get first dibs on the bacon. For all her sister's tall slimness and talk about holistic living, she always seemed to cave when bacon was thrown in the mix. Liv shook her head, which turned out to be a bad idea, and pushed herself fully up, heading to her own bathroom and the shock of the mirror at four-thirty a.m.

Looking in the mirror, she quickly averted her eyes

from her own reflection. *Won't be making that mistake
again at this hour.* Not without some moisturizer and at
least a little BB cream. And well, maybe a lot of eye
de-puffer. Something about this humidity and that Joy
Juice did not mix well with her skin. Coming back up
with her toothbrush in hand, Liv was forced once
again to meet her own thoughts as the night before
came rushing to the forefront.

Gosh, she was a total fool for getting on that bull
last night. Letting Rena egg her on like she did. What
was she, fourteen years old? In junior high? She sure
acted like it, but she knew exactly what it was that
made her get on that bull. It was looking across the
crowd and seeing Clayton Morris hanging with his
crew, trying his best to look too cool for school and
ignore the fact that she was in his airspace. So yeah,
she was an idiot, and yeah, she was all of fourteen
again acting like the silly little girl trying to catch the
eye of the most popular boy in class. And what did she
get for her troubles? She caught his eye all right, his
eye and unfortunately his misplaced sympathy to the
hilarity of the whole bar when he made a big show of
jumping the little makeshift fence and coming to her
rescue when she flipped bottom over top off the
mechanical bull after less than a second. She must
have looked a right fool. Butt high in the air, one
stiletto on, the other having to be handed to her by a
cute fireman after Clayton carried her out of the pit.
Talk about mortifying. Her hair had come undone,
and she looked like a frightful mess. Her blouse was
half twisted, and she was barely standing.

That was not the way one made an auspicious entrance back into town.

Liv leaned over and spit into the sink and then proceeded to rinse her face. Oh well, done was done, and

today was a new day. After wiggling out of Clayton's arms and only leaning for two seconds—okay, so it was two seconds on his rock-hard chest to right her body while she got used to the feeling of being on level ground once again—Liv did her best to regain her composure and her dignity. But it was hard. So very hard with him so close, his chest so firm, his arms so strong and solid, and his lips right there.

"That was the best thing I've seen all year!" Rena's joyous squeal was just what the doctor ordered and saved Liv from further humiliation.

Liv finally pushed herself away from Clayton and stood on her own wobbly feet. She looked over at her cousin. "Can we go now?"

"Just a minute," Rena said as she went over to Caleb Morris and collected what looked to be a crisp fifty-dollar bill and a warm hug.

"I can't believe that Clayton's brother bet for me to win or that you bet against me," Liv said.

Rena shrugged. "He knew it was a sucker bet. I think he wanted me to win. Caleb comes off as a hard-ass, but he's mostly a mush," Rena said, tucking the money away.

Liv slid her eyes Caleb's way and noticed his gaze was once again on Rena. For a second, she paused. It wasn't the gaze of a person who was just being nice or someone who was just covering for his boy either. But so far Rena seemed to be concerned only about what Troy was up to, so she seemed oblivious to the man at the bar sending soulful looks her way. All Liv could do was hope that Troy didn't continue to disappoint Rena the way he currently was. But if the past was any indication of his future behavior, she doubted he would change.

"What you gals doing up there?" Aunt Joyce's voice

came from downstairs. "We're headed to the shop to get cooking, not to the city for a beauty contest. Y'all got five minutes, let's get to going, otherwise I'll drive myself even if I'm not supposed to. I've already canceled my normal ride, so you are it."

Liv moaned as she caught her reflection in the mirror again. She gave herself her best put-on smile. "This is what you signed up for," she said. "This is what you came here for. Family, fresh air, and a good dose of what's real. Now it's time to embrace it. Get on downstairs and start living your life, Olivia Gale."

Breathtaking. That was her thought as the sleep fully washed away and Liv caught her first glimpse of the sun coming up over the lake as they made their way to the shop that morning. The silence was such a stark contrast to the sound of mornings in New York, which admittedly she'd always loved. It was much more of a quiet type of rush than life in the city. Yes, she loved the low hum of the cars as they made their way up Eighth Avenue, in Harlem, the metal clang of the store grates as they went up to shout out the beginning of the day. But this was somehow different; this was a gentler, more quiet type of signaling. Though somehow filled with just as much anticipation for her. The beautiful glow of the sun on the rippling water was inspiring, as it seemed to fill her with much-needed energy for the short drive to the shop.

Once in town, this time instead of pulling up to one of the metered parking spots, Liv brought the old sedan down the back alley to behind the shop, where Aunt Joyce usually parked. She turned off the ignition and Drea got out, helping Aunt Joyce as she went. Drea looked around at the back-lot area, pausing and nodding her head. "What you checking out so hard there, girly?" Aunt Joyce asked.

"I'm just thinking about what a nice space you got back here, Aunt Joyce," Drea said. "It'd be lovely with a few tables. I can see people sitting back here having lunch, enjoying the breeze, making an afternoon of it."

Aunt Joyce chuckled at that and went into her purse to pull out her set of keys. Finally, she poked a thumb Drea's way before pushing the back door of the shop open. "I see this one here is the dreamer." She shook her head and smiled wistfully. Reaching out her hand she touched Drea's cheek softly. "Reminds me of your mama. Always thinking of something. That gal would keep her head in the clouds."

Drea frowned. "Whose mama? I know you're not talking about mine. Not Mrs. Practical, that's for sure."

Aunt Joyce shrugged. "If you say so, but you don't know her like I know her. When it comes to imagination, nobody has one like my baby sister. But I'll just leave it at that." And that was how she left it, making her way into the shop quicker than a woman on a bum hip ought to. Leaving Drea and Liv no choice but to follow quickly to catch up as she went about flipping on the lights as they came through the back kitchen.

"Okay, girls, no time for fooling around. This is going to go kind of fast for the first few days, but you two are smart, so I'm sure you'll get the gist. Just mind what I say and we'll have time for questions after the morning's batches are done. Is that good?" Aunt Joyce asked, though the sisters both knew she wasn't really expecting any sort of answer besides an affirmative one.

Both Liv and Drea nodded, ready to head toward their respective tasks.

Grabbing a Goode 'N Sweet apron from a hook in the workroom, Liv was surprised by the overwhelming emotion she felt. She loved how well the plain muslin apron with its pink and brown logo on the front fit easily over her body. She brought the ties around the back of her waist and then over into a bow at her front, and smiled. Perfect. She remembered how the old aprons used to swim on her slim frame as a kid up until she was well past puberty.

Drea came over and gave her a look. "What are you grinning about so hard this early in the morning?"

Liv shook her head. "I'm just excited to get to work."

Drea pulled a face, giving her a skeptical look. Not quite as excited as her sister to be in her work apron. "If you say so."

Liv grabbed her tote and pulled out her cell. "Come on, let's take a photo. We look so cute in our aprons."

Drea shook her head at this, but let out a small sigh and smiled. "Fine."

The sisters posed together, Liv holding the phone high to get their best angle and show off their aprons to their best advantage.

Just then Aunt Joyce came around from the pantry. "Didn't I say we had a lot of work to do?" she snapped. "And here you two are doing a photo shoot!"

"Sorry, Aunt Joyce. We were excited to be in our aprons," Liv said.

Aunt Joyce tapped her good foot. "I tell you. You can't get good help. Well, come on over and let me get in the photo too. If you're going to do it, you might as well have the queen included."

Liv laughed. "Get on in here, then!"

They snapped their pics, then got on with what was

one of the busiest mornings of her life. By nine, both
Liv and Drea were about ready to cry uncle. Liv didn't
know how Aunt Joyce and Rena had been doing it.
They'd made three dozen honey biscuits, six banana
breads, four carrot breads, six apple pies, and three
cherry pies. And they had three pecan peach cobblers
going in the ovens, not to mention the mini tarts that
were chilling.

Beat didn't begin to explain it. What saved them
was how Aunt Joyce and Rena had had things prepped,
but even with that there was a ton of work.

By the time Rena came in at seven forty-five, after
getting her kids ready for school, her sister agreeing
to do the school drop-off—picking up the slack where
once again Troy fell short—Liv could see that both
Aunt Joyce and Rena were spread about as thin as
they came.

Liv could also see how a mistake could have been
made with the oven temperature, thus starting the fire
the other morning. There was no way Aunt Joyce
should be doing everything alone. Not anymore. It
was clear she needed help, and she needed it quickly
with the sheer magnitude of work they had going on
in the shop.

Morning business was steady from the moment the
doors opened at seven-thirty until about nine-thirty,
when folks were settled into their respective jobs and
had already made off with their morning treats from
Goode 'N Sweet. Though not great for profits, Liv was
thankful that they didn't have nearly as much business
at lunch as they did in the morning. She didn't think
she could handle it. At least not on her first day. But
she couldn't keep her business marketer's mind from
working overtime with thoughts of changes to the
menu and how they could pick up potential business

with just a few tweaks. Liv stopped herself though. She knew it was crazy thinking.

She couldn't go all out that way after just a day. Not when she wasn't coming up with any permanent solutions to them. And she wouldn't be doing that on this short trip. None of it mattered in that moment anyway, because she was exhausted, Drea was exhausted, and no matter how much she tried to hide it, she suspected Aunt Joyce was dog tired too. The only person not quite dead on her feet was Rena. The woman could clearly kick it back, ride bulls, take care of her babies, and somehow still work the bakeshop and not look any worse for the wear.

"I don't know how you do it," Liv admitted to her cousin when it was the first moment of quiet and some tourists had left happy with a couple of mini peach key lime tarts after sampling them.

Rena shrugged. "Listen, around here we do what we gotta do and that's all there is to it. No use slowing down, and there is no use worrying about the hows. It's all in the doing, so you just do."

Liv frowned to herself at the simplistic way Rena put it, something that was, in reality, so complicated that millions of people couldn't grasp it. She was thinking this over when Clayton Morris walked into the shop. Just great, talk about a reason to throw the whole not-thinking theory out the window.

He gave her one of those devastating smiles of his as he gave his greeting to the room in general. "Morning, y'all. I hope everyone is doing wonderful today."

"We're fine, Clayton," Aunt Joyce answered for the group.

"I'm glad to hear that, Miss Joyce." He turned toward

Liv. "And I'm hoping you're not too worse for the wear after your tumble last night."

With that, Aunt Joyce gave a short gasp. "What tumble? What you get up to last night that you had to take a tumble? Don't tell me you going and getting yourself hurt." She turned toward Rena. "Rena, what you get these girls up to last night? I told you not to get them into anything naughty."

"Naughty? Don't go getting your apron in a twist," Rena countered. "As you can see, Livy's fine. Besides, she's a big girl. She can handle herself."

Liv gave Clayton the harsh glare, and he gave her back a wobbly grin before mouthing "Sorry" and turning toward Aunt Joyce. "Yes. I was just teasing, Miss Joyce. Olivia is okay. I just saw the ladies up at Jolie's last night, and your talented niece here was trying her hand on the mechanical bull and, as always, that feisty old bull won out."

Aunt Joyce chuckled loudly at that and looked Liv's way. "Now, *that* I would like to have seen. Gal, you should steer clear of that darn bull. I've spent way more time on that bull's mat than I've ever spent on its back, let me tell you. You really want to know somebody who can ride it, though her stuck-up behind won't admit it, is your aunt Kath. I believe she holds some sort of record if you check the books for 1984."

Now, that was shocking, and not just to Liv, but to everyone else in the room too. "You have got to be kidding us," Drea said. "There is no way Aunt Kath would be getting on the bull at Jolie's."

Aunt Joyce leveled Drea with another look. "Girl, when you gonna start believing me? I don't tell no lies, and I don't talk just to hear my own voice. You can believe the airs Kath puts on if you want to. But a woman doesn't get the title Miss Sugar Lake just because she's so sweet. I'll give you that much. She's got to have some backbone to her."

Drea gave her head a nod at that one. "Well, I hear you there. Touché."

Liv frowned as her mind got to twirling. Aunt Kath riding a mechanical bull was almost too much for her mind to take, but then her mind went to her cousin Pearl and the fact that she was a former Miss Sugar Lake too, and the story Rena told about her being drunk came rushing back. Suddenly she had the feeling that if Pearl wasn't six months pregnant she would've been high up top that bull herself. She looked over at Clayton, and her mind twisted to places she didn't want to go. Bull riding, and the newfound revelation that Clayton was the one whom Pearl turned to when she got drunk and was feeling lonely. Liv shook her head. Nope, she didn't even want to go there. So instead she opened her mouth. "So, what brings you here this morning, Clayton? As you can see, we're all doing fine."

At that Clayton held up his hand and a small burlap bag. "Bees."

The one-word answer caused Liv to recoil. "Bees? You don't have bees in that bag, do you?"

Now it was Clayton who was frowning. He gave her an impatient look. "Why would I be walking around with bees, Livia?"

She gave him an impatient look right back as she folded her arms across her chest. "How would I know? There is no telling why you do anything you do." Liv sucked in a breath and told herself to dial it back. She had no right and she had no reason to snap at Clayton in such a way. *Way to go in the maturity redo department, Liv.* She tried to soften her comment with a smile.

"Sorry, just a little tired this morning. Carry on. Now, what do you have in that bag?"

"Sweetness."

The word dripped from his lips like syrup and decadence. But Liv wasn't buying it, and she narrowed her eyes, giving him an intense stare. He laughed. "No, I'm just joking. It's honey. I've got your aunt's usual order of honey."

Liv raised a brow. Honey? She knew he meant that he had honey in his bag because, yes, she remembered that Aunt Joyce said that he had some sort of organic honey-farming deal going on. Something else to add to his cachet of ridiculous perfectness, even if it was a bit odd. Come on. In order to get honey, one had to deal with bees.

Obviously, Aunt Joyce thought Clayton was laying it on a little thick too, because she chimed in. "Cut the flirting now, Clayton Morris, and quit teasing my niece. I'd like my order today."

"Yes, ma'am." Clayton said as he shot one last grin Liv's way before heading down the counter to Aunt Joyce.

Liv watched as Clayton pulled the amber jars of honey out of his bag, holding them up to the light that filtered in from the side windows. She enjoyed seeing the pride on his face as he tilted the jar left and right. He opened it with his long-tapered fingers as Aunt Joyce got a couple of her biscuits and brought out a spoon and knife from behind the counter. "You girls come on over here and taste this. I promise you you've never tasted anything like Clayton's honey."

Liv fought to keep her countenance placid as she walked over toward the rest, purposely taking a spot on the other side of the counter as far as she could get from Clayton.

Aunt Joyce cut a couple of biscuits in half and spread a bit of the honey over the top. "Now, I've used some honey from Lowers in the past, and it's all right, but I tell you, after you try Clayton's, you'll see why I had to give up on Lowers, which has made him right mad. But I had to do what I had to do." She gave Clayton a smile that was full of pride. "This boy here's got something special. And it has taken my honey biscuits to a new stratosphere."

She handed a honeyed biscuit to Drea, who took a bite and hummed her appreciation. "Wow, this really is good," Drea said, wide-eyed. "You've got something here. You take this to New York and you could make a mint."

Clayton laughed. "I don't think my small hive of bees could handle the pace of New York. Thanks. I'm good with what I've got here in town and the small surrounding areas. I do well enough," he said, giving a look to Liv, who couldn't help eyeing the biscuits suspiciously. She was sure that if she took a bite, it would taste better than anything she ever tasted in her life and she wouldn't be able to stop at just one taste. But then Aunt Joyce chimed in again. "What's holding you up, girl? It's not like the biscuit is going to bite you."

Liv blinked and looked up. *Promise?* There was Clayton, and he was now holding a biscuit up in front of her; the biscuit, dripping with glistening honey, was way too close to her lips. Oh heck, she had no choice but to take a bite. Not taking it would be rude, and besides, everyone was looking at her. Clayton, his eyes deep dark and intense, questioning, teasing, challenging her with their mirth. Liv had to lean forward and open her mouth.

It was soft, smooth, sweet, and everything honey should be, with a surprising smoky finish that had you instantly longing for your next taste. *Crud!* Liv knew tasting it would be a mistake. She looked up and met Clayton's eyes. Her lips spread into a smile that she didn't want to give in to. Leaning forward once again, she took another bite before she remembered where she was and the fact that they were surrounded by other people. Liv pulled back quickly, embarrassed as she tried to laugh it off. She nodded and looked away from Clayton toward Aunt Joyce. "Well, you didn't lie there, Aunt Joyce. That is some seriously good honey." She cleared her throat and turned to get a nearby napkin, then wiped at the corners of her mouth. She looked over at Clayton again. "Great job. You do have the beginnings of an impressive small business going. Good for you." She hoped her voice was at least one tenth as calm as she tried to make it out to be.

Clayton smiled. This time his smile didn't look particularly soft or genuine or welcoming. This time it looked quite flaccid and slightly cool. "Thank you. Coming from you that means a lot."

He was shuttered, and she didn't know if or how she'd somehow insulted him. She also didn't know why she felt twisted up about it or why she should even care. But she did. Just then, Clayton's phone rang and he picked it up. An anxious expression washing across his face. "Excuse me, ladies, I have to take this. It's my daughter's school." He stepped away from them, going to the far end of the shop, and she could tell he was concerned by his hushed whispers and the shaking of his head. Clicking off, he turned back to them.

"Is everything okay, Clayton?" Aunt Joyce asked.

Clayton ran a frustrated hand across the top of his head. "I'm sure it's fine, or at least it will be," he said to Aunt Joyce, then looked at Liv and Drea. Liv could see the signs of embarrassment move across his face.

"Sorry, but I have to run. I need to check on my daughter. You ladies have a great day. Don't stay up on that hip too long, Miss Joyce."

Aunt Joyce gave Clayton a small smile back. "Don't you worry none about me. I've got my girls. You just go and check on yours. Give her my love. And if there is anything I can do, don't you be shy about coming by and asking," she added.

Clayton was already halfway out the door, but he paused and gave Aunt Joyce a nod of thanks before he left.

Aunt Joyce let out a wistful sigh as she closed the top on the jar of Clayton's honey. "I swear that little gal gives her father more trouble than she ought to. I understand her being upset about her mother running off like she did, but really, it's no reason to be hard on her dad like she is. If you ask me, she's lucky to have a father as good as him."

"You're telling me," Rena said from where she was placing a fresh apple cobbler in the case. "I understand she's not happy about what her mother did, and believe me, her mama sounds like a right nutcase running out on a man like Clayton Morris, but still, she's a bit young to be dodging out on school like I hear she's been doing."

Liv was taking in the whole conversation, and it filled her with unease. Poor Clayton. And wow, those were words she'd never thought she'd say. But poor Clayton, and his daughter too. "Can I ask what could possibly be making the girl have trouble in school? Could it be more than just her mother running out on her?"

"Well, it could be, I'm sure," Aunt Joyce said. "You never know with these types of things. I mean, the girl has had her share of troubles, being uprooted from where they were in California, in the middle of the school year no less. All due to the fact that, from what I heard, one day her mother just decided that being part of a family wasn't no good for her no more. . . . Now, myself, I can get that. I feel all women don't have to be the mothering type. But I suppose that's something you need to come to terms with before you go off and have a child. Barely ten years after that child is up and in the world and you decide it's not for you? That type of thing just ain't fair."

"Nope, sure ain't," Rena said. "Not from a mama or from a daddy. It just isn't right. You can fall out with whoever you're with, but you sure can't fall out with the child or with your responsibilities. It just ain't done. It's too much for a young psyche to take." Rena let out a sigh, and it was the first bit of weariness that Liv glimpsed on her cousin's face since arriving in town. And in that moment, she wanted more than anything to go over and give her a hug, but she knew Rena and there was no way she would accept that type of sympathy. So instead she just agreed with her.

"You're right, it's not fair on the child or the parent left behind," Liv said.

"Yep, Clayton's got his hands full, all right. Being both father and mother to that girl of his. Plus, he's taking care of his mama and still checking on his recluse of a brother. It's a lot. But he handles it pretty well. I do say if he had a nice woman to help him out, someone to smile in his direction, maybe cook him a good meal now and again, it might do him a world of good." Aunt Joyce said these words and directed them toward the tart she was rearranging, but Liv swore she could feel the breeze flowing in her direction. Luckily, a couple of customers came into the shop; she was surprised to see that one of them was Deidre Clemens.

At first Liv barely recognized Deidre, she'd changed so much from the slim, tough-looking girl she'd known all those years ago with the hard eyes, tight rocker-type clothes, and tough attitude. In her place in walked this light-as-air, curly-haired woman with tanned skin and barely there makeup, wearing a floral sundress, holding the hand of an adorable little girl. She was accompanied by a tall, sandy-blond-haired man with a wild beard and soft gray eyes. Liv could tell from his eyes, which matched the child's, that this was the husband who Aunt Joyce had gone on about. She could also tell by the high man bun. That was a dead giveaway.

"Deidre Clemens!" Aunt Joyce exclaimed. "What brings you into the shop today? And with the whole family too?"

"Good morning, Miss Joyce." Deidre said. "And it's Walden now, remember?" she corrected. "We had a hankering for something extra sweet, and only one of your pies would do the trick. Why, my husband was just saying the other day how your pecan peach cobbler is the most perfect flavor. Between you and me, I'd love to know your secret."

"Well, wouldn't everyone," Aunt Joyce said. "But I'm afraid that's for family only. Some things you have to keep in house."

"Of course." Deidra nodded. "I surely do. We feel that way when creating new ice creams. Bless those family recipes. It's what we're made of. And of course we also wanted to see how you were faring after your fall."

Her husband chimed in. "Yes, we were so sorry to hear about it. It must be hard for you taking care of this shop and trying to get around. You let us know if there is anything we can do to help. Being business neighbors, we are here to look out for each other."

Liv saw Aunt Joyce's eyes narrow ever so slightly as her smile stayed firmly in place. This poor guy. He'd obviously been in town for quite a few years judging by the age of his daughter, but he'd always be considered an outsider by the locals. And here was Aunt Joyce not even getting his last name right. Liv felt the need to jump in and save him.

"Thank you," Liv said, coming over. "We really appreciate it. But Aunt Joyce is fine. I'm Liv, and my sister and I have come to help Aunt Joyce and Rena out for a bit."

Liv noticed Deidre's husband's eyes widen and then he smiled as Deidre chimed in. "Oh, hey, I remember you. It's great to see you again. This is my husband, Paul, and this little one is Molly," she said, indicating her daughter.

Liv looked down at the little girl. She was about three, well closer to four. She guessed not quite ready for school yet. But what did she know? Maybe they homeschooled her.

"We did hear Miss Joyce had family in town. That's wonderful. See there, Miss Joyce? Family to share those secrets with." Diedre continued, "How long are you staying?"

"Um . . ." Liv for some reason wasn't quite sure how to answer that question.

"Indefinitely," Aunt Joyce chimed in. "And I'm so glad they're here. Already Liv and Drea are just full of fresh ideas about modernizing the place."

With that, both Liv and Drea turned and looked at Aunt Joyce in shock. "We are?"

She gave them each a nod. "Why, yes, you are, and

I can't wait to get them going." She turned back to Deidre and Paul, who looked at each other just about as confused as Drea and Liv were over the talk of modernization. "Now, let me get your berry pie. I know you two need to be off to get your shop open."

As Deidre Clemens, now Walden, left with her pie, kid, and husband, Liv was left perplexed. Why had Aunt Joyce shuffled them out so quickly, and why was she suddenly so eager to do improvements on the shop?

Chapter 9

The weather could not have been more beautiful.
The sun was showing out in a glorious way, though it
was already late afternoon and still in the high seven-
ties. The fine mist of sweat on Liv's bare neck had her
fast remembering the extreme temperature change
once you were past South of the Border on I-95.
Goodness, Georgia sure could heat up. She was sure
back in New York the air was starting to catch a hint
of a pre-fall nip.

Liv put up her hand and gave a wave, knowing it did
little to nothing, and regretted not grabbing one of
Aunt Joyce's many sun hats, kept on hooks by the
front and back doors, before she headed out to the
backyard. After closing this afternoon, Drea had convinced Aunt Joyce to head out to the mall for a
mani/pedi. At first Aunt Joyce balked at the idea, but
it turned out she was an easy sway. Liv had a feeling
that though Aunt Joyce protested, she quite enjoyed
her a bit of pampering, and Liv was happy to let the
two of them go at it alone. Part of her felt bad taking
up so much of Aunt Joyce's time in the kitchen. Drea

was trying her best to help out where she could. It wasn't her fault that she really didn't have a culinary bone in her near perfect body. So this little outing might be a good thing for the two of them.

Besides, right now Liv was happy for the bit of peace and quiet. She hadn't truly been alone for any length of time since coming out to Sugar Lake, she mused as she made it out back and walked around to survey Aunt Joyce's garden. She took in the bounty of Aunt Joyce's crop. Cucumbers, tomatoes, peppers, lettuce, and greens, both mustard and collard. When the woman found the time to cultivate all of it and run Goode 'N Sweet was a mystery. The fact that Aunt Joyce considered such a thing no big deal was also astounding. Liv felt as if she was practically looking at the full produce section of her local New York grocery store and here it was, outside Aunt Joyce's back door.

It was funny, but only a few days in the sleepy town of Sugar Lake, jobless—well, except the predawn wake-up calls to get to the shop and get to baking and hanging with her extended family—and already New York felt like half a lifetime away. She barely missed her tiny apartment with her neighbor's loud reggae music coming through the living room wall. And she definitely didn't miss her four-inch heels and spending evenings sipping wine and mindlessly flipping channels while nibbling on takeout and looking over files for work the next day. Her biggest excitement for the week was if Damon would come over and join her in channel surfing and file flipping.

Walking around to the far back corner of the garden, Liv reached forward and ran her fingers over the smooth surface of one of Aunt Joyce's tomatoes. The color, a red so vibrant and bright it looked almost painted on. But no, this was all nature, no pesticides, no enhancements. And there had been no channel-surfing evenings for her here. For one, Aunt Joyce controlled the remote when they did watch TV in the evenings, and she was pretty set on her scheduled programs, and two, Liv found she really didn't care about what she watched or if she watched anything on TV. After getting up before the sun and spending a full day in the bakeshop, baking and then serving customers, which she'd come to learn meant a lot more than just serving—in a small town, this included quite a bit of conversation too—she was happily satisfied with the respite of the tiny twin bed when her head finally hit the pillow at night.

Plucking the tomato from the vine, mouth already watering, considering the salad she was going to make to accompany dinner that night, Liv suddenly felt heat bear down on her once more. But this time it wasn't up by her neck, it was down by her feet. It was hot. More than hot, it was burning, no, biting. Little poking, flaming needles going into her skin and burning her body from the bottom up. Liv looked down, then dropped the tomato and screamed.

"What is it! Are you hurt?"

She didn't know where he came from or that he was even outside to witness her undoing, but Clayton was at her side before her scream ended. No matter. This wasn't the time to be embarrassed. Not when there was a swarm of fire ants on her foot, traveling up her ankle with the deadly intent to suck her dry. She screamed, swatted, jumped, and howled. "Holy fracking crapsmoger, that hurts!" she yelled as she went at the ants, swatting in a frenzy.

"Livia! Don't jump and swat at them like that. You'll

only make them angry, and they'll just latch on tighter."

She looked up at him in shock, full-on panic about to set in. "Tighter! I feel like they are burrowing under my skin." She felt tears threaten the back of her eyes. Oh God, she did not want to cry in front of him, but goodness did this hurt. She was now jumping on one foot and was well aware that she must look like a complete idiot in her cursed flip-flops, cutoff jean shorts, and less than flattering overwashed and out-of-shape BAKERS KEEP IT SWEET tee.

But before she knew it she was off the ground and in his arms. Her next wail caught in her throat at the shock of being lifted so effortlessly. *Whoa! Is that what fire training did to a person? If so, oh my.* Clayton acted as if her substantial height and weight were nothing more than a grocery haul, while the feeling of being held—one arm behind her back and the other under her knees, with her shoulder against his firm chest— had driven away all thoughts of ants and had Liv feeling quite like a heroine out of a rom com. She blinked and let it wash over her for a second. But it was only a second, as the reality of it—and the stinging— came back.

"What in the world are you doing?" she said, hopeful that there wasn't any hint of damsel in her voice. She was a strong, assertive woman, gosh darn it. No matter that her arms had somehow wrapped around his neck of their own accord. She'd have a discussion with them later.

He looked down at her, his brown eyes sharp and serious while soothing and concerned. "I'm bringing you over to sit down and rinse off away from the anthill so you don't cause further damage."

"Oh," Liv said, finding no fault with the logic and

feeling a little silly that she didn't think of it herself when Clayton easily carried her over to the little planter's bench Aunt Joyce had on the side of the house. Thankfully it wasn't that far from the back hose, and she watched as he silently and quickly walked over to turn it on. He came back and kneeled at her feet.

Liv almost gasped and she froze, seeing him go down on one knee and then look up at her, eyes so deep that she could easily drown in them. When the icy water hit her foot, she was stung by the surprise of it and jumped up way too quickly, causing Clayton to rear back and splash himself in the face, hose flying, watering the both of them top to bottom.

"Seriously, woman! Do you have to be so squirrely?" he said, his voice now laced with a hint of frustration.

"Sorry, but it hurts and the water is cold."

"Good," he said, hose back firmly in hand as he grabbed hold of her leg. "Let it shock them. Now, sit and let me rinse you off. You want to make sure they are all gone. Some may have clamped on."

Liv sat down slowly. This was fine. So what that Clayton was kneeling in front of her, holding her leg as he carefully examined it, T-shirt now glued to him. And so what that she was in front of him, shorts now ridiculous soggy thanks to the hose gone awry, probably looking like something the cat dragged in. She started to laugh, and he looked up at her and gave her that gorgeous smile. Now, why'd he go and do that?

"What are you laughing at?" he asked.

She shook her head. "Oh, only just how ridiculous this all is. There I was in the moment in some stupid fantasy about fruit and how lovely things were out here and how peaceful everything is, and isn't it just like life to snap you out of it and crash you right back to earth, in this case in the form of fire ants." She frowned then. "I should have known there wasn't any real peace for me. It doesn't matter where I go."

Clayton's eyes grew serious, and she felt his hand loosen ever so slightly on her ankle. His voice was a little more tentative now. "I hope I'm not in any way the cause of you not finding peace while you're here in Sugar Lake."

Liv's heartbeat quickened at his direct question. Of course he was the reason, but could she dare tell him that? Was she even ready to face it? She quickly smiled. "No, of course not! It's just that I've got a lot going on right now. Being between jobs and all. Which is totally new to me, but it's all good." She forced herself to grin wider. "I really am taking this as a chance to reassess where I am in my career and what I want going forward."

Clayton nodded and looked down at her foot again. Long and hard. He examined it against the other, but something about the silence and all their past years of being friends let her know that he was deep in thought, and not about her foot. Finally, he looked back up at her. "So, it's just your career you're reassessing?"

Now it was her turn to pause, not that she didn't know what he was getting at. As if he had a right to ask her about her personal life. Finally, she spoke. "Pretty much. I was seeing someone back in New York." She watched carefully and caught the slight narrowing of his eyes over that statement. "But we're over now," she finally added. "I'm not looking to be in a relationship with anyone besides myself at the moment."

Clayton smiled then, clearly wanting to lighten the mood just as much as she did. "I can understand that."

She nodded and gave him a raised brow. "I bet you do."

Thankfully, he ignored her and looked at her foot once more, then back up at her. "Wait here, I'll be right back."

"I should just go and change. Thanks for your he—" she started.

"Just wait. Please."

Liv let out a head-clearing breath as he jogged the short way over to his house, and she listened as he went through his back door. What in the world was that all about? Did she really need this today? She should just go in and change out of these wet clothes, then put some ice on her foot. If Clayton came back and saw that she was gone, she was sure he'd catch the hint. But before she could properly get the thought out and contemplate it she heard his door open and close again. Darn, he was fast.

He was back and changed into a fresh pair of gym shorts and tank, and now he had a small, wet towel and jar of honey in hand. Liv pulled a face. "What are you doing with that?"

Clayton sat down next to her, casually picked up both her legs, and put them across his lap. When Liv tried to pull away, he clamped down on her ankles and held her firmly. "Just relax a minute. This will help so you won't have too much swelling. Honey helps inflammation and has been known to heal wounds. Alternate honey wraps with ice packs and you should be good to go. It doesn't look like you are allergic, but I can see a little redness. Just to be safe you should maybe take an allergy pill too, if you can tolerate it. Now, trust me, okay?"

Liv was once again stunned. She couldn't argue with his logic without coming off as irrational, but here he was, asking her to trust him, and he was the one person in the world she had the most trouble trusting. Though she felt her face pulled in a tight frown, she gave him a reluctant nod. "Fine."

Clayton smiled as he put the towel under her foot, opened the small jar of honey, and carefully poured some onto Liv's ankle and lower leg. She was mesmerized by his skill as the honey slowly drizzled down onto her skin and Clayton smoothly brought the jar back up and then closed the cap, not spilling a single drop.

"Now you're just showing off," she said.

He chuckled. "I may not have many talents, but I do know my way around honey."

Once again Liv's breath caught, but she tried to hide it with a roll of her eyes. "Yeah, I'm sure. Can we get on with this, please? As nice as this banter is, I have a feeling I might soon be going from ant bait to bee nectar."

"Don't worry, you'll be fine."

But she wasn't fine. Nowhere near fine when he reached out and gently rubbed the honey into her ankle with his long fingers. What in the world? This was supposed to be medicinal? Liv's toes scrunched up, and Clayton turned, looking at her quizzically. "You okay?"

"I, um, I'm fine," she said, looking out to try to focus on the lake. "I'm just a little ticklish. You think you can wrap this up?"

"Sure. No problem."

It took everything for her not to sigh in relief when Clayton finally wrapped her lower leg in the warm towel he'd brought out with him. She had to admit that the sensation was relaxing. The stinging pain was dissipating, and she was starting to feel calm.

"Sit here and keep it elevated for a while. You'll be all right," Clayton said, then looked out toward the lake.

"Thanks," she replied. When he made no move to let her feet go from their position, Liv spoke up again. "You can go, you know. You don't have to babysit me. I will sit like you instructed. I'm sure you have plenty to do. I'm sorry I disturbed you with my howling and ruined your clothes. Don't let me hold you up any further."

He didn't move, so she spoke again. "I will follow your directions. But you can go."

He turned his head toward her then. "You didn't disturb me or ruin my clothes. My clothes will dry, and Hope is at a friend's house."

"And your mom?"

His brows pulled together. "My mom doesn't need a minder."

She laughed at that, and he laughed too. "Though sometimes she thinks *I* do."

Liv nodded. "Well, good to see that some things never change. She did always keep a sharp eye on you. I tell you, back in the day I could feel your mama's eyes piercing into my back."

Clayton laughed. "Could you really?"

"Of course. Hey, not that I blame her. You were her precious boy. I'd be mindful of some New York gal sniffing around too, if I were her."

"Yeah, well it was nothing compared to the way your family watched you."

Liv balked. "What? Oh, come on. I could have spent the summer in a tree and no one would have cared."

Clayton snorted. "If you think so." He shrugged then, seeming to want to move on. "Hey, speaking of trees, remember that time you got stuck up in that old maple?"

Liv felt her face heat. "Oh God, do I. It was all your fault!"

"How was it? Nobody told you to go climbing up that high. It was madness."

"Well, nobody told you to go daring me to do it. I couldn't let your challenge stand. If you could get up to the fourth rung, then surely I could get to the fifth. How was I to know how high it would be once I got up there? Trees do not grow that tall in Harlem."

"For an eight-year-old, you sure were fearless."

Liv looked around then, taking in the yard, garden, the oaks, then the lake. All the nature churning around them and the perils seen and unseen. "Yeah, I guess I was."

Clayton started to laugh. "I thought the adults were going to have our hides. Boy, I didn't want them to know you were stuck. It took half a day to get you down."

She laughed, then looked back at him, their eyes connecting and in an instant traveling from the past to the present.

"But you did," she said softly. "You came up and you got me down."

He nodded. "Yeah, I guess I did. Though it probably would have been safer for both of us if I'd just bailed then. Gone to get help."

Liv felt her smile wobble at that statement. Just then, the gravel-crunching sound of a car approaching hit their ears, followed by Aunt Joyce's voice.

"Guess they're back," she said. "I'm going to head in and take that allergy pill you suggested. Thanks again." This time when she moved her feet, he loosened his grip and let them slide out easily.

Clayton nodded. "No problem."

She unwrapped the towel. "I'll wash this and get it back to you."

"You keep it," he said as he handed her the jar of honey. "And use this for the next few days."

She nodded. "I will."

They both stood. Liv slipped her flip-flops back on and headed toward the house while Clayton headed toward his home, but then she turned. "Hey," she called out to him. "Stop by the shop next time you get a moment and I'll give you a sweet treat as repayment."

But he shook his head. "No need. Haven't you ever heard of a little thing called southern hospitality?"

Chapter 10

"Ain't no party like a Goode 'N Sweet party cause a Goode 'N Sweet party don't stop!" Liv looked over at her cousin Warren, who was doing some odd version of the running man mixed with the robot. He started his wack rap over the portable karaoke microphone while her other cousin Wiley did his version of mixing at the makeshift DJ stand on the back of Aunt Joyce's porch. Liv shook her head in embarrassment, though she couldn't help the smile that quirked at her lips.

It was Sunday afternoon and the shop was closed. The whole family had come to Aunt Joyce's for a gathering to welcome Liv and Drea into town properly. They'd set the big farm table out back on the grass, adding the extension to make it long enough for the entire family. The table had been decorated with mismatched linens from their great-grandmother's stash, and Drea seemed to have the best time gathering flowers from the surrounding woods and putting them in vases and jars from around the house. Uncle Clint and Aunt Nori came over with extra chairs in the back of their truck so there would be enough seating for everyone.

At the moment, the party was just getting in full swing. Wiley and Warren had the music blasting, and Uncle Clint and Uncle Cole had dual grills going with ribs and chicken on one and fresh-caught fish from the lake on the other. All the sides were ready thanks to Aunt Kath and Aunt Nori, not to mention what Pearl and Rena brought by. There were fresh greens from Aunt Joyce's garden, potato salad, macaroni and cheese, seafood salad, and a host of other little dishes. Each meant to outdo the other, though no one would say whose was the best.

And then there were the desserts, all thanks to Aunt Joyce with a little help from Liv, which was a thrill. She was even able to sneak her berry swirl pie into the mix, which felt like quite an honor. She sure hoped it went over well with the family. Her dad was one thing, but the whole Goode clan, now that was another.

It felt nice seeing the family together, and not arguing, at least for the moment, but having fun, dancing, and chatting while the little ones ran around and played. The whole scene reminded Liv of the past and made her miss her parents and long for them to be there to experience this, even Elijah. But they were now off to Europe, her mother finally getting a chance to grasp some dreams of her own, and Liv was glad that she and Drea could help make that happen.

Liv was carrying a bowl of potato salad to the table when she faltered slightly, her gaze on the Morris family walking over from their property. Of course they would come to the gathering. Why wouldn't they? Still, Liv steeled herself as she took in the scene of Delia Morris flanked by her sons as they headed her way. Aunt Joyce and Mrs. Delia had never been neighbor-like besties. They got along well enough in a friendly rivalry of gardening, cooking, baking (that was always a moot point, but whatever), and in the southern way they'd always invited each other to family functions. It should have come as no surprise.

The surprise, though, was Clayton coming along too as if they were still kids. Didn't he have to be on call at the firehouse or something, and what was his brother doing here? As far as she'd heard, Caleb had quite the reputation as the family recluse. If so, attending backyard barbecues could quite ruin that. She sighed. Clayton said nothing about coming to their barbecue when she was hopping around like a fool on the anthill the day before. Wasn't that just like him.

But then the biggest surprise came into view a moment later, and thankfully Liv had put the potato salad on the table just in time; otherwise she may have dropped it and broken one of Aunt Joyce's coveted pieces of vintage Pyrex. Hope. She would have recognized the young girl anywhere, no matter that she was running out now at breakneck speed from behind Clayton's back. With her wide, dimpled smile; the same lovely, smooth brown skin; and deep-set soulful eyes, Liv had to forcefully tell herself not to tear up as Hope ran past her and into Aunt Joyce's arms. In that moment Hope swept her up in a momentary breeze that was full of the possibilities of what might've been and never would be.

"It's so good to see you, Miss Joyce," the young girl said. "I know it's been a while, but I'm glad to be here, and I sure hope you've got some peach cobbler today."

"Hope, is that a way to greet a person, asking for food straight out like you're starving?"

"Delia, you know that's what I love about this child. She's straightforward and honest, right to your face with it." Aunt Joyce answered Mrs. Morris and gave little Hope a one-armed hug and a kiss on the top of her head. Her hair was braided into two neat, long French braids that were thick and full and went just past her shoulders, then were gathered together into a low barrette. Liv couldn't help but wonder who braided the girl's hair. More than likely Clayton's mom did the girl's hair, but still she wondered.

"Hope." It was Clayton's rich voice that was reaching her ears now. "I'd like you to meet Miss Olivia. This is one of Miss Joyce's nieces from New York. She's an old friend."

At that odd declaration, little Hope, obviously no dummy, turned and gave Liv a serious perusing from her toes to the top of her head, then a look straight in the eye. Her eyes were so set and so serious and so like Clayton's that Liv almost burst out laughing; at the same time the temptation to squirm was strong. But she couldn't, not when she was under such scrutiny. "It's very nice to meet you," she said, putting out her hand formally. It was this show of respect that Hope seemed to appreciate. She took Liv's hand and gave quite a firm shake.

Hope gave Liv a nod. "Nice to meet you, too," she said, way more seriously than Liv was expecting from one so young.

"How's the foot?" Clayton interjected.

At that, everyone looked down and Liv immediately regretted wearing a sundress, hoping the redness wasn't all that evident. At least there wasn't any visible swelling, and she had on plenty of repellent today. She wouldn't tell Clayton in this crowd how effective his honey remedy was. She waved her hand. "It's fine. I'm okay."

Hope looked up at her. "What happened to your foot?"

Aunt Joyce sucked her teeth loudly. "She wasn't watching where she was going is what."

Gosh, why did he have to bring it up now? You'd think her aunt would have given her a bit of sympathy, but no. Liv had forgotten the country adage of nature ruling. When she went in with her bitten ankle, Aunt Joyce seemed to have more sympathy for the disturbed ants than her.

Liv looked down at Hope with resignation. "I stepped on an anthill yesterday. Stupid, huh?"

Hope's brows pulled together and she looked down at Liv's feet, then back up at her with concern before she broke into a grin. "Yeah, it was. But it's okay. I've done it too. Isn't it the worst?"

Surprising relief washed over Liv in finding this little ally. "It is. Thank you." She looked over at her aunt. "See? At least somebody understands."

Aunt Joyce shook her head. "I'm not saying I don't. I'm just saying you been out in these parts plenty enough to know better what to watch out for. This here is their country, not ours." She turned to Hope. "Now, Hope, why don't you run on and see if you can rustle up Rena's crew and the rest of the kids," Aunt Joyce said. "I can barely handle them without actin' like a witch, but they seem to listen to a poised young lady like you. You know how they admire you. Now, please help me out. The quicker we can get dinner out, the quicker you can get to that cobbler."

Liking what she was hearing, Hope looked up at Aunt Joyce and smiled. "Yes, ma'am." She started to run off again, but before she did she turned back to Liv. "You watch where you step now, Miss Olivia.

Oh, and get my dad to give you some honey to put on your foot. It's great for the pain."

Liv smiled, pushing down on a threatening blush as Hope sprinted away toward the lake, where the kids were to do Aunt Joyce's bidding. How smart. Liv knew that Hope wasn't all that much older than the other kids, but putting her in charge was a great way to send her off with the other children while still making her feel quite grown up. She made a mental note.

"It's good to see you again, Olivia. You're looking well," Clayton's mother said, pulling her back to the gathering. Liv knew it was meant to come out as warm, or at least Delia Morris's version of warm, so Liv took it for what it was and gave Mrs. Morris a nod.

"It's good to see you too, Mrs. Morris. It's been too long. But it's no telling that by looking at you. You look wonderful."

At that little compliment, Mrs. Morris smiled as she handed off her casserole dish to Aunt Joyce, who took it stiffly, which was about as much courtesy as she took any dish toward her table. Rena came out back, followed closely by Troy, who was late, but Liv could see Rena was glad he'd shown. With everyone in attendance, the music was lowered, the food was blessed, and Aunt Joyce declared it time to eat.

Liv was busy chatting and took the nearest seat. She shouldn't have been surprised when Clayton took the seat to her right, though she still looked up and gave him a slight frown, and Clayton returned her gaze with confusion.

"This isn't going to be a problem for you, is it? I mean, we are old friends; we should be able to share a meal." He laughed.

Liv's frown deepened, and she let out a resigned sigh as she waved a hand indicating for him to sit down.

Darn those ants! She shook her head. "Of course not. Good food is good food, and I can eat with just about anybody."

And this was supposed to be an easygoing dinner.

Fighting to ignore the prickly sensations over having Clayton so near her, Liv decided to just focus, really ridiculously hard, on her macaroni salad and not the man sitting beside her at the table. Having finished the salad way too quickly, she took a breath and went in on the ribs. She couldn't very well pick up a rib and eat it the way she really wanted to. Not with him right there. What would she look like with barbecue sauce all over the sides of her mouth? It looked really good. Glistening, warm, and sweet. Suddenly she thought of all the ribs, plates of spaghetti with rich garlic sauce, and any other delicious food that a woman is really not supposed to eat in front of a man she might want to impress. It brought flashbacks of Damon and all his little cracks about her body to the forefront of her mind. Why should she care what Clayton thought about it, or how she ate her ribs? Why should she care what any man thought about what she ate? They were her ribs and she'd eat them if she wanted to. Liv put down her fork and picked up her rib, going in for a hearty bite.

"I'm glad to see you've still got a good appetite." Clayton's voice almost made her choke on her rib.

Really? Who says something like that?

How is that polite lunch conversation?

To echo her thoughts, Liv turned to Clayton and posed that exact question with a sharp glare. For her reply, she got from him dark eyes and a shrug. "Well, at least I'm trying to make conversation. It's what people usually do at dinner," he said. "You're so silent, sitting here with your back all straight. Sorry, but I didn't know what to say."

He looked sheepish and grew quiet.

"Well, you could've said anything but that," she said after a hard swallow. "A woman doesn't like to be particularly reminded of her large appetite while she is at the table, eating. It gives her something to be self-conscious about, or feels suspiciously like policing."

Clayton gave Liv a quick up-and-down and then tilted his head to the side. "Oh, come on. Now, you are the last person who would have anything to be self-conscious about. With a figure like yours? Enjoy your rib." He reached down to his plate and picked up one of his ribs and moved it to her plate, then gave her a smile that was somehow more enticing than the rib. "Here, you can have one of mine too. Whatever you're eating, woman, it's doing you a world of good."

Liv was embarrassed by the heat that rushed up her body at his ridiculous comment. She supposed that he thought it was supposed to be a compliment in a roundabout, totally unobtrusive way. And she supposed that some feminist part of her should really be put out by it. Who did he think he was? Objectifying her like that, dang it! There was that look, those eyes, and that smile . . . and those old, familiar chills she'd thought were long dead, but now she'd come to find out the darned things were only dormant. Lying in wait for him to stir them again and bring them back to life. As if she needed or wanted any sort of stirring.

Liv reached over, plucked up said rib, and as tactfully as she could she dropped it back on his plate. With a splat, it landed in his potato salad. "Thanks, but no thanks. Not that I need your permission either way, but I'm getting full. Besides, I don't want to overstuff myself. I like to leave room for a little dessert."

Clayton smiled and nodded. "And you still have that sweet tooth. Glad to see that hasn't gone away either."

Liv closed her eyes, trying her best to hold on to a shred of control. Finally, she leveled Clayton with a hard stare and spoke with a low tone as she put on a cool smile. "You know, you don't have to have an answer to everything I say, and you really don't have to go out of your way to compliment me. Just because I'm here in town for a couple of weeks doesn't mean you should be nice to me. I'm not a kid anymore, and I got the message years ago about how you felt about me. Consider it water under the bridge. We're good."

At that, she saw something shift in Clayton's eyes and any semblance of light fade away. Liv caught a distant chill seeing his façade crumble in real time. When he looked at her now, there was no smile, no playfulness, and no spark. "Liv, I truly am sorry for the way I treated you all those years ago," he said, now completely serious. "But you don't know for a second who I am or what I am. I think—" He was just about to go on when everyone's focus was pulled to the far end of the table, where Rena's little boy, Justice, knocked over a large glass of juice.

"Oh, Mom, I'm sorry. I didn't mean to knock it over," the five-year-old said, looking up at Rena with his oversize brown eyes, which took up most of his face.

"It's okay, baby," Rena said. "I probably shouldn't have filled the glass so full. Let me quickly clean it up before auntie gets on me for giving you liquids before you finished your food, anyway," she said with a chuckle. But then Troy spoke up, his voice hard and cutting.

"I told you about coddling that boy, Rena. Giving

him all that juice. He'll be wetting the bed again. Got him acting like a mama's boy. He needs to man up!"

With that, the table went immediately silent. Everyone was taking in Rena's hurt and embarrassed expression, not to mention the look of distinct fear on young Justice's face.

Aunt Joyce gave Troy a look that could wither even the most hardened of giants. "You need to remember where you're at, young man. You're at my table, and nobody raises their voice at my table but me. So if you plan to continue, I expect you'll do it elsewhere. Secondly, you need to remember you're speaking to the mother of your child, not some dog in the street. Not that a dog deserves that tone, mind you."

Troy looked at Aunt Joyce, for a moment his eyes hard, and it seemed for a second as if he was about to say something when Caleb Morris opened his mouth, deflecting the situation. "You got that right, Miss Joyce. We all could use a little bit of a reminder from time to time. I guess the heat must have had Troy forgetting himself. It sure is a warm one today. He knows it was an accident. And accidents happen." He gave Troy a look that was both warning and censure, then he looked toward Rena. "But we can't let anything ruin this lovely day or this amazing meal. Y'all know I don't get out much from where I am up on the mountain, so I consider this a treat." He turned toward Warren and Wiley. "You guys going to have to come up and fish with me sometime; this catfish is delicious."

Wiley needed his agreement while Warren relaxed, but kept his gaze on Troy. Liv caught the nod Rena gave Caleb as she placed a kiss on the top of Justice's head and refilled his juice cup.

"Well, what's done is done. This is supposed to be a

party, and I'm so happy to have my nieces with me. Now, let's keep this thing going. Time to get to the desserts. I didn't do all this baking for my good health. Everybody go on and have a good time," Aunt Joyce said, indicating it was time to bring the desserts out.

Liv got up quickly to go and help, but was stopped by Clayton's hand on her wrist. "Wait, please, there is more I have to say," he said, looking up at her.

She shook her head. "No. I think we've both said more than enough."

Keeping his distance, Clayton eyed Livia over where she was standing by the dock having a piece of pie alone. It reminded him for a moment of how often he'd find her out there in that same situation when they were kids. Though there were usually tons of people milling about, she'd always found a way to pull herself away from the crowd. How she did it this afternoon was a feat within itself with so many people around. But since she did, he used the moment to his advantage and studied her. She looked beautiful, leaning easily against the old oak tree, looking intently out over the lake. Caleb frowned then, wondering what was going on in that head of hers.

There was still so much tension between them, so much animosity from the past, that no matter how cool she tried to act, it was clear she'd never quite forgiven him. When she hit him with that hot and haughty stare of hers back at the table, for a moment he didn't know who he was looking at. At times it was so clear that she was the same person he'd grown up with, learning and loving all those summers ago, but then when he truly opened his eyes and peered closer, the change of the years apart was so evident.

The hardness, the inherent lack of trust behind her eyes even when she was smiling. Clayton let out a low and silent breath. If he was the beginning of that for her, well, he didn't know if he could forgive himself.

Sure, he suspected a certain amount of jadedness coming from a city person like Livia, but she'd always had a natural innocence and a hopeful optimism that he'd come to thrive on and, silly as it was, somehow believe in. It's what he always loved about her. When she came to town she had a way of making him feel both worldly and brand new all at the same time.

The wind kicked up, and he watched as her sundress flew up in the breeze, exposing her shapely legs. He swallowed. And at the very moment she turned and looked his way, locking eyes with him. As if noticing his staring and his sudden response, her brows tightened with censure. Would she forever make him feel like the teenager he wasn't anymore?

But she gave him a slight smile, at least he hoped it was for him; it could have been for any of the guys around him. At the moment, he'd take what bone he could get. Clayton turned to Warren and Wiley and let them know he'd be back soon.

So it didn't look obvious that he was making a pilgrimage toward Livia, Clayton stopped along the way to check on Hope, who was playing with the other kids. He breathed a sigh of relief when he saw how happy she looked. Like a facsimile of her young eleven-year-old self. But he knew that sight was only temporary. That these moments were fleeting and rare. The other day when the school called, giving him the biggest fright, they'd let him know that she was missing from her sixth-period gym class, and he was just about two minutes away from putting out an Amber Alert. Thank goodness his biggest fears were squelched only five minutes later when they called him back saying she was found crying in the back of the girls' locker room.

The whole thought of what happened to her and how totally helpless and unskilled and unprepared he had been made him want to kick himself over and over again. She was only eleven and she'd gotten her period. Unprepared. All alone and without a mother to call on. She didn't even want the school to call him because she was afraid of how he would react.

Even at this tender age, she'd pegged him as an inept father and she was probably right. If he was any good, he'd have made it work with Celeste, at least for Hope's sake, and she wouldn't have had to go through this alone. As it was, all she had was her grandmother giving her probably antiquated advice and him doing the best that he could after practically buying out the feminine care aisle in the pharmacy and viewing YouTube videos for two hours. He did the best he could when Hope cried in his arms as he gave her the bags and told her it was all right and it was all perfectly normal. He told her he would always love her no matter what. But in the end, he knew it wasn't enough. He knew he would never be enough for her, but all he could do was try.

Hope looked up at Clayton and grinned, one braid going left, the other going not quite right. But he was still happy to see the light shining in her eyes. "Hey, Daddy, Uncle Caleb said he's going take me out on the lake later to fish."

Clayton's first instinct was to put the kibosh on this, but seeing Hope's face and her excitement let him know he couldn't squelch her dreams; he'd just be sure to tell Caleb not to let his daughter down. Hope loved fishing, and she liked spending time with Caleb.

He'd be sure to give his brother a reminder that if he made a promise to his daughter, he better keep it. He leaned down and put a kiss on top of Hope's forehead. "That sounds like fun, baby. I know it's been way too long since I've been able to take you out fishing, and your uncle Caleb needs to have a little fun. If anybody can get him smiling, you're the one to do it." Hope grinned wider before she was pulled back toward her game by one of the other kids.

Clayton let out a breath and turned his attention back toward where he was headed. Livia Gale. Might as well keep this party going. On from one temperamental woman to another.

Chapter 11

The view never failed to calm her, and after that meal, calm was definitely what she needed. That and this cherry pie. This pie of Aunt Joyce's was magic, the way it was soothing her nerves after enduring lunch sitting next to Clayton Morris. Really, the man could have chosen any of the twenty or twenty-five mismatched chairs today at that long farmhouse table, but he had to choose the one next to hers. Liv frowned. It was as if he knew exactly what to do to get under her skin. Was the fact that she was back in town some sort of new game to him? This thought pulled her up short, and her frown deepened. Though frustrated, Liv forced herself to smooth her features. At this rate, she'd age three years in the few weeks she was in Sugar Lake.

But the thought of Clayton Morris playing her for a fool was almost too much to take. Was he playing with her now? And more so, was what she thought they had when they were young just some sort of teenage game to Clayton, even back then? Just then, the wind picked up and she felt a prickly sensation on the back of her neck, and something, as if a strange calling, made her shift her head. Liv turned and glared. It was him. Of course. Well, she wouldn't let him know he was getting to her. Not this time. Not anymore. She sucked in a breath, let it out, and smiled before taking another bite of pie and turning back toward the lake. This time the sweet cherries tasted almost sickly syrupy and stuck in her throat as the memory of the bitter pain of finding out he was gone, possibly never to return, that summer when she'd just turned eighteen and had come back to Sugar Lake ready to rekindle their romance came rushing back to her in his gaze. As hard as she tried, she'd never forgotten all they shared. The promises made their last day and night together. Of love, of the future and forever. She swallowed down hard, determined to get the stuck bite down, when Clayton's voice reached her ears.

"I would say it looks like nothing's changed, but you know as well as I that that's not true."

She turned and looked at him, shocked to find him so near. But he wasn't looking at her as he spoke; instead he was watching the kids playing by the water's edge. Once again Liv marveled over how very similar Clayton's daughter was to him at that age. The vision gave her a conflicted knot in her stomach, and she hated herself for her intense, petty jealousy as shame engulfed her. How could she have anything but kind feelings and goodwill for Clayton's choices? Look at what it yielded him. He had a beautiful little girl and a chance at happiness in life. How could she deny him or anyone that?

So what, she was the idiot who believed in a teenage boy's lies? That was on her, just as it was on her for holding on to a dream of forever and fidelity for way too long. She couldn't fault Clayton for her own lack of judgment or for her lack of moving on. It wasn't up to him, or anyone else for that matter, to secure her happiness in life.

That was on her, and it was high time she realized it. She gave Clayton an easygoing smile. "No, nothing is the same, but that's okay. We are who we are in the end. I'm just happy to see you here now doing so well," she said lightly, hoping that even if she didn't quite feel her words, that in saying them she could make her heart believe they were true. She nodded toward the children. "And your daughter is beautiful. She looks so much like you. You should be proud."

Clayton's smile came fast and wide. "Thank you. I really am proud of her. She's the best thing I've got in this life."

His words, so sincere and true, brought Liv up short and, from anyone else but Clayton, Liv would be standing up and giving this man an ovation for showing such true and open love for his child, but still all it did was twist at her and highlight all she'd missed out on. Immediately, she felt like a million times a fool. And most embarrassingly, Clayton seemed to pick up on it.

"Oh, I'm sorry," he said. "I didn't mean anything by it." His gaze swept the ground in embarrassment before he looked back at her with sad eyes. "I really am sorry. It seems I'm putting my foot in my mouth over here."

"Stop. You have nothing to apologize for. Especially not when it comes to expressing how you feel about your daughter, and you really don't owe me any type of apology." She smiled at him and hoped it was convincing. "Please, don't worry. Just enjoy yourself this afternoon."

"Thank you for that," he said sincerely. "Though

I'm not sure I can agree with you. I feel I owe you a lot more than just an apology, but an explanation too."

Liv felt her heart rate begin to ramp up. She wasn't quite sure she was ready for this. Not today, maybe not ever. She looked back toward the house. Why wasn't Aunt Joyce giving her a call, or where was Rena with all her boisterousness when she needed her? "No," she said, trying to cut Clayton off. "You really don't."

Clayton stopped her, his eyes going serious, but his expression soft. Dang it, he looked good. Too good. "Like I was saying," he started, "I don't agree. I won't get into it all. Not here and not now, but I will start with apologizing for how I acted at lunch. I didn't mean to come off sounding so stern back at the table or coming on strong. That was uncalled for and frankly out of line. After all we've been to each other in the past, you deserve better."

With his words Liv had to remind herself to breathe, but she looked at Clayton, and he was looking so nervous that she didn't know who she felt sorrier for, him or herself. She gave a half grin to break the mood, and on nervous impulse, she stuck out her tongue.

"Lighten up, Clayton Morris. It's not that deep. If I recall, I was always the one out of the two of us who took things way too seriously."

Clayton's eyes went wide, then he grinned too, thankfully giving her a moment to let out a breath and think about her escape from this awkward situation. She was just about to make her exit when he spoke up again. His nervous tone was not quite hidden in the rich tenor of his voice. "Well, since we're talking and all"—he paused, way too long to be comfortable for either of them—"I was wondering, they do give me time off for lunch at the firehouse, so maybe we could meet for lunch or have coffee and I could hopefully give you that apology and explanation that's long overdue."

Liv couldn't help the frown that pulled at her brows again. She knew she'd talked up a big game, but this new leaf thing called for baby steps.

She fought to find the right words that wouldn't make her sound as if she were rowing backward. "You know, we really are fine. I meant that, but lunch, coffee? I don't know. Like I said, you don't owe me anything, no apology, no explanation. Nothing. Coffee or lunch may be a bit much for us." Liv shook her head. "At least beyond mixed company." She looked around, catching sight of his mother, who was sitting with Aunt Kath, both their gazes trained on where she and Clayton were standing. She gave her head a little nod in their direction. "Besides, you know how small towns are, and I'm only here for a short while. All my focus should be on helping out Aunt Joyce and getting her situated. I wouldn't want to go giving people the wrong idea."

Clayton's gaze went over to where his mother and Aunt Kath were. He seemed to catch his mother's pinched look and gave a short snort of laughter as he looked back over at Liv. He nodded. "Okay, I hear you, but the invitation remains open. You're right, this town is small, but just know you've always got a friend here in me. In case you need someone to talk to, besides the usual family, that is. I can understand how suffocating that may be."

It was then, as if on cue, a bit of that suffocating family came sauntering into their space in the form of Brent. Liv supposed she should've been grateful for the intrusion and breakup of the awkwardness of being stuck alone with Clayton, but honestly she wasn't.

Brent came over with his slick salesman smile coming on strong. He gave Clayton a quick handshake and threw a head nod Liv's way. "What's up, cuz?" He looked back and forth between the two of them and raised a brow. "You two picking up where you left off?"

Liv felt her eyes go toward the top of the trees.

"Not hardly, Brent, and don't go getting any ideas or spreading rumors either. I know how you can be."

Brent shifted his stance as Liv noticed a shift in Clayton. She didn't know if this posturing was a reaction to her quick comment dismissing Brent's words about them rekindling their relationship or if it was just to Brent in general, but something had gotten Clayton's dander up. Still Brent continued. "Yeah, cuz, I got you. Listen, you were always smart."

Liv pulled a face. "Am I supposed take that as a statement or a question?"

She heard Clayton chuckle from over her shoulder as Brent held up his two hands. "Oh, stop it, you know exactly how I meant it. I'm just saying you've always had a good head on your shoulders." He paused, giving a bit of a self-satisfied smile. "Like me, you're smart and you know a good deal."

Liv braced herself.

"So, I've been doing pretty well so far in the real estate business."

"Aren't you fairly new to the business?" Liv interjected. "I mean, that's what Aunt Kath seemed to indicate the other day."

She noticed a bit of tension around Brent's jaw, but he quickly softened it with his usual flash of a smile. "Oh, please, don't go listening to my ma. She's always one to underestimate me. I'm not half as new as she thinks, and I know a lot more than what she or anyone wants to give me credit for. Besides, you know how mothers are. They like to think their sons will forever be their baby boys. Am I right, Clay?" With that last comment, he gave Clayton a bit of a nudge in his bicep and didn't quite get a wholehearted affirmation back.

"If you say so, man," Clayton mumbled.

But Brent chose to completely ignore that response and focus on Liv. "Like I was saying, I'm about my business and I pretty much know what I'm talking about. The market around here is on the upswing. In high demand. Although some of the locals don't like the changes, tourism is up. Way up, due to urban migration. And that could be good for all of us. Why this spot we're on right now is worth way more than our parents, and certainly way more than our grandparents, probably ever even thought of."

Liv got a sudden prickly feeling. She had a feeling she knew where this was going and she knew she didn't like it. "So you mean gentrification?"

Brent frowned and was about to speak again, but Liv held up a hand. "I'm gonna stop you right there, Brent, though I pretty much don't have any say-so in the family's land, I'm sure if that's where you're going, Aunt Joyce or any of the other aunts or uncles would not like to hear any sort of land-selling talk."

Brent gave a dramatic eye roll. "I'm not talking about selling the land, or at least not all of it, and who's to say all the aunts wouldn't be on board? Sure, Aunt Joyce is a hard-liner, all about the family legacy and all that mess, but I'm sure your mother's more open. I mean, just think about maybe even renting cottages on some of it, or leasing part. We could be making a killing."

Liv shook her head; thankfully, Brent could tell she was shutting down. Lord, was he really doing this now? At a barbecue in front of Clayton Morris. "No problem, no problem, I get it. Like you said, you don't really have anything to do with it and this is supposed to be a party, we're not here to talk business. I'm just trying to open your eyes a bit to the possibilities of what's going on here in Sugar Lake. This is no longer the sleepy little town you left. A lot is happening with the new country club, and there's a mall not far away. We've got the best of both worlds. We've got your lazy sleepy town plus we've got something for the nouveau riche. There's a lot of potential here. Even with Aunt Joyce's bakeshop. Prime real estate like that doesn't come along often, and with her getting old, she needs to start really thinking about the future and what she wants to do with that location. That hip has to be whispering something to her about retirement."

Oh, the urge to go totally and completely off was so intense. The nerve of Brent! But Liv fought hard to appear calm. "Like I said, Brent, I'm only here to help Aunt Joyce out while she's getting back on her feet. I don't see any reason why things can't continue as they are." She gave him a hard stare. "I'm not here to add any more stress, and I don't think you should be either. But if you're feeling bold, why don't you head on over to her now and see how far you get with that retirement talk."

With that Brent looked over to where Aunt Joyce was sitting, not far from the action. She was pointing at Uncle Clint and clearly giving him an earful about something. Brent turned back to Liv. "Maybe some other time. This is supposed to be a celebration."

"Yeah, that's what I thought," Liv said as he walked away.

As he headed back to the house Liv tried hard to shake off the feeling that there was something more behind his words, but then again it was Brent and there really was no reason to put more weight on any words he gave out. Brent always had some sort of scheme going, and after that scheme fell through he was on to the next. This month it was real estate, next month who knew what it would be. They just had to ride it out. She suddenly felt for her own parents and Elijah with his never-ending studies and lack of commitment to a career. She looked up at Clayton and gave him a weak smile. "Sorry you had to deal with my cousin, he's always got something going on."

Clayton shrugged. "Hey, Brent is Brent. It's no big deal. Like many here, he doesn't change. But what he was saying about the town changing, that part is true, and what he said about certain people not being happy with the changes is true too. On the one hand it's good. The progress helps taxes and it helps infrastructure, but it's not all positive. It doesn't help the small businesses, and we've even noticed a small uptick in crime. Before you know it we've lost our small-town way of life. Not to mention property values. As they go up, the taxes get out of hand for the locals who live here. That's the worst part."

Liv could tell it was something that had been weighing on him. "I can tell you've been thinking about this for a while," she said.

"I have."

"Though I can't tell exactly what side of the fence you're on," she said.

He tilted his head as if he was weighing the pros and cons as he looked out onto the lake for an answer. "It's complicated."

"That's a Facebook status. You can do better."

He smiled. "Well, I see both sides, so I am a little bit torn, as you can tell by the way I'm talking. I get the side of progress and I can fully understand it. But my heart, for the most part, is with the townspeople. I can take progress, but not at the expense of others."

Liv nodded, understanding what he was saying, but something in his last line, the bit about the expense of others, hit her solidly in her gut. Was it something he truly believed, and was that something new for him? Did he think about the toll his leaving would have on her when he left without a word? Liv cleared her throat and looked down at her now totally cooled pie. She no longer had an appetite and no longer wanted to continue this conversation. "Listen, I better head on in and start helping with the cleanup." She felt herself bite at her bottom lip and quickly stopped when she caught it for the nervous tic that it was. "Like I was saying when you first came over, there is no reason to give people more of an excuse to talk. Despite what Brent is saying, the town has only changed so much, and it is still a small town. No need to fuel things. I'll see you around."

Clayton nodded at that, and Liv turned to join the party. But her nerves were too much of a jumble, and she forgot how rocky the terrain was over by the edge of the lake. So when her foot caught on a rock and she tripped over herself, it was like the cherry on top of a perfectly imperfect day. One moment she was upright and the next she was tumbling toward the ground, only to be stopped by Clayton blocking her fall with his hard chest as he stepped out in front of her, smashing her body flat against his own, her chest banging against his hard chest. The only buffer was a wet mash of cold leftover cherry pie as it smashed between the two of them. Liv let out a loud "Oomph!" as her eyes went wide meeting his and embarrassment enveloped her from head to toe.

But Clayton only laughed as his arm went around her waist, and he pulled her in impossibly closer, causing her to heat even more as he gave her that ridiculously dazzling smile. "As I was telling you, I'm here for you whenever you need me. I won't let you down. Not again."

Chapter 12

He was there for her. He wouldn't let her down? What kind of game was he playing now? Liv tried to puzzle out those questions in her mind as Aunt Joyce once again opened the bakeshop at the crack of dawn early on Monday morning. She knew she was wasting her time and energy though. Falling right into his hands, and falling off her game. This was probably exactly what he wanted. Clayton Morris wasn't her reason for being here in Sugar Lake. Aunt Joyce and the shop were. It was time to focus.

But how was one to focus when one's mind was still a jumble of sultry eyes, hard pecs, gorgeous smiles, and cherry pie, Liv thought as she followed Aunt Joyce and Drea inside the shop to open it. She went about what she was quickly learning were her usual duties as they got the shop ready for the morning's customers as the crushed pie incident stubbornly stayed in the forefront of her mind.

Oh gosh, she didn't know if she'd ever get over the mortification. First the ants, then crashing into him like some klutz, and *then* getting leftover pie juice smashed between the both of them. Now the topper, getting caught ogling the man changing out of his pie-stained shirt like some desperate overly hormonal spinster! The thought made Liv want to spend some time beating herself over the head with a rolling pin until her senses came back.

But goodness, that view was something else. She recalled thinking about how she pushed back from Clayton's grasp with a quick apology and talked about going to change. Once in her room and looking over her stained dress, she was over the idea of trying to look pretty, and she decided laid-back and comfortable was the way to go as she grabbed a pair of denim shorts and a white tank top. Going to close the curtain in her room, Liv thought about the days she used to glimpse out and see Clayton at his window. What a foolish young girl she had been. But back then just a glimpse of him would make her so happy. Sometimes he'd wave, then they would talk on the phone as if they hadn't spent most of the day together already. With a sigh, she went to pull the curtain shut and just about darn near passed out.

Whoa, talk about some things changing. Clayton Morris truly had changed. Liv swallowed down hard at the sudden buildup of saliva as she blinked and saw the vision of Clayton live and in color as he pulled over his head the cherry-stained T-shirt that he had been wearing. She clutched at the curtain's edge as the world seemed to suddenly tilt, taking Liv off her very axis as inch by glorious inch, one muscular pack of his six-pack—or it could be eight-pack—abs were revealed to her like some decadent, just out of reach, look-but-you-can't-touch temptation show. *Where did a man get abs like that?* Did he live in a permanent core flex or something? Liv's mind boggled as she continued to brazenly stare as if she were studying him like some sort of science before-and-after subject. Having the nerve to watch, she found her eyes following the T-shirt on its ascent as it revealed more of Clayton's glorious skin, up his chest, until finally the tee came over his impossibly wide shoulders. She watched the opening as it grazed his cheeks, catching on his slight chin stubble for just a moment, and then it slipped over his head.

Liv let out a breath then, one she didn't know she had been holding. She was just about to step back and move out of view when she looked up once again and Clayton leaned forward, his eyes connecting with hers dead-on, a devilish grin on that handsome face of his.

Oh god, no!

Stepping back, Liv shut her curtain tight. She quickly pulled on her change of clothes and headed downstairs, vowing that that would be the last time she watched Clayton Morris change from her bedroom window like a desperate not-quite housewife Peeping Tom.

"Earth to Livy. Earth to Livy."

"I swear I don't know what's with this girl this morning. Usually it's you who I have to get on about focusing, Drea. There is too much work to be done today for this lollygagging." It wasn't Aunt Joyce's words that brought Liv back to the present, but it was a clap combined with the flour that wafted around her as if sugar fairies were suddenly making snow that brought things back into semisharp focus.

But there were no fairies, only a not-so-pleased-looking Aunt Joyce, who looked poised to clap again, her floured hands at the ready in front of Liv's face.

Liv blinked and gave her head a good shake, focusing on her aunt. "Really, lady, was that entirely necessary?"

Aunt Joyce gave her a raised brow from the other side of the worktable. "It would seem it was. We've got about five dozen biscuits to get done this morning, and I don't have time for either of you girls to have your head in the clouds. Rena just sent a text saying she won't be in today. Her youngest is sick with a bug, so I need all four of your hands and your two heads on deck. We've got work to do."

Liv gave a nod and cleared her throat. "Yes, ma'am," she said. "I'm sorry about that. I'm here, ready to work and ready to focus."

Aunt Joyce gave her a nod back. "All right then. Good. I'm not saying you have to be a total worker bee. It's not like I'm running a sweatshop. I just want you to pay attention when it comes to these biscuits."

Liv tried to hold back her smile, but it was hard. She loved it when Aunt Joyce got all passionate about her baked goods. Most people would probably get upset, but Liv knew it was only because she wanted to serve her customers the very best. That she truly cared and took pride in her work and what she was presenting. She could appreciate and admire that. Besides, when Aunt Joyce got this way, you were bound to learn something good.

"Now," Aunt Joyce continued, "we got to have us an assembly line going. Especially when it comes to these honey biscuits. If these aren't done perfectly and on time, it will taste like you're chewing on a cement puck. And I will not tolerate cement pucks coming out of my place." She looked over at Drea, who was attempting to knead dough, and her expression turned grave. "Lordy, girl. How many times do I have to tell you? You've gotta put your back into it! You have to show it who's boss. The way you're rubbing it, you'd think you were angling for a proposal. Well, that's no way to treat dough or a man."

Drea pulled a shocked face. "Aunt Joyce!"

"What? Just because I'm old don't mean I'm dead. And don't think I don't just know my way around the kitchen."

Liv and Drea looked at each other, then burst out laughing.

"What?" Aunt Joyce said. "I don't see anything funny. You'd better get on that dough the right way, gal."

Drea let out a sigh, sobering up, and looked back at Aunt Joyce. "I am rubbing at it hard, Aunt Joyce. This dough is tough. I'm doing the best I can."

Aunt Joyce shook her head. "Girl, you call that tough? We haven't even added all the ingredients yet. Maybe your arms need a little building up. I thought everybody in New York took some form of kickboxing or something like that. Didn't y'all have to take some kind of martial arts class in order to ride the subways?"

Liv shook her head. "That's not right, Aunt Joyce; don't use tired stereotypes about how tough New York is to try to get weakling Drea here to knead your dough harder."

"Yeah," Drea said before she thought about what Liv had really said, and then she gave her sister a confused look. "Wait. What do you mean weakling Drea? I'm no weakling. This dough is tough. Why can't we use one of those two big electric mixers over there."

Aunt Joyce gave her a look as if she'd just committed blasphemy in the sanctuary. "Because those mixers are for other things. And not my hand-kneaded honey biscuits, that's why. My hand-kneaded honey biscuits are called hand-kneaded honey biscuits because they are just that. Hand-kneaded, and with love, mind you.

Like I always say, food always tastes good when it's cooked with love."

Drea gave her a shrug. "Well, I guess my food won't ever taste good, because I don't love to cook."

Aunt Joyce let out an exasperated sigh. "Bless her heart. What am I going to do with this child?" she said to the ceiling, the Lord, the universe in general, and then turned back to Drea and gave her a sweet, though quite menacing in its own way, smile. "Well, it's a good thing you have many other talents, dear. God don't put us on this earth without giving us talents. Yours will show themselves"—she paused, then added—"in time I'm sure. Now, head on over and start pulling out the ingredients we need, and let your sister do the dough."

Drea walked over to the pantry to gather the other ingredients. She paused after the butter and turned toward Aunt Joyce. "Wait, what ingredients are we going to need?"

Once again Aunt Joyce sighed, in that moment probably rethinking the sister's invitation and no doubt her initial trip up on the roof that got her into her predicament. "I'm gonna shout them out. You just prepare to pull 'em."

She then turned toward Liv and pointed her finger. "Okay, looks like we're shifting and you're up for double duty. How about you take some of those musings of yours out on the dough, and while you're at it add in the butter, sugar, and a pinch of salt. The honey will come later."

Try as she might, Liv couldn't get mad over the bit of chaos. It felt good having her hands moving, squishing in and out of the dough. Putting all her strength into something that would make people happy as well as nourish them. The rolling, then the precise measuring and laying them out for the oven. There was a clear satisfaction to it that she hadn't felt in a long time. Made all the better when she would look up and see her aunt and her sister right along with her.

"These came out delicious, baby!"

It was just before opening and Liv couldn't help feeling pride over Aunt Joyce's rave review over her batches of biscuits. In the end, she had given her a little more leeway over making them. And though Liv hadn't totally made them on her own, the fact that they were mostly by her hand made her feel pretty good.

"She's right, these are okay, almost as good as Aunt Joyce's. Give you a little more time and you'll be there, big sis," Drea said, finishing her own biscuit before downing it with the rest of her green tea.

Liv felt her lips tighten at Drea's backhanded compliment, but she'd take it anyway. Drea hadn't had the best of mornings, having been essentially shooed away from any sort of real baking by Aunt Joyce after her full-on display of lack of skills in the kitchen. But Liv had to give her credit for squeezing those lemons for all they were worth. In the short morning prep time, her sister had tidied up the pantry, then gone out and fixed up the counter and even rearranged the tables in a more pleasing manner. The best was that she took it upon herself to take down the old, worn curtains that had seen better days, pulled the old blinds all the way up so that the natural light from the street came in, and washed the front windows down so the whole place took on a new, bright cast as the morning sun started to stream in.

"I think it looks great, Drea," Aunt Joyce said.

"Though I would've appreciated it if you'd asked me before taking down my curtains."

"I'm sure you would have, Aunt Joyce, and I'm sorry about that," Drea said to her as she put down her teacup and then wiped down where it had been on the counter, then went to put the cup in the sink in the back. "But I couldn't risk your telling me no. Those old curtains had to go. Now, if you don't think I'm overstepping, I'd like those blinds to come down too. Maybe we can get that Errol of yours to come on in here and do that. I've got a few more ideas about changing the decor if you're open. I'm not much help in the kitchen. I might as well do something with my time while I'm here."

Liv took in Aunt Joyce's serious expression. She could tell that though she was a little put out, she still appreciated Drea's initiative, and Liv also could tell she liked that Drea had showed some real interest in the shop. But there was a part of it that gave Liv pause. She didn't want Drea giving Aunt Joyce false hope. They were only there for a short amount of time. They had already been there for a week and Liv could tell Aunt Joyce was clearly on the mend. She was starting physical therapy and would be her old self fairly soon.

Was it fair to talk about improvements on the shop and get her invested without leaving support in place? If they were going to really help out here, they'd have to do more than just making the shop look better. Liv would have to talk to Rena about getting Aunt Joyce more help for the future. Maybe she should just put Drea off this idea about improvements?

She had to figure out a way to balance helping Aunt Joyce with the shop and getting on with her job search. Before she knew it, she'd have to head back to New

York and get on with her own life, and she supposed Drea would have to do the same. "You did good, Drea. Everything already looks much brighter and cheerier, and I think doing a little something with the tables was a good idea too, but I'm not sure about bigger improvements. I'm not sure Aunt Joyce can handle much more new business. I mean, it's not like we're staying on to help her."

Liv knew immediately that she'd overstepped when she saw the stiffening of Aunt Joyce's back. Not to mention how quickly Aunt Joyce whirled around toward her. "Who said anything about you having to stay on to help, missy?"

"I'm sorry. I didn't mean anything by it. I wasn't trying to upset you, I just didn't want Drea to do too much and put more pressure on you when you didn't need it."

"Well, don't presume to know what I need or don't need. I know I called you for help, and I do appreciate it." Aunt Joyce softened her tone, but only slightly. In that moment, reminding Liv of her own mother and even a bit of herself. She could see every bit of the Goode temper rising up. "I think your sister has wonderful ideas, and I fully support them. Now, as to how they are worked out for the future, well, I for one will let the future handle itself. It all works out in the end. I have no worry about that. And you shouldn't either. Maybe that's your problem. You think too far ahead for other people when you shouldn't."

"Amen to that, Aunt Joyce." Drea was quick to chime in. "I've been telling her that for the longest time."

"Don't use this as an excuse to dump on me just because you don't have your life together."

Drea rolled her eyes. "Oh boy, here we go. The queen of deflection deflects again. I'm just gonna leave you to it and to yourself." She turned back toward Aunt Joyce and smiled. "Thank you for the vote of confidence, Aunt Joyce, and for being able to have the vision to keep your mind in the present instead of focused on ridiculous worries that you have no control over . . . or for staying stuck on the mistakes of the past." And with that, of course, Drea couldn't help but give a slick little side-eye toward Liv once again.

"Well, look at mister fancy over there," Aunt Joyce said, shifting the subject and bringing their attention to Brent, who was across the street with a couple of men in khakis and polo shirts with blazers. "He's out early too. I guess he's taking this real estate thing seriously. Those must be clients of his. I do hope he's getting his life together. Kath will be happy if he finally settles into something."

Liv frowned, remembering their conversation at the barbecue. "I'm sure. I wonder what property he's listing, or if he's just showing them the town. They seem pretty interested in this area," she said, noting how they were taking in the bakeshop and the surrounding storefronts from their vantage point across the street. When Brent noticed them watching him, he waved, and they waved back. Then he shuffled his clients farther down the block.

As quickly as Brent disappeared from view, Clayton appeared, walking into the shop looking like spring after a long winter.

"We're not quite open yet," Liv said without thinking, her voice sharper than it probably should've been.

"So this is how you're going to help me keep my business under control, missy?" Aunt Joyce hissed from by her side.

"Well, it's seven-thirty, and when I peeped in and saw you were all here at the counter and the door was unlocked, I took it upon myself to come in and say good morning. I hope that's not a problem, ladies."

Liv wanted to growl and at the same time she felt the heat of embarrassment as it rode up from her toes and wrapped around her body until it got to the top of her head. Why did he have to go and say something about peeking in? She looked up at him, expecting to see laughter in his eyes. A gotcha over her embarrassing Peeping Tom situation from the barbecue. She'd successfully avoided him by staying on opposite ends of the lawn and in totally separate spaces for the rest of the day after the incident. But still, for most of the rest of the afternoon, even though she would take peeks and not see him looking, she could still feel the heat of his gaze and his judgment. Had she ever been more embarrassed in her life? Probably not. Maybe not. Definitely not.

"Of course, you're always welcome, Clayton," Aunt Joyce said.

"And here, you've got to try one of this morning's honey biscuits. They are straight out of the oven. Liv made this batch herself and, if I do say so, she did an excellent job. Despite her lack of manners."

Clayton gave Liv a smile and a tilt of his head. "Made with your very own hand, huh? Well then, I definitely won't refuse."

Liv fought to stay neutral. It wouldn't do to be anything but kind. Besides, she'd already proven herself a bubbling idiot by bumping into him and smashing cherry pie on his shirt. She needed to once and for all show some type of smoothness in front of this man. "I've got a few skills in the kitchen," Liv said, hoping she came off somewhere near Cool Town and not

Dork Street. She caught a smirk from Drea and decided she probably got caught up somewhere on Geek Way. But then Clayton took one of her biscuits and put it to his mouth. He spread those deliciously full lips wide to take a bite.

He proceeded to chew, his closed-mouth smile causing his dimples to pop and creases to form in the corners of his eyes. Liv wanted to kick herself over the blossoming feeling of joy that came over her. Darn! She was not supposed to care about how Clayton felt about her freaking cooking. She let go of a breath. Maybe Clayton's feelings had nothing to do with it. Maybe she was just happy because somebody felt her biscuits tasted good.

"Just delicious," he said, looking Liv straight in the eye. "These are really good. You do have some skills, and here I was thinking you are just a pretty face and a brain. But then again, I should have known about your hidden talents, Livia."

Why did everything Clayton Morris say send her half into a tailspin? Thankfully, he turned toward Aunt Joyce. "Superb culinary skills must run in the family."

Liv inwardly shivered. The man should never say the word *culinary* again.

Drea snorted. "I wouldn't go that far."

Clayton turned her way. "Oh really?"

"It would seem I wasn't so blessed, but that's okay, I'm not crying about it." She put her arm around Liv's shoulder and brought her back to reality. "I've got my own talents and my sister has hers, and as you can see, she uses it well."

Clayton stared at Liv, mesmerizing her with his deep, soulful eyes. "Yes, she does." Just then two other customers walked in and Clayton cleared his throat. "Listen, I'll take two dozen for the guys at the firehouse. I have a feeling you're going to sell out today and I don't want to miss out on a good thing."

Liv raised a brow. "No," she said. "You definitely wouldn't want to do that." She turned away from him. "Let me just get those boxed up for you. Wait here. It won't be but a minute."

By the time she came back with the boxed biscuits, Clayton had already paid and was chatting it up with Drea. She resisted the urge to reach out and pull her sister back by the apron tie when she hightailed it to the other end of the counter as soon as Liv appeared with Clayton's bag.

"Here you go. I hope everyone enjoys them," Liv said. There, service with a smile.

Clayton lifted his hand slowly. He went to take the shopping bag from her, letting his index fingers graze over her own, sending the most intense zing up her arm. Liv pulled her hand away quickly and clapped her hands together in front of her.

"I'm sure they'll be a big hit," Clayton said.

"Thanks. Well, we'll be seeing you, I'm sure," Liv said, but ridiculously enough Clayton wasn't moving from his spot and heading for the door like a normal patron would be doing. Instead he stood rooted in his spot and continued to look at her.

Liv gave him an expectant look. "And is there something else I can help you with?" She hoped her tone let him know that there was nothing else she really wanted to help him with.

"As a matter of fact, there is," he said.

Of course there is. Why wouldn't there be?

"I was hoping you'd join me for lunch today. I'd still

like to give you that apology and that explanation that I talked about. It's kind of weighing on me."

The fact that he said it was weighing on him sent sparks of anger that Liv told herself shouldn't be there quickly igniting once again. "It shouldn't be weighing on you at all, Clayton, not now. You've had plenty of years to apologize and alleviate anything that had been weighing on you. So now that seeing me has brought up old feelings, well, I can't help that. I'm sorry but, no, I won't be meeting you for lunch today. Whatever it is you have to deal with, you just have to deal with it on your own."

She saw him about to speak again, in haste possibly, but then he seemed to think better of it. And he looked at her. In his eyes, she thought she saw possible pleading, but he never was one to be the pleading type; he was always too proud for that, so no, maybe it wasn't pleading in his eyes, but still there was a question there.

"Listen, all I'm asking is for you to please just think about it. I have a lot to answer for and a lot to explain. I'll be at Doreen's Diner between two and three o'clock, if you can get away. Just waiting, no pressure on your part. All I'm asking is for you to consider it." He gave her a broad grin, his countenance somehow shifting, and once again he looked every bit the easygoing fire chief she glimpsed when she first rolled into town. "Thanks again for the biscuits. I'm sure everyone will love them." He held up the bag again and made his voice a little louder this time so that Aunt Joyce and Drea could hear over the few customers that were now in the store. "Thanks again, ladies, I'll see you all around."

"Thanks, Clayton. Give my best to the crew and your mama too," Aunt Joyce said while Drea gave

a wave as she sauntered back toward Liv, giving her a
nudge with her hip.

"Not a word," Liv said before her sister could open
her mouth. "I don't want to hear one word on the
subject of Clayton Morris, not now and not ever. You
got me?"

"If you say so, big sis, but I have a feeling it won't be
me bringing up the name first." She exaggeratedly
looked at her watch. "I mean, two o'clock comes around
mighty fast."

Chapter 13

"What?" Liv asked when she looked up and found her aunt staring at her once again. "Why are you staring at me?"

Not moving, Aunt Joyce continued with her perusal, her eyes going from the old clock on the kitchen wall and back to Liv again. "I was just wondering why you keep glancing at the clock so much. I know you're trying to get this pie in the oven, but it's not a race. Now, if you got someplace else you need to be right now, maybe you should get to getting."

Liv frowned, then shook her head. She would not be put off her game. Nope. She knew her aunt was trying to get under her skin with that way-too-knowing stare of hers, but she wasn't letting her. She would stay focused on the task at hand, she thought as she shifted her gaze back to her trusty recipe book, frowning deeper when she caught the smatter of flour that had covered the plastic-covered pages. With a frustrated huff she reached for a paper towel to clear the mess, but only ended up smearing it. With a sigh she quickly turned the page and looked down to read the next needed ingredient in her not-quite-famous berry swirl pie.

"There," she said, "one teaspoon of cinnamon, three-quarter stick of butter, one cup each of strawberries, blueberries and raspberries." Liv looked back up at Aunt Joyce, purposefully ignoring her comment about the clock, preferring to keep the subject purely on the pie she was baking. "I'd love to try this with a bit of blackberries. I can never get sweet-enough ones in the city. Maybe if I checked the farmers' market here over the weekend I'd have better luck."

Aunt Joyce's expression changed to one of annoyance and exasperation. "Girl, don't think I don't know that you avoided my question about checking that clock."

Liv felt her lips tighten as her mind skipped around, looking for the correct word. Of course she couldn't tell Aunt Joyce that she was looking at the clock and once again checking the ridiculously slow-moving time. It was currently 2:04 p.m. Four minutes past the time she was supposed to—well, not really supposed to, but asked to—go over to the diner and meet Clayton for his apology-slash-explanation-slash-confession hour. And though she knew as soon as he gave the invitation that she was definitely not going to join him, she still could admit to herself that part of her had a desire to hear out what sort of excuse he'd planned on giving her to make up for breaking her heart.

But what could he possibly say to make up for all the years and the time lost? Not to mention the promises broken. She knew it was a waste, and she knew that this meeting was really nothing more than something else to cover up for his own guilt. So why give him the satisfaction? She wouldn't do it. She'd much rather stay here in the relative calm of the kitchen

baking her pie instead of listening to whatever excuse
Clayton Morris had cooked up.

Still, something in Liv's stomach turned. The
thought of him sitting, waiting for her, even though it
was just for an hour and not for a full summer as she
had done back when she was eighteen, she was ashamed
to say the thought gave her a perverted sense of . . .
she didn't know, glee or satisfaction from getting a
little bit of revenge? Yeah, all of that, while at the same
time it just didn't sit right with her spirit.

Liv swallowed down hard before looking over at
her aunt. "I don't know what you're talking about,
Aunt Joyce. I'm focused on what we're doing right
now. Actually, trying hard to focus as much as I can. I
want to do well for you by showing you one of my best
recipes." She poked her finger carefully down at her
book, and to her utter shock Aunt Joyce snatched her
recipe book right from underneath her flour-covered
finger and slammed it tightly shut.

"That's the problem right there. You are and you've
always wanted to do everything so right and so perfectly that you always followed things by the book.
Why, I'd wager that you know every recipe in this
book already inside out. You know the measurements
and every ingredient by heart." Aunt Joyce laid the
book aside, put her right hand on her chest, and gave
herself a pat. "But do you know the recipes in your
heart? That's the question I want to know the answer
to. I reckon you don't need this book at all. Like I said
to your sister earlier, when you're baking you need to
do it with love. When you do it with love, it shows, and
that's when you truly bring magic to your food."

And then to Liv's distinct shock and horror, Aunt
Joyce took her precious recipe book and, without any

sort of fanfare, picked it up and dropped it right into the trash can.

Liv gasped and went diving after her recipe book, fishing it back out quickly and brushing it off. She placed it gently on the edge of the worktable before looking back at her aunt with wide eyes. "How could you do such a thing? I've been working on this book for years. Don't you have a care about other people's work and what they do?" Liv said, raising her voice, for the moment forgetting that she was talking to her aunt.

But Aunt Joyce just waved a hand in front of her face and laughed. "Oh, girly, I knew you were going to go after that book and probably nab it before it hit the bottom of the can. There was no way you would let that thing go. Besides, if I really wanted to get rid of it, I would have snatched it without your knowledge. Don't worry, your precious book is safe. I just wanted to illustrate the fact that I don't think you need it. You've got all you need already up there in that brain of yours, and I suspect you really do have it in your heart. Now, if you want to show me something for real, you just keep that thing closed and get to baking. I've seen what you can do so far, and I always knew you had talent. Now, prove me right and make me something sweet that will knock off these horrid orthopedic socks I'm wearing." With that short but effective speech Aunt Joyce turned away from Liv and went over to where the rest of the fruits were stored, pulling out a few more berries for Liv to add to her pie. Thankfully the rest of the hour went by quicker and less tense than the first few minutes, and Liv got through it by focusing less on her stress and anxiety over not joining Clayton at the diner and more on making the best berry swirl pie she'd ever made.

* * *

Clayton sat in a booth at Doreen's Diner and took another sip of his now cold coffee. "You sure you don't want to go on ahead and just order something now, Clayton? It's been over forty minutes; I don't think your friend is gonna make it."

He looked up at Doreen, who was smiling down at him, coffeepot in hand to once again warm up the cup of coffee he was nursing for all it was worth. Doreen, the patron and owner of the diner, looked at Clayton with her soft green eyes, and Clayton could tell that, though Doreen was all sweetness and light, she wanted more than anything to know whom he was currently waiting for. Petite and still somehow quite statuesque with an open smile and an easy laugh, Doreen came on as everybody's favorite confidant, but one had to be careful when it came to sweet ol' Doreen. Like a vampire who lived on blood, Doreen was fueled by the town's gossip. Some thought it's what made her still so vibrant at her undeterminable age. The woman didn't look a day over fifty, though some of the older town residents had her pegged at seventy, if she was a day, and she'd buried three husbands already, each eighty and above.

That he'd asked Livia to meet him over at Doreen's, Clayton now knew, was probably not the best idea. But then again, where else could they meet for coffee? The town was only so big, and the new chain coffee shop didn't seem quite like the place to have the type of talk they needed to have. Maybe he should have asked her to dinner. Something and someplace fancier, like the country club. She was a city girl and probably used to finer things. But really, who was he fooling? Finer things or not, she still would have turned him down. She didn't even want to sit with him at a casual backyard barbecue.

Clayton rapped his knuckles on the table. It was a moot point now. He needed to come to terms with the fact that she wasn't showing up, not now and probably not ever. He gave Doreen a look of resignation and a nod. "I'll have a cheeseburger deluxe, Doreen. Thanks a lot."

Doreen stood for half a second more than she needed, probably hoping he'd give her more talk, more explanation, than just his cheeseburger order, but he wasn't in the mood, not today. Just his food please and he'd be on his way. Food and his own thoughts, that's all that he needed right now.

But apparently asking for just sustenance and his own company in that moment was too much, because just as Doreen walked away, Clayton looked out the window and locked eyes with his brother coming down the street. Caleb gave him a quick nod and then shocked him by turning and heading toward the diner's entrance. Crap. Would he really not be able to sit by himself and stew in his misery?

And what was Caleb doing out in the middle of the afternoon, in polite society, anyway? First, he decided to make an appearance at Mom's, obviously taking what he said at the bar to heart, and then he topped it off by staying for the Goodes' barbecue. It was all disarmingly out of character.

Clayton was in a mood with Livia not showing, so he had a hard time keeping his cool when Caleb, without as much as a "how do you do," took the seat opposite him at his booth.

Quick as a whip, Doreen came scampering over with her chipper attitude and a big smile. "Hey there, better late than never," she said to Caleb before turning to

Clayton. "Isn't this great. And there I thought you'd be dining alone." Though Clayton very much wanted to stand up and clamp his hand over Doreen's mouth, the last thing he wanted was for his brother to know he had been sitting for forty minutes waiting for a no-show from somebody, but of course he couldn't keep Doreen quiet. All he could do was sit and watch while she talked and the wheels turned in Caleb's head as he caught on to the fact that Clayton had indeed been stood up for his lunch. "Yep, I'm glad to see you made it. Your brother was sitting here looking a might fit to be tied waiting on you, and it takes a lot to get him to lose his sunny disposition." She smiled even more broadly, having done all the damage she needed to, Clayton guessed. "Well, what can I get you? He's already ordered a cheeseburger so won't be long before it's up. Can I do the same for you?"

Caleb gave him a half-sly grin that said he had indeed put two and two together, but then he quickly looked back up at Doreen and gave her a smile. "A cheeseburger would be great, Doreen, medium for me with pepper jack cheese please and extra fried onions. Oh, and I'll have a chocolate shake to go with it, thanks."

"No problem," Doreen said, and hurried off to put in Caleb's order.

With that, Caleb turned back to Clayton and placed an elbow on the table, tilting his chin in his hand. With his non-prosthetic hand, he drummed his fingers expectantly on the table.

"What is that look all about?" Clayton said. "And what's with the finger drumming? And what's with you out in the light of day anyway? You showing up here in the daylight might ruin the whole 'man of mystery' thing that you got going."

Caleb gave his head a shake when Doreen brought over his milkshake. "Very funny, lil bro. Stop being so suspicious. I come out in the daytime plenty. People just don't happen to see me because I'm stealth. Also I happened to have business in town that needed to take place before five o'clock. For some reason, they still like to close banks before five in this godforsaken town. But hey, check this out, you get to be the beneficiary of it and enjoy my company at lunch."

Clayton let out a snort. "Yeah, lucky me."

"Don't look so thrilled about it. I could tell from Doreen's speech and your reaction that I definitely wasn't your intended lunch date today."

Clayton wasn't taking the bait. It was none of Caleb's business who he was meeting for lunch. "So what business did you have to take care of before five o'clock at the bank? Is everything okay? Anything I need to worry about with you and finances?"

Caleb raised a brow and shook his head. "You don't have anything to worry about with me. Not now, not anymore. I'm working, doing a decent job at the bar, being a semiproductive part of society." He raised his prosthetic limb slightly and gave it a little twist. "As you can see, me and my little friend here are doing just fine. Sure, I could use a bit more mobility, but this is about as state of the art as my insurance is going to get me, so I'm grateful for it. Things could be worse."

Clayton looked at his brother seriously, for the moment thoughts of Livia pushed to the back of his mind. "Or they could be better."

He saw briefly a hint of impatience spark in Caleb's eyes, and it looked as if he was getting a flash of something. A spark, maybe of a memory. "Like I said. They could be worse."

Clayton thought it best to drop the subject. At least

his brother was out. He was right, they could be worse. He'd been such a recluse since moving back home, and for a while there, Clayton and his mother were really worried about him. By moving out to the other side of the lake and not connecting with any of his old friends or doing any of the things that he used to do, it was as if he'd left a good hunk of his personality back on the battlefield in Afghanistan with his lost limb. Clayton knew his brother was changed the moment he'd seen him at the army hospital, but he didn't know how much until he'd been discharged and had come back home to presumably start his old life again.

But there was no restarting his old life, not for Caleb, and as Clayton would soon learn, not for him either. There was no going back. His brother taught him that. Maybe that was the lesson he needed to get into his head now with Livia back in town.

Doreen came back to the table with their burgers, and the two brothers proceeded to eat silently. The silence wasn't wholly uncomfortable or unwelcome, but Caleb broke it by speaking up once again. "So, you going to admit to me that it was Olivia Gale who had you sitting here looking sad and lonely with no lunch date this afternoon?"

Clayton stopped chewing mid-fry and gave his brother a harsh glare. "Why should I admit to any such thing?"

"Yeah, why would you? That might mean you admitting defeat, and we know that's something you never do." Caleb took a lazy bite of his burger, which made Clayton want to rush through his that much faster. Besides, he'd been away from work long enough and needed to get back to the station house. Thankfully there hadn't been any real emergencies today, but he had plenty of paperwork he could get done in his office, and if not paperwork, getting home early enough to help Hope with her homework tonight wouldn't be the worst idea.

"Listen, I really don't have time to talk about this," Clayton huffed out. "So what if Livia is the person I was waiting on?" Why did he just admit that?

Caleb nodded his head as he put another fry in his mouth and gave his brother a half grin.

"I swear if I get one slick word from you about Livia or about women in general, I'll take the other half of that burger and smash it in your face."

Caleb's smile went wider. "As if you'd really do that right here in Doreen's and ruin your perfect reputation. No way, for a do-gooder like you."

Clayton could feel the steam rising in his body, and he was sure he was about to start sweating through his T-shirt. He took a couple of final, determined bites of his burger and then downed his full glass of water. "Doesn't matter anyway. So what if she didn't join me for lunch? I was only trying to be nice to her with an invitation. You know, make her feel welcome back in town once again."

Caleb laughed full out, then took a long swig of his milkshake before speaking again. "Yeah, I bet you want to make her feel welcome, all right. You want to make her feel welcome from her head right down to her pretty little toes."

Clayton felt his fists clench into tight balls. "I'm warning you. You're taking this way too far."

"Then stop making it so darned easy," Caleb said. "It's just too much fun pushing your buttons. I mean, you've got them all out and exposed like flashing

Whac-A-Moles. Cut me a break, I'm enjoying seeing
you show some emotion for a change. It's better than
watching bad reality TV. I should go over there and
give Olivia a right proper thank you. Maybe offer
her a round of drinks at the bar on me tonight for her
and her sister."

"Don't you dare. The last thing I want is Livia tangling
with the likes of you."

Caleb put on a face as if he was somehow put out.
"Why? Are you afraid if she hangs out with me she
may learn some secrets about the real you?"

Clayton felt his brows pull tight. "You talk like I have
secrets."

Caleb let out a slow breath and shook his head. "If
you don't think you have any secrets, then I suspect
they are buried deeper than I thought. Maybe it's best
she didn't join you for lunch. I don't think you're
ready to handle Miss Gale just yet."

"What are you talking about? Maybe you've been up
in the mountains way too long. And I don't have any
secrets I'm keeping from Livia or myself. I was meeting her to just be nice. Nothing deeper than that. The
past is the past and what's done is done."

Caleb shrugged and his voice lowered as his expression grew more serious. "The past may be the past, but
what was done didn't have to be. Like I said, it's nice
to see you getting all riled up like this; it's been way
too long. And it's good to see a little spark in your eyes
again. I only see it now when you smile at Hope or talk
about her. I know I've never seen any joy or passion
when you talk about Celeste."

Clayton frowned deeper. "Man, I don't know what
you are talking about. None of this has anything to do
with Livia."

"Doesn't it? And that's why you keep calling her by the name only you called her back then."

Clayton was taken aback. He shook his head. "Nah, man. That's just old habit. I wanted to meet with her, sure. To talk to her maybe about some things that have happened in the past, maybe to make amends, I don't know. But any sort of feelings I may have, um, had, that thing is long gone and long in the past. I'm sure any feelings she may have had for me are long over too. She's made that perfectly clear. Besides, she's here only for a short while and I'm a father, single father of a daughter who needs me to focus on her and my responsibilities to her."

"You may be single, but you are not dead. And you're single for a reason," Caleb said.

"Yeah, I'm single because I couldn't figure out a way to make it work with my ex. And she decided I wasn't worth the work anymore."

Caleb shook his head. "Listen, you did everything too fast, too young and too impulsively. And believe me"—he looked down at his prosthetic hand and back up at Clayton—"we've both made those kinds of mistakes. I would do anything in my power to change my part in my own and in your impulsive decisions."

"Don't think like that," Clayton protested. "You lost a limb out there. It was me who made the decision to enlist after you had your accident."

"But I should have stopped you. I should have found my voice and spoken up."

Clayton didn't think he could hear this, and he didn't want his brother putting any more on himself. "You couldn't have stopped me back then, even if you'd tried." He let out a sigh. "I know it was reckless, and maybe a part of me was running from—" He thought for a moment, and the image of a sweet, young Livia came to his mind. She was looking at him as if he had the power to give her the world, and all he felt in that moment was powerless. He looked at his brother again. "—Everything. It was reckless getting drunk and hooking up with Celeste and then marrying her. But none of that is on you. You left enough out on the battlefield, you can't be responsible for me and my stupidity too."

Caleb nodded. "I get that. Well, at least part of me does. The rest of it I'll have to work out on my therapist's couch later. But you have to figure out a way to move on too. You were young, impulsive, and so was your ex. But neither of you are young and impulsive now. Now she's older and selfish. And you're older and being a martyr, and neither of you are doing your daughter any good. Now is the time for you to heal yourself and find some happiness."

"Fine, I hear you, but I still don't get what this has to do with Livia."

Caleb shook his head. He took another swig of his shake before looking back at Clayton. "Don't you? You know as well as I that nothing happens without a reason. She may be here just for a short while, but don't let whatever short moments they are go to waste without you bringing some sort of peace and closure to the left-open relationship that started all those years ago. Besides, maybe Celeste walked out of your life because you were kind of a jerk and a little bit of a stick-in-the-mud and most likely a pain."

"Thanks," Clayton said. "You're doing my ego tons of good."

"Or maybe," Caleb continued, "she walked out of your life because she knew that if she stayed, she'd only be a placeholder for a woman who you've been telling yourself you were not in love with for the past twelve years."

Clayton could do nothing more than look at his brother in stunned silence. What had brought this man off the mountain in the warm light of a late afternoon to come down here and ruin his lunch like this?

Clayton looked down as his cell went off with an alert for a 911. Part of him was suddenly grateful for the reprieve. That was until he answered and found out that once again he was headed to a fire call at Goode 'N Sweet.

Chapter 14

Clayton took one look at Olivia Gale in the arms of Braxton Lewis and declared that indeed this was an emergency. Though not the type he was expecting.

Sure, his heart was racing a bit when he saw that the 911 he'd gotten was for yet another incident at Goode 'N Sweet, but when he'd made it to the back of the shop where all the action was and saw Lewis with his arms around Olivia, his Livia, all thoughts of any fire danger went right out of his head. There had better be a professional purpose or the younger man was going to pay. The guy had one arm around Liv's shoulder and the other one closely grasped about her waist while Livia was leaning back and looking up at him with a slightly stunned, or maybe it was admiring, expression—crud, he didn't know—while silky smooth Braxton Lewis was looking down on her with too cool a grin.

"You mind letting her go and focusing on the situation at hand?" The words came out of Clayton's mouth before he could stop them, and worse, they came out way more clipped then they should have.

Clayton watched as both Livia and Lewis swiveled

their heads his way, and their expressions went from confused to clearly something else. Livia's slipped into annoyance, and Lewis's, well, his was something that Clayton hoped wouldn't be a problem later on. It was a combination of both amusement and embarrassment. No matter, Clayton's words clearly worked, because Lewis carefully removed his hand from around Livia's waist, though he didn't remove his other arm from around her shoulder as he looked down at her and asked, "Are you sure you're all right? I wouldn't want you putting any undue pressure on that ankle until it gets checked out."

It was Clayton's turn to look confused. Wait, was she hurt? Had he gone and read the situation wrong? See, this was why he kept himself free of any entanglements, not that Livia was an entanglement. She was far from one, but this was why he kept himself nonattached, in his mind and his heart. It was better to stay focused on business, his family, and his daughter. That way he didn't go around making dumb assumptions like the one he'd just made.

Clayton took a step forward, still peeved over his emotion-fueled misstep, and he hated to admit it, a part of him was pissed that Livia had needed help and he wasn't the first on the scene there to give it to her. Instead he was stuck over at Doreen's having a nonsensical conversation with Caleb. He paused as the irrationality of his thinking hit him and shame crept up his neck in the form of unwelcome heat. He needed to deflect. Clayton quickly scanned the situation and was relieved when he didn't see evidence of a serious fire. No flames, no dark smoke. But there was still the smell of smoke in the air and light-colored remnants indicating that a fire had been recently put out in the Dumpster.

"Are you hurt? What happened here?" Clayton asked.

Livia gave a slight push away and out of Lewis's hold, and Clayton was embarrassed over how much he appreciated seeing her move out of the other man's embrace. She looked at him. "I'm fine, though just as klutzy as normal, it would seem. I took a bit of a stumble over one of the parking stalls when I rushed back in after noticing we had a fire in the Dumpster."

Clayton glanced back over at the Dumpster again. Yes, it was contained, but he got an uneasy feeling in his stomach. So, two fires now at Goode 'N Sweet? This *was* getting weird. There hadn't been any incidents at the bakery for all his life, so why two so close together? He knew this needed further investigation. But he stared closely at Livia. "Are you really okay? Lewis here is right. If you tripped, you really should get checked out just to make sure that you don't have a sprain or anything worse. You came down here to help out your aunt. You wouldn't want to end up being the patient, now, would you?" He looked at Lewis. "Please take her to Avery for a once-over."

Livia sighed. "That really is not necessary." She glanced over toward the bakeshop's back door opening, where her sister, aunt, and their cousin Brent were milling about. Clayton frowned. He guessed Brent must have been in the area and heard the ruckus. He looked around. There were more than enough people from local businesses looking on. That's how it was around here. Not much happened, so when there was any sort of action, everyone came out.

As per her usual, Miss Joyce was looking annoyed at the intrusion on her day, while Brent looked as if he were trying to reason with her and not getting too far. Meanwhile he caught the fact that Livia's sister's attention seemed torn between her aunt and a few of the rookie firefighters huddled on the far side of the lot with a couple of Sugar Lake officers who had rode by to see what the excitement was all about.

"I really need to just get back to work and get my aunt calmed down. She's not happy about this at all. And it looks like I need to save Brent. He can be a bit much at times."

That brought Clayton's antennas up. "Is he being a bother? Can I help?"

Livia shook her head. "No, he's fine. He was in town on business and noticed the commotion so stopped in to check on us. I'm sure it's fine. He's harmless."

Clayton gave the scene another glance before turning back to Livia. "What happened?"

She shrugged. "Drea threw out the trash about an hour ago, and then just a little while ago we started to smell smoke. Of course, the first thing we thought was that the ovens were faulty again, but no, everything was fine. Thank goodness I thought to go and look outside." She let out a sigh and brushed back some wayward curls that had fallen into her face. For a brief second Clayton's breath caught over how beautiful she looked doing that small gesture, her eyes fluttering and her lips puffing out in frustration. *Focus, man, you're supposed to be working here.*

"And tell me what happened when you came out. Did you see anyone else out here?" he asked, trying to get himself back on track and back to work.

She gave him a frown. "No. There was nobody here. Why would there be? When I came out I was shocked though to see the beginnings of a fire inside the Dumpster. My heart nearly stopped dead cold. I don't know what could have caused the fire." She paused and looked pensive, her front teeth worrying at her bottom lip. "I didn't see anyone, but maybe someone threw a cigarette in the Dumpster? I don't know. I don't think it could've been anything that we put in there. There wasn't anything strange or combustible in the trash. And it's not overly stuffed, well, not too much. I know trash is not due to be picked up until tomorrow, so there are quite a number of things in there that could catch. Do you think the heat could have done this? It's strange and kind of shocking."

Clayton's brow knit as he considered what she was saying. "Well, you're right it's both. There has never been anything like this, as far as I know, happening in Dumpsters around here. If it is someone just being careless and throwing a cigarette into the Dumpster, then I'm furious about it. And if it's something else we need to investigate and find out. It could have possibly been a combination of some sort of improper handling of ingredients mixing together, but that's a stretch."

Livia looked at him with confusion in her eyes, and he could tell she was thinking it over. "I'm not sure about that. I mean, it probably is a stretch. I know Drea was doing some cleaning earlier, but I'm pretty sure she put whatever was recyclable in the recycling bins and not in the Dumpster. I'll ask her though, just to be sure."

Clayton looked over at Alexandrea and Miss Joyce again, then he shook his head. "You just go and get checked out for now and get the all clear. I'll look around in the Dumpster to see if we can get to the bottom of things. I'm sure it's all probably just an innocent mistake. Don't worry too much over it, and tell your aunt not to either. We will inspect everything and make sure all is up to code. You guys just get back to doing what you do best, keeping the town happy and in a sweet mood."

Livia looked up at him, then narrowed her eyes. "Is that supposed to somehow be funny?" she asked. "Because if so, you've got a long way to go before you get even halfway there."

Clayton gave her a deadpan look. "Maybe I'd be a little wittier if I had enjoyed my lunch and had better company."

He wasn't supposed to say that, was he?

He watched as her mocha cheeks bloomed with color. "I would say I'm sorry about that, but it wasn't as if I didn't tell you I wouldn't be coming." She gave him a deadpan stare of her own. "At least I afforded you that courtesy."

"Wow. Knockout punch in the first," Clayton said. "You've got a deadly right hook there, Livia," Clayton said as he gave a grin. "Finally. At least now I finally get one real answer out of you. It may have taken three conversations, a lunch stand-up, and a Dumpster fire. But finally, you're starting to get real."

Livia shook her head and let out a low breath. "And you've got a sneaky left." She threw up her hands. "You know what? I don't know what you're talking about, Clayton Morris. I've been nothing but real and honest with you. I was real back then, and I'm real now. And I'm not here to have lunch or play games with you. I'm here to help out my aunt with the bakeshop and be on my way. Nothing more and nothing less. Now, I have to go. You were saying something about me getting my ankle checked out."

And with that Livia walked away just as proud and as beautiful as the woman he'd always known her to be.

"Well, at least this time it wasn't the ovens, so your pie didn't get ruined. As a matter of fact, both of these are delicious. Let's hear it for small miracles," Aunt Joyce said.

They were back home and trying to semi-relax after the fire at the shop that day. Liv was trying to get Aunt Joyce to put her feet up, but as usual she was kicking up a fuss. "Just let me do what I do. Really, I am feeling fine."

"Come on, Aunt Joyce, sit back and relax," Drea said. "It's been a long day for all of us. With the fire and everything, I think it's taken a toll. All this excitement. And if it hasn't, still do us a favor and humor us and just put your feet up for a while. Come on, we can watch *The Bachelorette* and see who gets booted off next."

Aunt Joyce gave a reluctant nod. "Okay, if you say so. I did call you all here to help me out, so I guess I might as well accept it." She looked over at Liv, who was clearing the dishes and tidying up the kitchen. She waved her fork in Liv's direction. "Why don't you leave those for now, Livy, and sit and join us. Your pie is delicious, and so are those sweet little blackberry pocket thingies you made up. We need to come up with a name for those and sell them in the shop." At Liv's astonished expression, she grinned wide. "Don't look so shocked, girly. I know how to give a compliment when it's due. You've got something good there. Besides, I think I can take some of the credit for your talent. I'm glad to see you are paying attention. If you're still here for the fair, I think we should enter a few of your pieces in the pie competition along with mine. Might as well hit them with all we've got."

Liv shook her head. She couldn't believe what Aunt Joyce was saying. Number one, the woman didn't give compliments that freely, and two, she definitely didn't give compliments about other folks' baked goods.

Maybe Liv really did have baking talent, or maybe she was still loopy over her encounter with Clayton earlier. "You really think my pieces were that good?" Liv asked.

"Now, you know me," Aunt Joyce said with a certain amount of annoyance. "I don't mince words and I don't hand out compliments lightly. If I said it, I meant it. So expect to be extra busy tomorrow. You'll be making a lot more of those little pockets come the morning since I want to officially add them to the menu."

Liv let out a long sigh, but she still grinned. "Well then, I think I better head on up, grab my shower, and skip the TV tonight. Sounds like I'm going to need all the strength that I can muster."

Liv had just showered and changed into a T-shirt and some casual sleep shorts when a rustling and a flicker of light outside her window caught her attention. She ignored it for a few moments, but then the shift of light happened again, causing her to look up from where she was sitting on her bed, about to flip through classifieds on her laptop. There's no way he was actually signaling her; that'd be stupid after their encounter this afternoon, but for some reason she felt the need to go to the window to look.

She got there and, not quite opening her curtains, but just peeking through the side opening, she glanced over to where she knew his window would be. It was dark. With a yawn, Liv turned to go back toward her bed. But then, just as she was starting to walk away, something caught her eye at the window just over from Clayton's.

There was a curtain open, and a small foot in a white sneaker and blue jeans was coming out of the window, as easy as pie heading down the ivy-covered trellis on the side of the house. It was Hope Morris and the eleven-year-old was, for some reason, sneaking out of her house at nine-thirty p.m. Liv moved the curtains aside and leaned forward to see where the child was going.

She watched as Hope quietly and expertly jumped down from the trellis, looked left, and then looked right. For a moment Liv thought she might be headed toward the road, but then she saw Hope turn left and head toward the lake. She felt a knot form in the pit of her stomach as she wondered what to do. Her first thought was to immediately call Clayton, but then she thought of what she'd heard about the girl being teased and having trouble at school, and her heart began to ache. This must be so hard for her. She seemed like such a sweet girl at the barbecue, and Clayton clearly loved her. There had to be something to her doing this. Liv quickly looked around, and her eyes zeroed in on the napkin with the cherry smudge on the end and Clayton's number scrawled in the middle. She grabbed it, then snagged her phone, and pulled on her sneakers and headed for the stairs.

On the way out, she yelled to Drea and Aunt Joyce, who were in the den. "I'll be right back. I'm just gonna grab a little air outside for a second."

"Grab some air?" Aunt Joyce yelled. "I thought you were going to bed, and what about your ankle?"

"My ankle is perfectly fine. I may be clumsy, but I bounce back. Besides, I'm feeling restless right now. I'll be back in a minute."

She could hear Drea mumbling something about her weird sister as the door slammed behind her.

She slipped out, went toward the side of the house, and headed the way she saw Hope go. The girl couldn't have gotten too far. There were only so many trails along the lake; it was either left or right, so Liv had a fifty-fifty chance. She sucked in a breath, said a silent prayer, and decided to go left. The trail was a little more secluded there, and she remembered when she was younger there were a couple of spots that she liked to go to in order to find a little peace and quiet when she used to come for the summer and family got to be a bit too much. But still it was late and dark. Liv told herself that if she didn't find Hope within the next five to ten minutes she'd go ahead and call Clayton and let him know what she'd seen. She could not keep a parent in the dark about their child longer than that. Her conscience wouldn't let her do it.

Liv walked fast, her eyes quickly scanning the area for any signs of Hope. She stayed on the well-worn path, as it was late at night and so long since she'd been out there that she didn't trust herself to veer too far from the trail. Liv had been walking for only a couple moments when she caught sight of Hope's white sneakers peeking out from behind a tree. For a moment, her heart caught; she thought the girl might be in danger, but then she saw her toes make a tapping motion and her head came into view. Liv let out a relieved breath. Hope was just leaning against a tree looking out on the lake as she listened to music.

But then a lump formed and socked her in the middle of her chest when she noticed the girl's free-flowing tears as they coursed down her cheeks. Ugh. Liv suddenly felt all sorts of intrusive and, for a moment, she wanted to turn and go back to her aunt's home, but she knew she couldn't do that. She couldn't leave Hope out here crying and alone, and why was she out here crying anyway? Not wanting to scare her, since she probably couldn't hear her with earphones on, Liv stepped back a few paces and made a big show of coming around so that she was in Hope's field of vision. She waved her arms and kicked her knees up as if she was somehow jogging, which was the strangest thing because why would she be jogging with no socks on and in her sleep shorts, but she hoped that young Hope wouldn't look too closely at her attire and somehow give her a pass.

She watched Hope quickly wipe at her face, trying to cover up the fact that she'd been crying, and look up at Liv, pulling her earbuds away from her ears. She somehow looked older tonight than she had at the barbecue, as if whatever was worrying her had the power to age her with its weight. She cleared her throat as Liv waved and pretended to pull up short. "Hey, what are you doing out here?" Liv asked as nonchalantly as she could.

Hope stared at her for a moment, bewildered, and then she shrugged. "I was just listening to some music and thinking. I like to come out here sometimes."

Liv nodded as if that was cool and perfectly normal, but she looked around and then glanced back at Hope. "Well, it's kind of late to be sitting out here alone, don't you think?"

Hope looked at her, her eyes full of skepticism, and gave her a quick up-and-down. "Well, it's also kind of late to be jogging, but you're doing it." She frowned then. "And I thought your foot was bothering you from your ant thing the other day."

Liv laughed nervously. "Well, you got me there," she said as she looked down, then gave her foot an exaggerated twirl. "But I'm okay, as you can see. How about you? Tell me, does your father or grandmother know you're out here?"

Hope pushed from the table and brushed off the

back of her jeans while shrugging. "Yeah, sure they do. They've got no problem with it."

Liv stared at Hope long and hard, trying her best to give her the same stare that her mother gave her so many times before. "You sure about that?" she asked.

Hope sighed and looked at the ground. "Okay, fine, maybe they don't know I'm out here. But I just needed—" Hope paused, obviously searching for the words that would cover her, and then she looked back up at Liv, her eyes full of what looked like mistrust. "I don't know, whatever. I'm going back home."

Suddenly Liv felt like an inadequate mess. She didn't know what to do. She didn't want to be the one to rat out this girl, but she also knew she couldn't let this go without telling Clayton what she had seen. "Hope, wait, please," she said.

Hope turned around, her impatience and frustration clearly evident. "Why? Wait for what? You're of course going to tell my father, and he'll of course be disappointed in me. Like he always is disappointed. He's never happy anymore."

What did she mean by that? The one time Liv had seen Clayton light up was when he was talking about his daughter. "I'm sure that's not true. Your father loves you very much. And I know I've been here only a short time and may not know him like you do, but he seems pretty happy to me, especially so and proud too when he's talking about you."

Liv couldn't help but notice the girl's eye roll, even if it was hampered by the moonlight.

She looked around, suddenly feeling suspicious. "Wait. Were you out here waiting for somebody?"

Once again Hope let out a frustrated sigh. "No! Of course not. It's not like that. I really did just want some time to myself. Some time without people asking me questions like you are right now. I just needed to breathe and think things over, not have anybody judging me. But of course, as usual, here I am with somebody judging me."

Liv looked at her and tried her best to soften her gaze. "I'm not judging you at all. It's perfectly normal to need time to yourself. Heck, that's why I am out here too," she lied. "We all need a little space sometimes. I understand it can be hard to feel like all eyes are on you. But trust me, everybody feels like that sometimes, and since everybody's feeling like that, more often than not, the everybodies are thinking about themselves and not looking at the other person."

Hope stared at her, and Liv could tell she was contemplating what she just said. Part of Liv felt as if she was overstepping, intruding into the girl's personal life, but then she knew being out alone, especially for one so young, just wasn't safe. But still, something churned in her belly. Liv wasn't sure. She was torn about what to say to Clayton. She didn't really know what to do in this situation.

Just then a mosquito came up and nipped the right side of her arm. She slapped at it hard and then looked back at Hope, catching a smirk that looked so much like her father's. "Listen, how about this, I understand you don't want your father or your grandmother to know that you are out here, but it's really not all that safe by yourself, especially with them not knowing. Let's say, I won't tell your dad." She saw Hope's eyes brighten at this, as if she felt she'd had her, but then Liv added the rest of her conditions. "If you head back with me now and walk through the front door letting them know that you went out on your own to walk by the lake."

Liv watched Hope's expression collapse. "I can't tell them that. They don't know that I snuck out without telling them."

"Well, don't you think it's better coming from you than coming from me?"

Hope gave a small groan, and Liv saw her weighing the pros and cons over in her mind. "I guess it's better coming from me," Hope finally said.

Liv put her arms around the girl's shoulder. "Your father is not going to like hearing that you were out. But trust me, he'll respect you for telling the truth, and then I'm sure it will all blow over. You're his daughter, he'll love you through anything. It's a law. It was written the moment you were born and he got his first glimpse of those beautiful brown eyes of yours." Hope gave Liv a soft smile, almost causing her heart to split in two before they proceeded to walk back toward the houses together.

Chapter 15

"See there, I knew your little blackberry pockets would be a hit. The lunch rush is not even over and we're already about sold out. And folks are raving over your Berry Good Swirl Pie too. I think you should definitely enter both in the Founders' Day contest. Maybe with you entering, I'll finally have some competition. Even if we are on the same team. It will be fun. We'll just see who takes home the top prize. Shoot. I don't mind as long as the ribbons all stay in the family."

Liv glanced over at Aunt Joyce. The woman looked positively giddy talking about the upcoming Founders' Day baking contest. Her skin was glowing, and her smile took up most of her wide face as she packed up the near end of the blackberry pockets for a couple of guys who'd come over from the hardware store.

Liv smiled back. She was happy to see Aunt Joyce so happy and thrilled herself over the praise for her work. It felt good getting this response. Though she had been confident in her work when she was back home in New York, she honestly didn't expect for it to go over this well here. But entering the bake-off against some of these seasoned southern cooks? The thought gave her a twinge of fear. "Thanks, Aunt Joyce, but really, I don't know about entering any contest. That's a tall order, and besides, family against family? Don't you think that might be getting us in a sticky situation?"

Aunt Joyce just waved a hand at that as the hardware guys left. "Of course not. We can handle it. There are no rules against it. It's families cooking together all the time. And we need to be a little more creative anyways. That darned Delia Morris thought she was so slick adding in a minis category last year. I think because she was just tired of me winning in pies and cobblers so she thought she could slip her pecan twirls in. Now, I'll admit, they are tasty, but they can't hold a candle to these blackberry pockets of yours."

Liv nodded. Great. So now she wanted her going head-to-head with Clayton's mom. The woman didn't like her all that much when she was a kid. Beating her in a town bake-off was sure to keep their relationship frosty. Oh well, why should she care? It's not like she'd have anything to do with Delia or Clayton Morris once she headed back home.

It had been days and she hadn't seen or heard from Clayton. She knew she should be happy with that. She was the one who sent out the strong back-away signals. And she was the one who had stood him up at lunch letting him know, in no uncertain terms, that she didn't want or need any sort of apology or any rekindling of their friendship. But still she found herself glancing up each time a tall male figure walked by the shop's window. And worse, she'd found herself longing to see his smile, that twinkle in his dark eyes, or hear his deep rich voice once again.

Thinking of it all frustrated her to no end. Maybe she should just text him, she thought. Inadvertently, after her encounter with Hope she did have the perfect excuse to check in with him.

Part of her thought she would see him after that encounter, have a reason for him to walk over and say something to her, possibly give her an update, but no, he didn't, and she had to admit that worried her a bit. It wasn't that she hadn't heard from him at all, and she knew that Hope was doing okay, at least on the surface she was. After she'd walked her home that night, there'd been no more, to her knowledge, bouts of her sneaking out through the window. Liv saw no more fluttering besides the normal catches of the breeze at Hope's window. And she also saw, not that she was looking all that hard, no more activity at Clayton's window either.

That night, she'd gone back up to her room after sitting with Aunt Joyce and Drea for a few moments while they finished the television show. She told Aunt Joyce about seeing Hope down by the lake and the fact that she'd walked her home. Aunt Joyce let her know how worried she was for the young girl, whose mother hadn't been in town for a visit in the past year that they'd been in Sugar Lake, and the thought of that saddened Liv. No wonder Hope felt a bit lost, and she had every right to in the predicament that she was in. But Liv also had to wonder what could possibly have gone wrong in Clayton's relationship with his ex that would cause the woman to not only leave their marriage, but walk away from her vulnerable young daughter? Liv was relieved when Aunt Joyce's cell phone pinged that night with a message from Clayton, thanking Liv for sending Hope home. He told Aunt Joyce that Hope was fine and that there was nothing to worry about. Liv had watched expectantly as her aunt texted Clayton back with astonishing speed, and when she pressed her for more information, her only response was a way too smug, "Ask him yourself." A moment later, Liv heard her own cell pinged with what she knew was Aunt Joyce forwarding Clayton's text. It was amazing how savvy this older generation could be with technology when there was a point to be proven.

Like a coward, Liv never reached out. She told herself it was enough that she already knew Hope was fine.

The bakeshop's door opened, pulling Liv's mind to the day's work at hand, and she was surprised when her gaze met Clayton's. He nodded at her, turning back to hold the door, and gave a greeting to Mrs. Comfrey, who was just exiting as he was coming in. He greeted Aunt Joyce, who was seated on a stool by the register, and Drea, who was clearing the front table. She nodded and gave him a half smile before walking toward the back with the dishes she had just cleared, and she gave Liv a knowing side glance.

Clayton came forward, walking straight toward Liv, and for some reason she found it even harder to find her voice. "Hey there." She hoped that was normal, though she never was one to pull off a *hey there* in her life.

"Hey there to you, too," Clayton said. "So." He looked around and then down at the display case as if searching for something before his eyes came back up to meet Liv's. "I hear the town's all abuzz about these new blackberry pockets you all are selling. I had to come and find out about them for myself."

"Well, it took you long enough!" Aunt Joyce said

from where she was sitting by the register. "Any longer and you'd have missed out."

Liv couldn't help the glare she aimed Aunt Joyce's way or wonder if there was any sort of double meaning to her words. But Clayton was standing in front of her, so she put her direction there. "My aunt is right, you did almost miss out; luckily we have two left. Can I get them for you?"

He grinned, that little half smile lighting up his face and sending small shards of pleasure radiating throughout Liv's body in a way she didn't know how much she actually craved.

"Well, it looks like I made it just in time. Yes, please," he said.

Liv couldn't help the narrowing of her eyes. Why did he have to speak? And why did everything he say always remind her of feelings she would rather forget? She put the two pastries in a bag and handed them to him, careful this time to not make any contact with his hand. Clayton took the bag with a nod. "Thanks," he said. He glanced at her, a bit of uneasiness in his eyes. "Listen, I probably should have come over here earlier, but I was a little busy and we had a couple of emergency calls, and then I had so much paperwork, and well . . ." He stopped rambling and looked her in the eye. "It doesn't matter. I should have come over here earlier," he said.

"You don't have to explain yourself to me," Liv countered.

But Clayton swallowed and continued. "I do. It's the least I can do. Thank you for what you did the other night with Hope. She came home and told me about sneaking out to go walk by the lake, and she also told me that it was you who brought her back home and convinced her not to sneak out again. Whether she

needs space or not, it's not safe. I can't tell you how
much I appreciate that."

Liv held up a hand, slightly stunned by his words,
but so very happy to hear that Hope had told him the
whole truth. "Really, you don't have to thank me.
Anyone would've done it."

"No, anyone wouldn't have, and I . . ." He looked at
her, clearly searching for the right words when Aunt
Joyce chimed in from by the register.

"Hey, Clayton, you wouldn't happen to have any free
time this afternoon, would you?" The way she asked
out of the blue caused Liv's brows to pull together and
wonder what the woman was up to. It seemed like such
an odd request when Clayton had clearly just stopped
by to grab his pastries and be on his way. Liv felt a
setup in the making.

Clayton turned toward Aunt Joyce at the same time
Liv did, confused, but Liv could tell he was clearly glad
for the intrusion on his awkward conversation. "I did
and I am. It's my afternoon off today, so I have some
time. Is there anything you need doing around here,
Miss Joyce? I'll be happy to help out."

"No, not really, I'm good. It's just that, you won't believe we're already running low on honey, but with the
girls here and Liv's new recipes, it seems we've created
quite a stir and can't keep up with orders."

Clayton stared at her, clearly even more confused,
not quite knowing why what she was saying had to do
with him being off that afternoon, and frankly neither
did Liv. "Well, usually I don't collect until the weekend for your order and for the farmers' market, but
I'm sure I can gather up some more for you this afternoon and have it for you in the morning."

Aunt Joyce clapped her hands with a huge smile

"Now, that was just what I was hoping you would say. Isn't he the most accommodating, Liv?"

Liv smiled, but still looked at her aunt skeptically. What in the world was she up to?

Thankfully, she didn't have long to wonder, since Aunt Joyce decided to move in swiftly with her killer shot. "Well, since we got that straight, seems like no time like the present. It really is amazing how you get all the honey from that little crop of bees you've got. Why, Livy, you ought to see it. It is something to behold. As a matter of fact, Clayton, why don't you take Olivia right now and show her your hives and how you collect the honey. I'm sure she'd find it fascinating."

"I'm sure I'd not," Liv said, then caught herself and turned back toward Clayton, an apology in her eyes. "Sorry, it's not that, it's just that, well, it's probably best to stay here and help out with the shop. I don't want to leave my aunt, and we've got plenty of work to do."

"We have no such thing," Aunt Joyce said. "Rena will be back in a few minutes when she picks up her little ones from school, so she can take over then, and Drea is with me now, so I will be fine."

Really, did Aunt Joyce have to go on? There was no reason for her to go up and see Clayton's dusty old beehives. It didn't matter how good his honey was. Clayton, his hives, and all that went with them were not her business, and Aunt Joyce needed to understand that.

She turned to Aunt Joyce. "It really is not necessary," she said. "And besides, I remember seeing those old hives years ago when we were kids. Clayton showed me how they work. I'm sure not that much has changed."

Clayton chuckled from where he was standing.

"Well, that's where you're wrong; I have made quite a lot of improvements in the time that I've been here, and things have changed since my dad's day. The developments really have been quite fascinating. But really, it's no big deal, Livia." He turned toward Aunt Joyce. "She's right, Miss Joyce. Being around the hives can make some people quite uneasy. You've got to have a pretty strong constitution and nerves of steel to be able to handle them. Some people are just not up to the task."

"Excuse me?" Liv said. She was sure there was some sort of put-down in Clayton's seemingly benign remark and it got her fired up, though at the same time part of her felt intrigued to see what improvements he had made, and a part of her also couldn't help feeling a bit of sadness over thinking of him taking over where his late father had left off. But for the most part, the petty part, was stuck on the fact that he thought she couldn't handle his hives. "What do you mean, not everyone is up to the task? Are you trying to call me some type of wimp or something?"

"Of course not. Why would I do anything like that? I'm just saying that it's not the type of situation for someone with anything but the strongest of constitutions, and if you've got any sort of aversions to bugs, it may not be your thing. Besides, it's been a while since you were a kid running around in the fields. And let's be real," he said, giving her a swift up-and-down. "You've been in the city a long time. And my hives are set quite a ways back. Who knows if you're up to that kind of rugged terrain?"

Liv frowned. "I know where your hives are. I remember your father used to keep hives off by that old fishing cabin of his. Isn't that where they are?"

"Yes," Clayton said with a bit of curtness to his

voice. "That's where they are. Like I said, it's been a long time since you've been out there, and like I said, the terrain is rough. It's changed quite a bit. I'm not sure it's something you can handle or would even care to try."

Okay, he and his attitude were really starting to get on her nerves. Liv gave him a sharp look. "How would you be able to determine what I'm up to handling and what I'm not, Clayton Morris? I'll have you know, I can handle pretty much whatever is sent my way. And I've never been afraid of any kind of bugs, be it spiders, lizards, or what have you." She paused then. What was she arguing about? It wasn't like she wanted to hang around a bunch of bees. Who would? But then she looked up at Clayton and thought about his words and realized it was the principle of the thing. Liv went for the front tie of her apron and proceeded to untie it. When she was done, she looked back up at Clayton. "I'd love to see your hives. Aunt Joyce needs some honey, and you've been saying you wanted to talk, so let's get to it. Might as well kill two birds with one stone and all that." She looked over at Aunt Joyce and gave her head a tilt. "Is there anything else you need, perhaps something that doesn't require folks to get into a situation where they might get stung?"

Aunt Joyce let out a chuckle and shook her head. "Nope," she said, "the honey is about all I'll be needing. You kids go ahead and take your time. Drea and I have it from here. As a matter of fact, I'm sure we can find our way home and just meet you there."

At that, Liv's eyes went wide and she gave Aunt Joyce an incredulous look. "Really, there's no need. I'm sure this won't take very long, and I can get back and pick you all up in time for closing."

But Aunt Joyce shook her head once again as Drea walked out from the back room. "Nope, like I said, we're fine. Just leave the car keys and we'll make our way. You go on and see about those hives with Clayton."

With that, Liv tried her best not to give a huff and add in stomping her feet like she really wanted to; instead she tried to continue to hold her head high as she looked over at Clayton, who at least had the wherewithal to give her a sideways glance and look back down at the ground as he shuffled his feet, still holding his bag with the two blackberry pockets. She noticed a small butter stain start to form on the outside of the bag. He gave Liv a half shrug and walked over to Aunt Joyce, going into his pocket to pull out a few bills. Aunt Joyce waved him away. "You take those on me, Clayton. Just be sure to take good care of Livy while you're over there by those hives. I wouldn't be happy at all if she did happen to get stung."

Liv came around to the outside of the counter, putting her purse over her shoulder and tapping Clayton on his. "Oh, you don't have to worry about that, Aunt Joyce. I'll be extra careful; nothing is going to sting me."

"Ever get the feeling you're being set up?" Clayton looked over at Liv as they stepped out into the bright light of the afternoon sun and he took in her annoyed expression. Annoyance aside, she still looked beautiful with her hair pulled back in a high ponytail, showing off her lovely brown skin, high arched eyebrows, sparkling eyes with full lashes, strong regal nose, and full lips that today were covered with only a hint of gloss. Clayton fought the urge to stare, so he turned his gaze forward, but not without noting that she was wearing a cute, sleeveless striped T-shirt and tight stretch ankle-length jeans. He couldn't help the joy it gave him to see that on her feet were once again well-worn Converse sneakers. At least she hadn't grown out of that style choice.

"Yeah, I'd say we were totally set up on this one," Liv agreed. "Sorry. You know how my aunt is when she gets a bee in her bonnet, no pun intended. She doesn't stop until she's fully satisfied."

They started walking toward the firehouse, which was just a few doors down and across the street from the bakeshop. Clayton turned to her, having already noticed a couple of glances from a few inquisitive eyes. As they passed Doreen's Diner, Doreen openly gawked at them, and he swore that she would have overfilled her current patron's coffee cup if Cletus Jones hadn't stopped her with a poke in her arm.

He turned to Livia. "Listen, you really don't have to come and see the hives if you don't want to. I can just take you and drop you off at your aunt's house and go and extract the honey myself. She wouldn't be any the wiser, and you'd have a free afternoon. I don't want you to feel that you're obligated to hang out with me." He held his breath for a moment, suddenly nervous as to what she might say.

Livia glanced up at him as they were just reaching the front of the firehouse. She seemed to be taking him in, studying his expression as if looking for any hint of subterfuge. Finally, she shook her head. "It's fine. Honestly, seeing beehives wasn't topping my list of things to do when I got up this morning, but I'm sure they are quite fascinating. And besides, if I don't have that honey when Aunt Joyce gets home, there will be all heck to pay, and to top it off, I have a feeling she'd know if I didn't actually go and see the hives myself. She has a way of making me feel like a teenager all over again. She might even give me a pop quiz or something."

Clayton let out a relieved breath. "Honestly, I wouldn't put it past her. She is quite determined. Come on, my ride is out back. We better get going. Depending on how the honey taps, it might take a while to actually fill a jar."

Livia followed Clayton around the back of the firehouse to where his truck was parked, and as he walked her over to the passenger side to open her door, he caught her admiring the Harley next to his truck. For a moment it seemed as if she was about to reach out and touch it. "You like it?" he asked.

She looked up at him with a hint of admiration in her eyes. "Oh, yeah, I guess I do. Not that I'm one for motorcycles all that much. It just reminded me a little bit of the one you used to have when we were kids. Although this one is the more modern version. So much more put together than the one you had as a kid. No rusted-out tailpipe."

"Hey, I thought you loved that old bike of mine. Rusted bits and all." Clayton couldn't help but laugh. He'd run that old bike into the ground, but he loved it and was proud of it. Snagged for all of $350 and missing its most vital parts, he'd spent the better part of the summer restoring it. Once he got it together, he couldn't wait to zoom around town, and he was the proudest when he'd finally convinced Livia, after much cajoling, to take a ride on the back with him. She'd been so afraid, having never been on the back of a bike before, but when she finally did, she was hooked. Constantly egging him on to go faster, really get the wind in her hair. He'd loved how fearless she was in her innocence. It was such a surprise to him after seeing her only as the quiet city girl he thought she was.

He looked back at Livia. "You want to take a ride?"

Once again, she looked up at him with shock. "This is yours? I didn't think you still rode. I mean, all I've seen you drive since we've been in town is your truck, so I assumed you'd given up the motorcycle for your new life. You know, being a dad and all."

Clayton put his hand over his heart and feigned being wounded. "Ouch, that one hurt. I'll admit I don't ride all that much. Mostly it's just been parked here at the station. Mama says it's too much racket and it's easier to shuttle Hope and groceries in my truck, but hey, are you trying to say that a dad can't still be cool?"

"Oh yeah, you're a regular road warrior," Avery said, suddenly coming up behind them and interjecting herself into the conversation. "Don't believe anything he says, Olivia. He hasn't been on that bike in I don't know how long." Clayton shot her a harsh glare, which she laughed off. "Well, you haven't. I was wondering if you're thinking about finally selling it. I know a couple of people who would happily shell out the big bucks for that bike."

"I'm not selling anything," Clayton said, "and don't you have reports that are due tomorrow?"

Avery shrugged her shoulders and looked from Clayton to Olivia. "I guess I've been dismissed. You two carry on. I'm off to do my reports. Have a wonderful afternoon, Chief."

He turned back toward Livia knowing that, come tomorrow, when Avery handed in her reports, she'd be expecting a report back on what was going on with him and Livia, as if something would be going on. He tried to brush off the sudden feeling of hopeful feeling of unease and gave Livia a casual smile.

"She seems nice. Like she's a good friend and uh . . . colleague," Livia said.

Clayton turned, looking once again at Avery's retreating back. "She is, though at times she can be pushy and blur the lines."

At Livia's frown he was quick to add, "What I mean is, she is a good friend and just that. But she is always on me about things like my bike and getting out, having more fun."

Livia nodded and looked away, as if she were embarrassed about inquiring.

"So, about that ride," he said. "Do you want to?"

She glanced from him to the bike, then back at him again, and he could tell once again she was weighing the idea of what she wanted to do with her trust in him. "Look," he said, "I know Avery said it's been a long time since I've ridden, and well, maybe it has, but you have to know you're safe with me." He reached into the back of his truck and pulled out two helmets, handing her one. "So, are you game?"

Livia gave him a halfhearted smile. "Sure," she said, her lips looking sweet and inviting while her eyes still held a hint of hesitation. She took the helmet from him and brought it over the top of her head. "How can I refuse an offer like that?"

Chapter 16

The ten-minute ride out to the lake felt both too short and somehow like an eternity, Clayton thought, with Livia pressed against his back. Why he thought it was a good idea to offer her a ride on the back of his bike, he'd never know. In what world did he think he could handle the pressure of feeling her so near, so close, and still find a way to keep his cool? The idea was unfathomable. It took all of Clayton's skills just to keep the bike steady and upright as they sailed down the winding roads that were so familiar to him, but seemed to take on an all-new danger with Livia's arms clasped tightly around his waist.

He could've sworn even with his erratic heartbeat that he thought he could feel her shivering slightly behind him, and she tightened her grip just a little bit more when he picked up speed on a flat, open stretch that ran parallel to the lake.

"Are you all right?" he yelled over his shoulder, not knowing if she could hear him. But she must have, because he could feel her nod her reply, but still her grip tightened all the more as she scooched in just a bit closer to him, her thighs locking more solidly around his own.

Finally, they pulled up onto his property and he brought the bike to a not-quite-as-smooth-as-he-wanted stop, jerking them both slightly forward before coming to an unsteady halt. Clayton turned around, removed his helmet, and gave Livia a shaky grin. "I hope that wasn't too bad for you," he said.

She removed her helmet to reveal bright eyes and cheeks flushed with excitement and a surprisingly wide smile. "No," she said. "It was fine, though I will admit at times I was scared out of my wits. It's been at least ten or twelve years since I've been on the back of a bike." Her gaze went skyward as if her mind went somewhere far away, glancing back up at him, and this time when she spoke it was a little bit softer. "Thank you," she said. "It's been a long time since I felt that kind of excitement."

Clayton went temporarily still. What could she mean by that?

"Oh, come on, you must get all sorts of thrills and excitement in the big city. But I will accept the compliment; it's been a long time since I've given a beautiful woman a ride."

It was then that he saw something shift in her, and her eyes seem to shutter with his compliment. Did he go too far? He didn't mean anything but the truth by the nice words. It had been forever since he'd had anyone on the back of his bike. Celeste didn't go for riding. She was actually terrified of his motorcycle and had banned him from ever letting Hope on the back. And truth be told, it didn't really bother him one bit that Celeste didn't want to ride with him. Honestly, he hadn't met anyone in all these years with whom he felt he wanted to share that feeling of letting go, of

being free, since those years that he used to ride with
Liv. But she just stared at him and he wanted to do
something, anything to break the awkward mood.
"Well, we better get a move on and head out toward
the hives if we're going to get that honey tapped for
your aunt. Like I said, it's no telling how long it may
take. It all depends on how things are flowing. Are you
ready?" he said, trying his best to make his voice light.

Livia looked up at him, a little bit of her normal
brightness and energy now back in her gaze. "Lead
me to it," she said. "I'm a woman on a mission."

A mission? Yeah, right. More like she was trying to get
through this afternoon without completely losing her
cool and not getting stung by a bee and making a fool
of herself. That was her mission. Liv got off the bike
and tried her best to steady her legs and keep her
knees from shaking as she took off her helmet and
looked up at Clayton. How she let her aunt get her
into the situation she'd never know. But here she was,
out in the middle of the woods all alone with her
childhood crush, playing nicey-nice about seeing the
man's beehives.

Liv looked up at Clayton nonetheless and smiled,
saying some nonsensical words as she got her legs
together and followed him along the uneven terrain
toward his little shack in the woods. For the first time,
the danger and the absurdity of it hit her, and Liv
looked at Clayton's back with unease. Nah, she was
just being overly skeptical. There was no way Aunt
Joyce would send her out here with Clayton if she
didn't have full trust in him. Besides, after that ride
and leaning against his ridiculously muscular back
while holding on to that firm waist and feeling his

rock-hard abs, it wasn't Clayton that she should be worried about, it was her own out-of-control hormones. That was what she needed to get in check.

In that moment, Liv faltered and tripped slightly on a rock, once again her innate grace shining through as she bumped into Clayton's back. Thankfully this time her hands stopping her before her whole body crushed into his. He turned around quickly.

"Are you okay?" he asked, his eyes full of concern. "You better watch it here, like I said, the terrain is a bit rough. Nobody really comes out here but me, so the path is not that well worn."

He took her hand, quite matter-of-factly, as he continued to lead her through the forest on the way to his cabin. But even with his casual demeanor, Liv couldn't help but feel a tingle radiate from her hand, up her arm, and straight to her heart. Nope. No way, she told herself, she wouldn't let herself feel this. She couldn't let herself feel this. On instinct, she tried to pull her hand from his grasp, but he only tightened his grip and looked at her, his eyes soft and still somehow stern. "You'd better let me lead you, at least until we're on more solid ground. If you get hurt on your way out here, I'll never hear the end of it from your aunt. And believe you me, I don't want to have to feel the wrath of Miss Joyce."

Liv let out a low growl as she gave Clayton a half-hearted nod. He was right, nobody wanted to feel the wrath of Aunt Joyce. She continued to follow along, trying not to focus on the out-of-control sensations of her mind, heart, and body, but instead take in the quiet beauty of the forest, the cool breeze as they got deeper into the trees and the sun shone through only in dappled light and secret spaces. It really was beautiful out here. So very peaceful if only one would stop to take it in.

Finally, they reached a clearing. "We're here," Clayton said. "I know it's been a long time, but has it changed all that much to you?" he asked, his voice full of expectation. Liv didn't quite understand how he wanted her to answer.

She looked around, taking in the small fishing cabin. It was pretty much just a little shack not wider than two people with their hands spread apart. It was set a few yards back from the lake in a little alcove, not all that far off, but far enough from the Morris's main house to be a bit of a trek and afford privacy.

The familiarity of it hit Liv as she was noticing the changes that had been made since she'd seen it last. It was still the same sturdy log cabin build, but Clayton had gone and done some improvements, giving the window trimmings a fresh coat of deep green paint. He'd even accented it with a softer moss green, giving the shack a sweet, welcoming quality that it didn't have before. Liv couldn't help but wonder if that touch had something to do with his wife or with his being a dad. Either way, it added a nice appeal to the old structure.

Looking to the right, she could see the remains of the old canoe in which they used to spend so many lazy hours on the lake fishing. It was leaning on a tree, flipped on its side, clearly rotted out, pieces of moss growing over it, and vegetation poking through it, now becoming one with the landscape. Not far from it was a much newer vessel, and Liv could just make out the name HOPE ETERNAL painted by hand. The vision of it made her smile. She turned her gaze to Clayton. "It's beautiful. Just as I remembered. But I can see you made quite a few improvements. I mean the paint job and, is that an outdoor shower you put on the side of the house? Wow, you got it pretty fancy out here, Clayton."

He laughed and seemed to have a look of relief as she watched him visibly exhale. "Yeah, I did make a few improvements, but the shower was only because my mother put her foot down and refused to have me tracking fish guts back in her house." She noticed how nervous he seemed. As if he was really waiting, no somehow hoping, for a favorable reaction from her. Why did it matter what she thought? She'd been nothing to him. So much nothing that he'd walked away from her without a word. Liv let out a frustrated breath. "So where are these hives my aunt can't stop going on about? Might as well take me to the stars of the show."

"Hold on a minute there, we can't go just so fast. You don't want to go running up into a swarm of bees, now, do you?"

Liv's brows pulled together with the thought of running into a swarm of bees. He did have a point. "No, you're right about that. So what do I need to do to prepare? I don't suppose bug spray will do it in this case?"

Clayton chuckled. "No, you're right, this is not a spray type of situation, and I wouldn't like spray around my bees anyway. Bees go into attack mode only when they feel threatened, so we don't want to make them feel threatened or get them agitated. And in order to do that, I'm going to need you to stay calm, keep things easy, and for the most part just don't worry. I've got a suit for you to put on over your clothes as well as a mask so you'll be fully protected when I go to show you the hives, and despite what you may think, the bees are pretty well contained. I just have to untap and start the flow for the honey to get going for your aunt, and then we only have to wait. Easy-peasy."

Liv raised a brow at him and tried her best to squelch the unease that was starting to creep up her back. "Okay, if you say so. Let's get to it."

She followed Clayton down toward the shack, and along the way he pointed toward three hives that were set out a couple of yards toward the left of the cabin. "Those are the hives over there. I don't put them too close to the house. As you see, I changed out the ones my dad had for more modern ones that I found on the Internet. You'll see the changes once we get you outfitted and closer. Really the suit is more of a precaution for your comfort because, like I said, everything is mostly enclosed."

Liv just nodded and followed him over to the shack, her mind less on the hives now and more on the old fishing shack and memories of a lost time. As they got to the doorway, Clayton suddenly stopped. When he looked at Liv his eyes softened. "Um, if you want you can wait right here and I'll bring the suit out to you. You don't have to come inside."

Liv was pulled up short, suddenly stunned by his caution over letting her enter. Was he haunted by the same ghosts she was? Having the same stirrings? Feeling the remnants of the same old memories. She let out a long breath as the urge to face her feelings head-on gripped at her. She then barked out a laugh that came out probably much harsher than she meant it to. "No, it's fine, I really want to see how the old place looks." She looked up at Clayton with a bit of a challenge in her eyes. "You don't have a problem with that, do you?"

He looked down at her and shook his head. "No, no problem at all. Come on in. Make yourself at home."

Pushing down on her trepidation, Liv stepped into the small dwelling that she hadn't set foot in in over twelve years, letting her eyes adjust to the dimness. She inhaled, taking in the masculine smell of pine as it mingled with the hint of disinfectant and evergreen of the cottage. As her eyes adjusted, the memories came flooding back to her—how she'd first seen the little one-room dwelling. Not much had changed. The makeshift kitchen area was still to the left with the old sink and side slab work area and tiny window with the checkered curtains. Circling around she could see that Clayton still had his dad's fishing reel display stocked with at least ten poles ready and waiting to cast out at any moment on the lake and bring in the day's catch. Toward the back there was a small curtained-off area that functioned as a little bathroom, and she couldn't help but wonder if it had been modernized or if it was still nothing more than a glorified out-house, just a seat and a small door that opened to the back of the house, convenient for easy disposal. She remembered being horrified when Clayton proudly showed her when they were kids how it actually worked and how they would do the dumping of the refuse out in the woods. But she was avoiding the biggest elephant in the room, which really wasn't so big at all. There it was, the little twin bed on which she'd given her heart, her body, and her soul to him. That felt like a lifetime ago. The same bed where he'd made her the promise of forever. Where he'd asked her to be with him, love him, to be his as he in turn promised to be hers. And like a fool she believed him, to return the following summer expecting to find him

waiting there as he said he would be, but only to find
an empty shack and hollow promises.

It was a clearing of Clayton's throat that brought Liv
back to the present, and she was relieved to find that
she hadn't embarrassed herself fully by shedding the
tears that were burning the backs of her eyes. "Here
you go," he said. "Slip this on over your clothes, and I
promise you'll be fine."

Clayton was standing in front of her holding a white
hazmat-type suit. She half expected him not to even
be standing there, since the last time she'd been down
at that little cabin she was there all alone, just herself,
her sorrow, and her tears trying to make sense of why
he would've gone away and not left any word for her.
But instead of asking him why he did what he did, Liv
just reached her hand out and took the suit from him,
putting it on without a word.

She stepped outside and was happy to feel the sun-
light on her face once again. It was almost suffocating
inside the cottage, and she could admit to herself that
it wasn't just the small size, but the overwhelming
memories. Liv swallowed, then sucked in a deep breath.

"Are you okay?" Clayton asked.

"I'm fine. Come on, let's do this. You said it might
take a while, so let's get started."

"Okay, okay, I just wanted to make sure you were up
for it. You seemed . . ." He paused, and she could tell
he was reaching for his words. She could also tell he
was hoping not to insult her. She decided to throw
him a lifeline.

"I said I'm fine, let's get moving." Liv was about to
walk when for the first time she noticed that he hadn't
put on a suit himself. "Wait a minute, what about you?
Where is your suit? Don't tell me I get the only one."

He shook his head. "No, I have another, but I'm

fine. I don't need a suit. Like I said, the hives are mostly contained. There are barely any bees buzzing outside the hives. Everything should be fine."

Liv shot him a glare. "It's the *should* part of that sentence that I don't like. If you've got another suit, just do me a favor and put it on to make me feel better?"

He gave her a long look for a moment, and she could tell the second he decided to acquiesce and not argue. He nodded and moved to go inside the shack. "I'll just be a second."

While he was gone Liv took a seat on a little bench on the front porch and looked out on the lake. She rubbed one hand inside the other for a moment, remembering how it used to feel when his hand clasped hers, that excitement that she got from just that small gesture. It had been so long since Liv had felt that way, and she wondered if she'd ever feel that way again.

"Okay, I'm ready. Let's do this, Livia."

She looked up at him smiling down at her with that easygoing smile of his, saying her name as if he'd been saying it for the past ten years. She gave him a half-hearted grin and a nod as she got up and let him put the protective mask over face, and the world went a little bit fuzzy, taking on a strange, soft diffused hue. Once again, Liv let out a much-needed breath and followed Clayton Morris toward the unknown.

Liv was trying hard to concentrate and watch what Clayton was doing. It was fascinating really, but she had to admit she was completely distracted being in the situation that she was in. She told herself to focus on his words, focus on the task at hand. *Come on, get it together, girl. There will be bees around you, for goodness' sake,* she said to herself as she watched Clayton expertly explain to her the ingenious way he was extracting the honey from the cool, new hives he had gotten.

"If you look to the side over here—" Liv watched as Clayton opened a window on the hive and showed what looked to be hundreds, maybe thousands, of bees congregating around a comb, doing the work, and she could see the sweet orange nectar emanating from them into the comb.

Part of her was a little squeamish and a little horrified, but the other part was fascinated by the ingenuity of it all. "In the center and down toward the bottom is the queen, and everyone congregates around her where she's laying her eggs. It's really amazing how, out of this one little box, I can get so much honey." He closed a little window once again and looked at her proudly. Then he went toward the front of the box and opened up another little window.

"And if you see here, all I have to do is just open this section and we've got all the cells where the honey collects. Look here. There are three empty cells from where I collected honey over the past month, but these two are already just about full. So I use this little key to open the flow and put in this shoot right above the jar, and all we have to do is sit and wait while the jars fill."

Liv was stunned when he turned a long metal key and suddenly, from the little tap, slowly but surely, rich golden honey started to flow from the hive and down into the mason jar below. It was slow and steady, but still the jar started to fill. "That is truly amazing. I can't believe it." She shook her head. "I was expecting the old boxes that your father used to have, and those rectangular cards that you'd have to pick out heavy with bees eager to swarm us. This is nothing like that."

Clayton shook his head. "No, it really isn't. Not that there's anything wrong with that method. And that method has worked for so many years. This is just something new and quite inventive, though it is a bit controversial. I just find it works for my lifestyle, and it's a lot less intrusive. And it's a way that it's even got Hope interested in nature without being overly put out by it."

"Well, that's great. You'd want to get her involved and interested in something like this. I tell you, when I was a young girl there was no way you'd get me around any sort of bugs. To have her involved in nature and biology, I think it's wonderful." Liv caught his wistful smile and wondered what he was thinking, if he was worried about Hope and her sneaking out the other night. "She really is a great girl," Liv added.

"Yeah, I think she is too." Clayton looked at Liv, his eyes full of concern. "But I will admit, I do worry about her. I want to thank you again for leading her home the other night."

Liv shook her head. And noticed a couple of bees buzzing right in front of her face. She scrunched up her nose and recoiled on instinct.

Clayton smiled at her calmly. "It's fine. Remember, you have protection." He looked down at the jar and took out a small piece of cheesecloth from his side pocket and went to cover the top of the jar. "This is to protect the honey so the bees don't fly inside and get at it before we can." He expertly sealed the top with a rubber band. "Looking at the way this is flowing, it may take a little while. It usually takes about an hour or so. If you want, we can head back to the shack, sit out on the porch, and grab something cool to drink. I may have something in the icebox."

Liv felt trepidation creep up her spine again as she looked at the slow-moving honey easing its way into the Mason jar; she knew she had no choice. She was out here for the long haul. She looked back up at Clayton with a nod. "It will be nice. Besides, it's running slow and it's hot. That dock seems sturdy and shady. Why don't we sit and cool off a bit?"

Chapter 17

Clayton handed Livia the soda with what he hoped was a steady hand and took a seat next to her on the edge of the fishing dock. She'd rolled up the hem of her jeans, and her feet were swaying lazily back and forth, skimming the top of the water. Her pretty toes were painted a bright pinkish color, peeking out of the top of the water playfully each time her foot arced up. Clayton felt as if he could stare at those toes forever and just be happy sitting right there with her next to him, saying nothing. The sun started to set, giving the world a soft, mellow golden filter that made everything seem almost like a dream.

But it wasn't a dream. Clayton knew he had a lot to explain. As he rolled up his own pant legs and dipped his feet in the water about a foot away from hers, he remembered how, when they were kids, he'd teasingly kick over and splash her, causing her to squeal in feigned annoyance. He knew he couldn't do that now. Now, he didn't know how any of his overtures would be accepted. Cripes, she barely would tolerate him sitting next to her. If not at the urging of her aunt there was no way she would even be out here. He gazed at her, still so beautiful, probably even more so, her profile regal, and even though she seemed to blend perfectly with the untamed beauty of the lake in the forest, some part of her always stood out. Like she was better than it. Better than the simple life it held. Better than him and the life he could give her.

Clayton had always known it too. Deep down from the moment he'd fallen in love with her, he knew she wasn't for him. Even before he'd overheard the scolding she'd gotten from her family that night that she'd given herself to him and gone back to the Goode home with their youthfull promises of a future of forever still fresh on their lips.

He'd been so full of hope just moments before. Believing, at least in the moment, that they could conquer anything, that he could conquer anything as long as he was with her and she was by his side. She'd made him feel like he was more than just the accomplished athlete that they'd made him out to be. Better than just the commodity of a talented body. He remembered how they'd sit on the edge of the lake and he'd tell her dreams about wanting to start a business or farming, and she'd sit and listen and tell him he could do anything he set his mind to. Why, she had him even thinking that he'd use his football scholarship to take business and biology classes. But who was he fooling? With his grades, how would he ever live up to what she expected?

Clayton looked at Liv and knew the silence needed to be broken and he needed to fess up to the reason he wasn't there when she returned for him the following summer. "So, about those fires at your aunt's shop." *What the heck? That is not what I am supposed to be talking about. Get it together, man. I don't even have any leads on the fires at her aunt's shop. Why am I talking about this now? A backbone, Clayton, you're supposed to have a freaking backbone.*

Livia turned to him with concern in her eyes. "Do you have any leads? I have to tell you, my aunt might be getting older, but I really don't think anything was wrong with her oven. She had her handyman, Errol, come in and give it a check, and he found the ovens to be perfectly fine. And when she says she set them properly, I believe her. I haven't noticed anything wrong with the facilities since I've been here. And then that fire in the Dumpster? I don't know, Clayton, it seems pretty odd to me. When you guys checked that out, did you come to any conclusion about how it started? Was it due to something that we threw in the trash?"

Clayton frowned. Well, he started this line of conversation, might as well go with it. "No, it's kind of odd. We didn't find any evidence of any cigarette butts or anything like that, but we did find remnants of burned newspaper, and it looked quite twisted as if . . ." Clayton paused. He didn't want to cause her any real concern or give her any reason to fear.

She gave him a sharp look. "Come on and spit it out, as if what?"

"As if it was prelit and thrown in the trash," he said. "I don't know, maybe someone was burning their newspapers and then tried to put the fire out? I'm not sure. But we definitely will watch things a lot closer now."

Livia, her expression dark, looked back out at the water. "Why would someone throw burned newspaper in our trash? It makes no sense. There is a recycling bin right on the opposite wall." Clayton nodded, and once again silence engulfed them.

Livia turned back his way. "Why do I get the feeling there's more you're not telling me?"

He got prickly tingles along his arms. Clayton didn't know what to tell her and what not to tell her. He couldn't possibly tell her that he felt the fire in the Dumpster was suspicious. Or that he now had suspicious feelings about the oven fire too? Not without any evidence. No, he just had to watch things closely and hope that there would be no more mishaps, but if there were, he hoped like all get-out he caught whoever was starting them before any real damage was done or anyone was hurt. And more than anything he hoped it wasn't who he thought it could be. Clayton shook his head. "Don't worry about it. I think it's probably just one of those weird mishaps that sort of happened at around the same time and same place. You all just be extra careful and keep a close eye on things and everything should be fine."

Livia frowned, but nodded her agreement as she took a sip of her soda and let her feet sway in the water a little more before she turned back to him once again. "Well," she said. "Now that that's done and you've got me out here against my better judgment and my aunt's extensive schemes, you said you had something to apologize for, so I'm willing to hear it. You want to tell me why it is I came back looking for you, expecting you to live up to your word and your promises and all I got for my troubles was nothing but an empty shack and not even a Dear Jane letter?"

Clayton was almost surprised by her bluntness and the swift change in subject. But for all his being surprised, he should have expected it, because Livia was pretty much fearless when it came to calling him out on his bull. He'd bet a dime for a dollar that she'd known he was stalling when he was talking about the fires before. Just giving him his time to dance around the big elephant in the woods.

Clayton put his soda down beside him before looking back at her, meeting her intense gaze. There would be no turning away, no hiding from her scrutiny. "Liv," he said, "I really don't know what to say to you besides, I'm sorry."

He saw anger spark in her eyes. "Oh, come on, you've already said that, Clayton. You didn't have to bring me all the way out here for an 'I'm sorry.' I'm looking for more. I'm looking for a reason why."

"What does it matter? The reason why? Shouldn't 'I'm sorry' be enough? Shouldn't the fact that I messed up and I was completely wrong be enough?"

She shook her head in frustration, placing the soda beside her and motioning as if to get up. Desperate, as if on reflex, Clayton moved, bringing his hand out to still her, then he pulled back quickly when her eyes looked down at his hand in dismay.

"Please wait," he said. "I'm sorry. Wait. No, not I'm sorry. I know you need more than that. Just give me a chance." He swallowed, trying hard to push down the fear over her leaving frustrated with his unsaid words. "Just give me a chance, Livia. I'm not prepared for this, though I've had more years than I deserve to prepare."

He was way more relieved than he expected to see her sit back down on the dock. But still she glared at him with hard eyes.

"Okay," he started, "you already know I'm sorry, for what you don't know. I was stupid, foolish, and a big part of me was a coward back then."

Clayton watched as confusion ran across Livia's expression. Her beautiful brows scrunched together, and her eyes clouded with uncertainty. He continued. "When you left, a part of me left with you. And it wasn't just when you left to go home at the end of the summer. It all started when I dropped you back at your aunt's that last night we were together."

Clayton looked down and saw that she was tightly holding one hand inside the other, clasping almost for dear life. A big part of him wanted to reach out to her and just touch her, put his hand over hers. He practically ached to do it, but when he made the smallest gesture to move his hand her way, he saw her almost imperceptibly shrink back, so he moved back and instead continued to talk. He decided not to look at her, but to train his gaze on their feet back in the water. "So I don't know if you remember that night."

"I remember," she said softly.

He cleared his throat and continued. "Well, after I walked you home and left you out back with your family, your mother, your aunt, you remember, it was one of your family's usual gatherings. What you don't know is when I walked away, I doubled back just to tell you one last good-bye, and that's when I heard what your aunt Kath and your mother were saying about how they hoped you were not getting your head all twisted by hanging out with me. How they thought you could do much better than any boy from these woods. That you had plans. Big plans. Much bigger plans than the likes of me and a place like Sugar Lake after you left for college in the fall."

He heard Livia's intake of breath as she looked up at him in shock. "No, Clayton, you can't have believed that. You got it all wrong," she whispered. "So very wrong."

"Oh, come on, Livia, did I? I'm sure I didn't. And

even if I did, they were perfectly right. You didn't dispute them. I heard you tell them that you had your head on straight and you already looked into early admittance at some Ivy Leagues. And that was okay. You were better than me and what I could offer. Always so much better than our small-town teenage dreams."

"How could you say such a thing? You knew about me going to college. And you said you would wait. You were talking about college too. But you always said you'd wait for me. Besides, what was I supposed to tell them? Was I just supposed to blurt out that I just came from your father's fishing shack where I had given my everything to you? How do you think that would've gone over? My father would have had your hide. That's how it would've gone over. I can't believe you let one overheard silly conversation change your entire perception of me. If that's the case, then you were just looking for an excuse to get out."

She looked furious, and Clayton could tell he more than messed up, but it didn't really matter. He knew that in some ways they were right and so was he. "Like I said, I'm sorry and I know I was stupid and I know I was wrong. But I also know that deep down I was never quite good enough for you. Look at the mistake I made. Look at the mistakes I continue to make. It wasn't just that one overheard conversation, that conversation just brought up the innate fear that I had inside of me. The silly impulsiveness, the feeling that I was never quite enough for you. I knew it then just as I know it now. And it all came to a head a few months later when my brother got wounded. I was lonely and I was angry and I wanted a reason to run. So I used him as an excuse. I know that now. I saw my brother lying in a hospital bed without a limb, and I said I would make myself worthwhile by somehow avenging him."

Livia stared at him with such a stunned expression that in that moment, the folly of Clayton's eighteen-year-old declaration was expressed on her face. He shook his head. "I know, I know it was ridiculous. Believe me, it was totally and completely ridiculous. Caleb told me I was a fool for doing it then, and I live every day now with him and my ex-wife as a reminder of what a foolish mistake it really was. The only good thing to come out of my enlistment was the practical life lessons I learned and the fact that I have my beautiful Hope to show for it. But the price, Livia, the price was also high, and one I'm not sure I'd be willing to pay again."

He noticed her eyes begin to water as she swallowed. "Don't say that, Clayton. Don't ever say that."

"I can't not say that. There has not been one day in all these days we've been apart that I haven't thought of you and haven't thought about what might've been if I just stood firm and kept my promise to you."

Clayton was shocked when Livia jumped up, water splashing him to silence. It was so quick that he wasn't prepared to stop her, and she started to walk away. He scrambled after her, reaching for her elbow, and was stunned when she turned on him, her tears clearly flowing. "I told you, don't say that!" She turned to start back up the uneven pathway.

"Where are you going?" Clayton yelled. "Wait a minute. Livia! You don't even have any shoes on."

Livia stopped with a frustrated huff and doubled back to get her sneakers. She looked up at him with anger burning from her eyes. "Don't talk to me about what you've been feeling for the past twelve years or your regret. Do you have any idea what I've been feeling?"

Her words hit him like a punch in the chest, leaving him breathless. All these years he'd thought she moved on with her life and was somewhere totally and completely happy and better off without him. That's the way people think when they feel they're not good enough or don't live up to the expectations of another person. He stared at her, searching for the words. "No, I don't have any idea. I always hoped, no assumed, you were happy, so much happier than I was. And that was good enough for me."

The tears flowed steadily down her cheeks, and she swiped at them. "Well, you assumed wrong! How can anybody be happy with unanswered questions in their life, Clayton, tell me that? Just how?"

Seeing her like this, crying, but still so strong and so beautiful, did something to Clayton, and all of a sudden it was as if everything were breaking apart inside him, spilling out, and he could no longer hold onto himself. Clayton reached out to her at the same time she held up a hand. Still he couldn't stop himself, and he pulled her to him and brought his lips down on hers in a desperate crushing moment. It was more of a plea than anything as he surrendered his heart to her in a kiss.

And surrender he did. His whole world shattered and then was pieced back together in the moment that she let go and yielded to him. Moving in ever so slightly, easing into him on a breathy sigh, Liv's lips were sweeter than any honey he'd ever harvested. Clayton felt like everything in him went liquid and he had to steel his core to keep himself together.

God, would this woman always have this effect on him? How could she still make him feel this way all these years later? One kiss from her and he was gone. Transported to another realm where the air was sweeter, the colors brighter, and life suddenly worth living that much more. Clayton leaned in farther as he breathed in some much-needed air, wrapping his arms tighter around her waist, but he stilled when Livia stiffened and pulled back.

"No," she said softly.

"No?"

She shook her head.

"No."

"Then tell me," he asked, "why are you still holding on to me so tight?"

They both looked down at the same time and saw the hand that Livia had put up. It was between them and tightly grasping his T-shirt.

She looked up at him, her lashes spiked with tears. "Because right now I don't know how to just let go."

Clayton felt his voice come out in a hoarse whisper, and he forced his gaze away from her to the lake as he took in the low-hanging sun, threatening to soon sink behind the trees. He told himself he should be strong for the both of them. If she wanted to let go, but didn't know how, he would show her. He was good at good-byes. Letting go was his specialty. But when he looked back down at her and she looked up at him, her eyes full of every dream he'd ever secretly held, his voice came out as a hoarse plea. "Then don't let go. Even if it's only for this afternoon. Don't let go, and neither will I. Let's hold on. We've still got each other and the sun is still shining, for now."

Clayton leaned forward once again, this time kissing Livia with all he had while picking her up. His mind briefly went to the honey jar that he was sure was nearly filled. He knew it was probably near over-flowing and would be by the time they went back out to check it. But then Liv reached up and touched his lips. "The sun will be setting soon," she said as she pulled back.

Clayton leaned in more. The honey wouldn't be a problem for another hour. Right now he had Livia Gale in his arms once more, and there was no way he was letting her go. Sure, he knew there would be a mess to clean up later. But later would have to take care of itself. "Soon," he said. "But not yet."

Chapter 18

Liv stood at the kitchen sink and once again wiped down the jar of honey before placing it back on the kitchen counter as she looked out the window over the sink. "Okay, enough is enough," she said to herself as she pushed the jar back a little farther from the edge and stepped away from the counter. Unconsciously she put her fingers to her lips and closed her eyes as she swallowed.

Why did she fall for it? Why did she fall for *him* once again? She went to the lake with Clayton knowing there was an attraction, but she thought she had a handle on that, she thought she at least had a handle on her own emotions. All she wanted was to hear his apology, find out his stupid excuse for letting her down like he had, and finally get closure. But what did she do? She went and let him kiss her, and like an idiot she kissed him right back. Falling for his sweet desperate words, soft eyes, and honey lips like a lovestruck teen. Liv let out a frustrated groan. Never again. Nope. Not ever again.

It didn't matter that in the thirty seconds of that one kiss it was as if her whole being had been reborn, set anew by the beat of his heart against her chest. That it felt so good that she wanted to keep the feeling going and wanted to hold on to it with all she had.

None of that mattered. What mattered was that she knew the reason he walked away and left her, sad as it may be, silly as it may have been, she now knew that it was something that they both had to live with and move on with their lives. She had and he had to take what they shared this afternoon as a final good-bye. The one they should have had.

She had her life in New York—speaking of that, she needed to get busy and up her job search—and he had his life here with his daughter, with his family. He'd gone on just fine without her and would continue to, despite whatever tales he was telling himself, now that she was back for the short amount of time. Liv hadn't been around noncommittal men all these years to not know the lies they told themselves and how good they were at convincing themselves that those lies were true.

She shook her head and turned toward the fridge, pulling out fixings for the night's dinner. She needed to keep herself busy. To not focus on Clayton. She needed to come to terms with the fact that today was in no way a beginning, but a long-drawn-out end.

And it was time to put it behind her. She had just a few weeks in town, and she would make the best of it. She could and would get on fine knowing that Clayton was around and would be a part of the periphery of her life for these few weeks. She could be mature about that, and they could be cordial; heck, they could even be friendly. Though nowhere near as friendly as they had been today. She hoped she'd made that clear to him.

Liv turned as the front door opened and Aunt Joyce's voice rang out. "We're home!"

Liv cleared her throat and unconsciously ran a hand across her face and hair as if trying to tidy herself up, hoping that Aunt Joyce couldn't read any of her anxiety across her face. Liv pasted on her best bright smile and yelled back, "I'm in the kitchen!"

Drea and Aunt Joyce walked into the kitchen, both looking at Liv with expectant expressions. Immediately she tried to brush them off. "Hey, you two," she said brightly, "how'd the rest of the day go?" She stared more closely at Aunt Joyce. Searching for hints of fatigue. "Why don't you go on in the den and relax? It's been a long one for you. I'm thinking it's about time you got off your feet."

"Oh, please, girl. Things quieted down quite a bit after you left, so I spent the better part of the afternoon off my feet. I have way more energy than I probably deserve. Besides, I'm feeling fantastic. I can't wait to see my doctor next week. You two being here has been just the spark that I needed. I'm sure he's going to say I'm doing great." She waved a hand and gave Liv a close, way too close for comfort, inspection before turning and looking at the jar of honey on the counter, her cheeks broadening in a wide grin. "You got it! I'm so glad. Let's get dinner going so you can tell us all about how it went over there by the hives."

Liv shook her head. She should know that talking about her trip to the hives would be the very first thing on Aunt Joyce's mind and there would be no putting her off. She reached in the fridge and pulled out some leftover grilled chicken from the barbecue. There were some fresh vegetables that Drea had picked up at the farmers' market the day before; she figured stir-fry would be a quick and easy dinner tonight. She and Drea had been taking turns with dinner—well, as much as Aunt Joyce would let them—in order to find ways to force her to relax in the evenings. It wasn't an easy task, and it took quite a bit of arm twisting, but with a little bit of guilt they'd come to find out that Aunt Joyce could be persuaded.

Liv shrugged. "There's not all that much to tell. Though I will say I'm proud of myself for not completely freaking out being around so many bees. You're right though, Clayton has quite the little setup there." She hoped more than anything that her voice was light and easy and didn't show any hint of the turmoil she was actually feeling. "He's modernized it so much it's really ingenious the way he can tap the honey and get it to flow out without really disturbing the bees and their work. And I have to admit, you're right, he does have a superior product." She wasn't lying about that. Clayton did have something good there, and the thought of it actually made her that much sadder to hear him say that any part of him didn't think he was good enough for her, or smart enough. It was ridiculous. Liv paused as she was getting a pan out for the stir-fry. She hoped she conveyed that properly in her dealings with him today. She didn't want something like that weighing on him, because for someone to go around feeling in any way that they were any less amazing than they truly were, well, it was more than a shame. It was a waste.

"You going to get that pan on the burner anytime soon?" Drea asked, bringing Liv back from her thoughts. "We're hungry over here, you know."

"Oh," Liv said. "Sorry about that. I was just thinking about something. But let's get dinner going. I'm hungry too, and we all have to get up bright and early

in the morning." She flashed a smile. "Those pies are
not going to make themselves, now, are they?"

"No, they sure aren't," Aunt Joyce said. "Not with
tourist season fast approaching. I'm starting to get
really excited about what we can really do. I say after
dinner we do some serious planning on our game
strategy. If they think I came to play last year, they
don't know what I'm bringing to the game this year
now that it's Team Goode 'N Sweet 2.0."

Liv looked over at Drea with wide eyes and shook
her head. "Oh, why do I get the feeling we've created
a bit of a monster?"

Drea gave her a head shake right back. "Hey, don't
blame me. I'm not the one with the mad baking skills.
All I do is make things pretty. You're the one who
brings the sweet."

That night Liv couldn't help sitting in her old spot
on the old window seat. She had her laptop open,
looking for leads on a new job and uploading her
résumé to a popular job search site. Just a few minutes
before, she had deleted an annoying message from
Damon. He had the nerve to send her something
about a job lead. As if she'd want to hear from him on
a job lead. And he had the nerve to send it so casually
after the way he'd moved out on her. The only thing
she wanted to hear from him was that he was returning her TV; besides that, she wanted nothing more
from Damon Harding.

Talk about a cherry on top of a completely confusing
day. At this point in her life Liv felt that she should be
feeling great about herself, on solid ground, have it all
together, be accomplished and all that, but no, here she
was sitting in the same spot she had been sitting as a
teenager, filled with the same uncertainty and unease
that she felt back then. Thinking about the same man

she was thinking of back then. She was a completely hopeless case and she knew it, but still she couldn't get her mind off Clayton and what he'd told her earlier that afternoon. And worse yet, she couldn't get her visions, or her out-of-control feelings about their afternoon and how it rocked her world, out of her mind.

For all her strong self-talk, if she was truly honest with herself, she was now more confused than ever. She looked out the window and glimpsed what she knew to be his bedroom and took in the fact that the light was off, noting there was nothing but darkness coming from that room. Glancing at the rest of the house, she noticed each room was illuminated, including the room that she'd seen Hope shimmy out of. She wondered where Clayton was at this time of night. It was late, so late that she probably should be asleep already, having to get up at four-thirty in the morning. But where was he? Did he go back to work an overnight and sleep at the firehouse, or did he go back to the fishing cabin and sleep there? She'd remembered him mentioning that sometimes he did stay out at the cabin when he needed to gather his thoughts and get a little privacy. She wondered if tonight was one of those nights, but then she let out a long breath and shook her head. What good was it wondering things like that?

"What are you still doing up?" Drea's voice had her turning her head toward her bedroom door in surprise.

"I could ask the same thing about you," Liv said softly as her sister entered the room and took a seat opposite her on the window bench.

"I was thirsty." Drea shook her head. "Nah. Let me not lie. I was sneaking down to get a taste of your leftover berry swirl pie. It really is good. I can't believe this newfound sweet tooth of mine. I stay here much longer, I may actually have to take on some form of exercise, and you know how much I detest manual exertion without any payoff, but all these sweets are doing nothing for my hips."

Liv looked over at her sister, taking in her still perfectly proportioned figure. "Trust me, you have nothing to worry about in the hip department. Not that a little exercise is a bad idea for anybody."

Drea tilted her head to the side at that and then glanced out the window. "So, you gonna tell me what's keeping you up?"

Liv let out a sigh, hit a few keys, then closed her laptop. "I was just filling out a few job applications. Aunt Joyce seems to be doing a lot better than we expected. So I need to start seriously considering what I'm going to do when I get back to New York. It may take me a while before I find something that's a good fit."

Drea nodded. "I hear you on that," she said. Then she let out a soft, almost imperceptible breath. "I guess I should be getting on there too."

"You guess? It doesn't sound like you've given it much thought," Liv said.

"No, I've given it quite a bit of thought," Drea said. "I just haven't come to any conclusions yet. Honestly, I've been floundering for so long, hanging my hat on the singing and acting thing that hasn't quite panned out, that I don't really know what I want to do or what I'm qualified to do."

"Oh, honey, you're qualified to do so much. And I don't think you should totally give up on your dream of singing or acting if it's really what's in your heart. But it doesn't hurt to have a backup plan if things don't work out the way you want them to, or just to have something to keep you floating until that does work out. Why, just seeing your work with Aunt Joyce has shown how incredibly talented you are."

Drea looked at Liv skeptically. "Get real, taking down some curtains and changing a few runners, that doesn't take any real talent."

"Oh, come on, you've done so much more than that. Stop selling yourself short. In no time, you've given the shop a whole new look and a whole new brightness. And that came to you completely innately. It takes true talent to do something like that. Not to mention you are amazing at customer service and have been a true draw to the shop. In just the couple of weeks that we've been here, Aunt Joyce has already seen an uptick in business and I'm sure that's not due to just the few pies that I've added to the menu. I know it's got quite a bit to do with how you've brightened up the place. Maybe you should think about something in customer service or in styling. I don't know, but I know you've got a lot of talent and you shouldn't let it go to waste."

Drea looked at Liv a lot more intently. "And what about you?"

Liv pulled back, surprised by the question, not quite knowing what her sister meant. "What about me?"

"Have you only been applying for marketing analyst jobs on the web? I could say the same about you and the improvements you've made to the shop in these weeks, not to mention the changes I've seen in you personally since you've been in the kitchen baking. There's a new lightness to you. I haven't seen you smile as much in the last two years as I've seen you smile in the last two weeks."

"I smile plenty, I'll have you know."

"Yeah, that plastered-on smile that you do so well. I'm an actress, remember? I know the truth from what is just a put-on. Not to mention you're my sister. I've been watching you perfect that fake smile for most of my life. I know when you're trying to pull one over, Liv. Just like you were trying to pull one over on us by pretending it was all about the hives with Clayton Morris this afternoon. And no big deal. Come on and give me a little credit. One look in your eyes and I could tell that man showed you way more than his hives."

Liv's eyes went wide over her sister's frank talk in the way she'd totally read her from the inside out. "Get outta here. It wasn't anything like that. He did show me his hives, and it was just like I said. Well, almost. We might have had to air a few things out about the past, and I might've got a little upset, and things got a little heated, and well, maybe he might've gotten a little out of control himself and kissed me, but it doesn't matter because nothing is coming of it. Absolutely nothing."

Drea grinned and nodded her head. "That was it, huh? Well, that sounds like a whole lot of its and nothings to me."

Liv reached over and gave her sister a light whack on her thigh. "You are the worst," she said, but couldn't help the smile that tugged at her over the way Drea put her anxiety in perspective. It was honestly just the bit of levity she needed at that moment.

"I know I am," Drea said, "but I'm probably just the right amount of worst you need right now." Drea got serious, her voice sobering. "Listen, I know you and I know you're probably beating yourself up over the kiss and nothings that happened this afternoon, but I'm here to tell you to stop. Like you said, it was just a kiss, but it was probably just a kiss you needed at that time. Everything happens for a reason."

Liv shook her head at her sister. "Not this. Definitely not this. There can't be a reason for this happening. Not now. If there was a reason for this, it would've happened twelve years ago when it should have."

Drea leaned forward and put her hand over Liv's. "And there you go. My ever-controlling sister. Thinking she has the power over time and space. Like I said, everything happens for a reason, and it all happens in its due time and in its due season. Maybe this kiss was just the wake-up call you needed to let you know that you weren't ready for it to happen all those years ago. Maybe he wasn't ready for it to happen all those years ago."

What in the world was Drea talking about? This was the absolute worst time for it to happen. Liv had a life in New York, and Clayton had a life here, not to mention a life here with his family, with his daughter. She didn't see any room for her in that. "I love you, Drea, and I love you for coming here and being here with me and supporting me now, but I have to tell you, I think you're wrong. Clayton and I, well, that ship has long sailed. I'm here for the short while and then I'm going back to my life in New York, leaving him to his daughter and I hope a very good life here. He made his decisions back then, and now I'm making mine for the best future I can."

Drea got up with a stretch and a yawn. She leaned forward and gave Liv a kiss on the top of her head. "Okay, dear sister, if you say so. But if I were you, I'd stop staring out that window at his and go on ahead and get some sleep. The future starts tomorrow bright and early at four-thirty a.m. Good night."

Chapter 19

"We keeping you awake over there, Chief?" Clayton looked up at Braxton Lewis from where Clayton was sitting at the head of the conference room table in the firehouse. He had his head cradled in one hand while he was staring at the spreadsheet in front of him, honestly not making heads or tails of the uptake in food in the past six months. He wanted to point fingers, but the only change had been the addition of the new guy, Ducky Waterford, who had come on in April, and there was no way pint-size Ducky could be putting it away the way this paperwork had described. Still, Clayton had to admit it wasn't the numbers that had him transfixed, and yes, Lewis had caught him halfway on his way to a nap and not really listening to what the crew was going on about as they did their weekly roundtable recap.

He spent another restless night tossing and turning, going over his encounter with Livia down at the fishing shack. Encounter. Like he could call what they'd shared just an encounter. Though he was sure that was how she would like to categorize it. An encounter with Clayton Morris that she could put in a box and file away, pretend it never happened. Well, he had news for her: It happened, and if he could help it, it would not be the one and only time. He'd like to have her open up a permanent spot for him on the desktop of her mind for many, many more files.

He gave himself a mental head shake. The thought of that seemed almost insurmountable. Not after the way he'd botched up his so-called apology. He was, for the most part, fine as long as he wasn't rambling on to her. Doing that was nothing but a recipe for disaster. He'd never wanted to admit his feelings of insecurity, or in any way make her feel as if she was responsible for them. But he was afraid that he had, and that wasn't really on her, that was on him. And once again, he found himself feeling guilty and needing to make amends for his own stupid blunder. That was, if she'd even want to listen. Now there was a big rub. Probably no way she would after all his droning on about his feelings. Worse yet, after his droning on about his oversensitive feelings, he had the nerve to—without permission or real provocation—go and kiss her. Not that he could or would regret that kiss. No, there was no way he'd have any regrets when the result was so earth-shatteringly amazing.

Clayton forced himself to focus on the business at hand as he looked over at Braxton. "Yeah, Lewis, of course I'm awake. Don't be such a smart mouth." He looked around the rest of the table, taking in a myriad of confused and expected expressions. He could tell they were all judging him, trying to figure out what was going on with his mood, but today he just wasn't in the mood to entertain any questions. For once he wanted to keep to himself and not have to deal with anyone's unsolicited opinions. "If there are no further points of business, let's adjourn and everyone can get

to their assigned tasks." He gave a nod and attempted
a smile that probably came out as little more than a
halfhearted grimace. With any luck they'd all think he
had a bout of the stomach flu. "Thank you for your
time, and as always, remember safety first. You are
your crewmember's keeper."

With that Clayton rose and gathered his papers in
order to head out. He purposely ignored Avery's look
of concern as he made his way toward his office. He
noted she was just about to say something when
thankfully his cell phone pinged with a message.

Dad, I'm stopping off to get ice cream after school
with Alisha. I told grandma. Will call you later.

He gave a nod and a smile as he wrote a quick
answer back to Hope letting her know that it was okay
to go with her friend for ice cream after school, but to
indeed not be too late and to call him for a ride
home. School was just about up for the year, and
though he was still worried about her, he had noticed
in the past two weeks that she seemed a little bit happier, and he was thrilled that she was getting out and
engaging with some friends. With the busy season
picking up in town, though, he couldn't help but be
a little concerned about his daughter getting to the
age where she would be hanging out on her own in
town. Being the overzealous father, he made a mental
note to take a little stroll along Main Street at around
three-thirty just to be sure everything was all right.

But as three-thirty came around, something told
Clayton it probably wasn't the best thing to do,
strolling by the ice-cream shop and embarrassing his
daughter when she was just starting to get out and
make friends. He was sure she would hate him for it.

Maybe it would be best if he just hung back and waited for her call. He paced by the entrance to the firehouse, clutching his cell phone, at a loss for what to do. It was then that he looked up and straight into the eyes of Olivia Gale.

Just great, here he was completely perplexed about the eleven-year-old in his life and now he was face-to-face with the nearly thirty-year-old that had him twisted inside out.

"Hi." *How is that for enlightened introductions?*

"Hi," she said back. She sure looked pretty today, no, more than pretty; pretty was for beauty queens and Hollywood starlets. With the way she looked and how she halted his breathing and confused his mind, breathtaking was the only way to describe her.

She was wearing a lovely, simple, sleeveless yellow knit sundress that hit above her knees and showed off her sleek legs and beautiful brown complexion. She gave Clayton a smile that was sweet and easy and still slightly cautious, which made his heart ache a little bit.

"What are you doing here?" he asked.

Her look clouded, and he wanted to kick himself over his poor choice of words. It was then that he noticed that he wasn't alone standing in front of the firehouse. Now four other guys suddenly had urgent in front of the firehouse loitering business. Like he didn't know they were there to watch him talking with Liv. As if his speaking with her was somehow a watch-worthy event. "Well, I happened to step out of the shop for a moment since it was quiet, and when I looked up the street I saw you over here pacing, which looked a little odd, so I decided to come up and say hi. I hope that's okay."

Suddenly extremely self-conscious, Clayton nodded.

"Sure, it's more than okay. Though I'm sure the pacing did seem a little weird. I, um, was just waiting for a call from Hope. She's out with a friend getting ice cream down the street, and I was wondering if I should go check on her." He rubbed at his head and looked over at her. "I know it's silly, and I'm probably being overly protective. But she doesn't go out with friends much, and for her to say she's going out . . . well, I just wanted to make sure she was having fun."

Livia nodded and smiled at him, her eyes softening. "I totally get it, and you're not being overprotective at all. You're just being a good father." She turned and looked down toward the ice-cream shop. "Hey, I just passed the shop on my way here and gave a glance inside. I saw her sitting there with two other girls. She looked fine to me. But if you want to take a walk down, I'll walk with you."

Clayton shook his head, letting out a sigh of relief. "No, you telling me that bit of news makes me feel a lot better. I don't want to walk past and embarrass her. Make her feel like I'm checking up on her. Let me just type this quick text and tell her that I'm available to bring her home whenever she's done."

Clayton sent off the text to Hope and felt relief after it was done. He looked at Livia and admitted he was slightly surprised to find her still standing there. He'd wanted to see her and talk with her so much since their afternoon together, but she'd given him strict rules that he didn't need to and she didn't want him to reach out to her. It felt so wrong that it was making him nuts, but he had no choice but to play by her rules.

So why was she really here now? Did he owe her another apology, one for pacing in her line of sight? Oh whatever, she was here, and he shouldn't question it, but be grateful for the chance to talk.

"Listen," he said. "It's kind of quiet right now, thankfully no emergencies. If you have time, you want to grab a quick iced coffee at the new coffee place? I'm sure my going there will send Doreen into a full-on hissy fit, but when I next go to her for my usual cheeseburger, I'll just place the blame firmly on you and you being a New Yorker. I'll say something about how New Yorkers need their coffee on steroids or something. That should do it."

That pulled a chuckle from her. "Sure, it's been so long since I've had my usual octane, I'm way over-due. You actually won't be lying to Doreen if you tell her that."

As they headed down the street, Clayton tried to quell his rapidly beating heart. He could do this. He could be normal and they could be just two old friends having a coffee; it would be fine. Along the way they passed Redheart, the old movie theater. At the same time, they both looked up at the old vintage marquee, and he saw Livia give a wistful smile.

"We had some good times there, didn't we?" she said.

He nodded. "We really did. Those were some days. Back then it seemed like summer would go on forever right up until the very end, when it all came crashing down way too fast."

She nodded. "It did feel as if it would go on forever. And now summer just feels like another month on the calendar, and those months go so fast they barely feel like weeks. One day melting into the next. It's a shame, really. I will say though, I'm surprised the old theater is still here."

"Me too," Clayton agreed.

"It's barely in use. As you can see, it's closed today. The only reason it's still in existence is because of the determination of Mr. Kilborn, its owner. He and his wife are such fans of classic movies that he refuses to bend and sell it, despite the many offers I hear he's gotten over the years. Just about all the young folks go out to the mall and the new multiplex anyway, so Mr. Kilborn now solely opens for matinees on the weekends. One Saturday night showing. Usually it's whatever he or his wife is in the mood to run, which is pretty hilarious. It's a surprise potpourri movie night of sorts."

Livia looked at him in shock. "You have got to be kidding me? How does he stay in business doing that?"

"Oh, don't feel bad for the Kilborns, they do just fine. Not only do they own this movie theater, but they are huge landowners in these parts and have their hands in all sorts of other property investments, from what I hear. The old man is quietly a financial wiz. This theater is just their tribute to old Hollywood and holding on to what they feel is the way of life that they love."

Livia nodded. "Oh well, I get it, and I can't say I don't admire their way of doing things. I'm happy to see the old theater still here. I wonder what they're showing this weekend."

Clayton felt his heart stop for a moment and all judgment go out the window as he once again threw caution to the wind. "Would you care to come with me on Saturday night and we'll see what the showing is together?"

At her immediate wide-eyed expression, he was quick to throw in, "As just friends, nothing more. I promise not to do anything crazy like try to kiss you. I heard you loud and clear the other day."

Livia gave him a sideways glance. "Yeah, that would be crazy." She then blinked and gave her head a little shake as if she were shaking off her own comment as she looked up at him with a smile. "Glad to hear you were listening. So just friends, huh?"

Clayton gave a quick nod and attempted a smile, though everything in him was saying that just friends was the last thing he wanted to be when it came to her.

She finally nodded back at him. "Well, when you put it like that, how can I possibly refuse? Now, come on, you talked of this coffee so much, I'm actually quite thirsty." She started to walk ahead of him, leaving him no choice but to follow.

Clayton looked up at the marquee of the old theater. "Thirsty doesn't even begin to describe it."

"It's just a movie," Liv said to Drea, who was sitting on the opposite twin bed as she changed out of the purple sundress she was wearing and flipped the black one over her head.

"Yeah, honey, you keep telling yourself that. Meanwhile this is the fourth dress you've tried on. I always change my outfit four times when it's *'just a movie'.*"

Liv gave her sister a sharp glare as she took in the air quotes that Drea had put around "just a movie." She didn't need the added pressure tonight. She didn't need any pressure at all. It was bad enough she accepted the date—no, not date, the meet-up. No, not quite a meet-up since he was picking her up outside the house and they were going together. Well, maybe it was a meet-up because he was just meeting her in front of the house, so technically she could call it a meet-up. Right. Either way, she didn't need the added pressure of Drea teasing her over the fact that she was indeed going to a movie with Clayton Morris tonight.

Just as the dress skimmed over her hips, the doorbell rang. "Dang it! What is he doing ringing the doorbell?

We were supposed to meet outside, and on top of it he's five minutes early," she said. "This is gonna make it look like a date. If Aunt Joyce opens the door and lets him in and starts chatting with him, this is totally going to make it look like we were officially courting or something." She started waving her hands at Drea, shooing her. "You run downstairs and play interception, beat her to the punch. She's got a bum hip. The woman can't be that fast."

Drea was jumping up from the bed and Liv was trying to wedge her feet into sandals while putting on some lip gloss when they both heard Aunt Joyce greeting Clayton at the front door. "Why, Clayton Morris, don't you look the dashing picture tonight," Aunt Joyce said, her voice loud and exuberant as it trailed up the stairs to their ears.

Liv groaned and Drea fell back on the bed in a fit of laughter. "Cut it out, it's not that funny," Liv said.

"It's kind of hilarious." Drea giggled. "You'd think you were a teenager the way you are acting and the way she's going on down there. I feel like we're something out of an Austen parody novel. It's cracking me up. This is seriously turning into the best trip ever."

Liv picked up her crossbody purse and slung it over her head. "Well, I'm so glad one of us is having a great time. Let me get going before Aunt Joyce comes up with an imaginary dowry for me and really pawns me off on the man."

Drea started laughing all over again as Liv hit the staircase. "I won't wait up!" she yelled. Liv growled in response. Yet she knew she'd made the right decision agreeing to go to the movies with Clayton Morris tonight, that was for sure.

Chapter 20

Liv rushed down to Clayton, interjecting herself into his conversation with Aunt Joyce. "We better get going if we're going to make the movie time," she said, not really leaving any room open for debate from Aunt Joyce.

Aunt Joyce's clear disappointment couldn't be missed. "Well, I guess you kids go and have fun. Though I was hoping to at least offer a bit of refreshment to Clayton before you all left," Aunt Joyce said anyway.

"Thanks so much, Miss Joyce. I'll have to take you up on that next time," Clayton said, and Liv couldn't help giving him a side-eye glance. Next time? Not so fast, buddy, this was just a movie between friends. It wasn't like there would be so many next times. But she wouldn't get into that now. Now it was time to get them both out the door and on their way.

So quick to get them out, Liv didn't get to know what anxiety was until they were alone together in Clayton's truck. As he shut the passenger-side door behind her, it really hit her how much this felt like a date. She watched nervously as he walked around the front of the truck and got in on the driver's side. He looked good dressed up, though still quite casual in jeans and loafers and a button-down shirt. She could tell he made the effort. Something about him made her want to smile, but also gave her a little pain over the fact that he'd gone to so much effort over what he would wear tonight. She looked across the dashboard and gave a quick glance to the interior of his truck. It was quite clean and well kept, though the truck was clearly a few years old. She could see that the dashboard was polished to a high sheen, and there were no extra frills in the interior. She took a deep breath and instantly regretted it as his masculine scent hit her nostrils, putting her body on full alert.

Clayton started the truck and she rolled down her window, letting the welcome smell of the woods into the cab of the truck as they started down the road.

"I'm excited to see what they're showing tonight," she said, hoping her voice sounded bright and easy. "I hope it's something fun."

"Me too," he said. "Hope it's not too dark or too deep. You never know with Mr. and Mrs. Kilborn; it's a toss-up. Like I said, it totally depends on their mood. You'll forgive me if this turns into a bust, won't you? If it's totally something you don't want to see, please just let me know and we can scratch it or we can go to the multiplex down at the mall and see something more current." Liv noticed the worry in his tone.

"Don't worry, I'm totally game. I'm sure whatever they're playing should be good. Besides, there's nothing out right now that's striking my fancy. Everything seems like more of the same. I don't know if the Kilborns still have that old popcorn maker; I'm sure you're looking forward to that. Popcorn with lots of butter, just like you like it."

Clayton started to chuckle as he continued his drive down the road.

"What is it? Why are you laughing?"

"I'm just laughing over the popcorn. Can I be honest with you for a second?"

Suddenly Liv didn't know what to expect. Nothing good ever came out of that "Can I be honest" question. But she nodded, "Go ahead, though I admit, I am kind of nervous as well as curious."

Clayton glanced at her, his eyes dark and shining in the moonlight, before he turned back to the road and kept driving. "I was never a fan of butter on my popcorn like that. Heck, I only kind of like popcorn. I only got it because I knew how much you liked it. This is embarrassing, but I went with it just so I could happen to touch your hand in the popcorn bucket."

Liv couldn't have been more stunned if he told her he was some sort of alien from outer space. But then she started to laugh at the absurdity of it all.

Clayton turned to her with confusion in his eyes. He shook his head. "Wow, you really do go for a guy's jugular, Livia. Though I guess it is funny finding out how truly over-the-top crazy for you I was. I know I was a total and complete sap during those days."

Liv shook her head and held up a hand at him. "No, that's not it. That's not it at all."

Now he was even more confused. "What are you talking about?"

She snorted and shook her head even more. "You probably won't believe this, but I don't like popcorn with butter either. I mean, I like popcorn just fine, but with just a little salt and a hint of butter. I only ordered it that way because I thought you liked it."

Liv watched as understanding dawned on Clayton's features, and she started to laugh once again. "I guess we're both total and complete saps, or at least we were back in those days. Teen love is quite the thing, isn't it?"

"You can say that again," Clayton said as he continued to ride into town, this time both of them lost in their own thoughts about young love and sacrifice.

At the concession stand Liv ordered a medium popcorn, no butter, but Clayton insisted she add a bit and he tacked on M&M's and the vintage red lace candies they had, and she was surprised to see they even offered freshly baked pigs in a blanket. "Yum, I love pigs in a blanket. Those smell delicious. Mrs. Kilborn makes them fresh."

Liv was astounded. "Only in Sugar Lake would folks even show off their culinary skill at the movie concession stand."

Clayton laughed and, balancing what he could, stepped aside, making space for Liv as he lead her into the theater.

Along the way Liv whispered, "I can't believe that Mr. and Mrs. Kilborn dressed as aliens tonight. They really know how to get in the spirit of things." Liv found it tough to keep a straight face while accepting her Coke from Mrs. Kilborn, who was indeed dressed in full alien regalia for the night's showing of the original *Independence Day*. The petite, elderly woman with the eager smile could barely keep her antennae from falling off while trying to balance them atop her purple bouffant wig. And her husband was equally as

funny, looking like a mashup of *Forbidden Planet* meets
Dr. Who meets *Cocoon*.

It was so cute, and she was a little more than grateful for the easy lightheartedness of it all. To say Liv was
relieved at the choice of movies being screened was an
understatement. She was nervous expecting that they
might be playing something that was overly romantic,
making both her and Clayton feel quite uncomfortable. But *Independence Day* had always been one of
her favorites, so she was actually excited about seeing
it again.

"Yes, they really do go all out and get in the spirit of
things," Clayton said as he ushered her into the theater. Although she wasn't surprised, Liv was still a little
sad over how empty the theater was. There were only
four other patrons—two middle-aged men close to
the front and another couple off on the left side.

"Well, it looks like we've got our pick of seats," Clayton said.

"Yeah, I would say so. Which is kind of sad. I really
don't know how they keep this place open," Liv said.

"Remember what I said about how well they do with
their other properties, so I think they're okay. And
besides, this is opening weekend for the big horror
thriller that everybody's talking about, so I'm sure
that's where most of the crowd is tonight, down at the
multiplex."

They settled into seats toward the back midsection,
and Liv was surprised to see that, though it was the
original theater, it wasn't as run-down as Liv imagined
it would be. Sure, it could use some updates, but it was
clean, the old seats looked to have been reupholstered,
and there was fairly new carpeting in the rows. She
could tell that the Kilborns really loved either this
place or each other very much. She bet that both

weighed pretty heavy. It felt somehow magical seeing a movie in a place that still had such fine architectural details. She didn't even miss extra leg room or stadium-style seating.

"Wow, it's even more beautiful in here than I remembered," Liv commented as she took her seat.

Clayton nodded as he helped her balance her snacks and get settled. "That it is. I guess they figured since they were keeping the old place open they wouldn't let it just go to rot, which we all can appreciate. As you can see, though it's small, at least a few still come here," he said. "They even rent the place out for parties and small festivals," he added.

Liv couldn't help being impressed, telling herself that all would be fine while she fought to push her earlier anxiety aside. Besides, so far things were working out well.

As Clayton took a seat beside her and the previews came up, she settled in to enjoy herself.

But as she sat uneasy in her seat munching on her third handful of popcorn, Liv wondered, since when did *Independence Day* turn into such a highly charged romantic movie? There were aliens, for goodness' sake. Aliens and fight scenes galore. She wasn't supposed to feel so much sexual tension during this movie. But as she sat there trying to concentrate on the big screen and enjoy her not-too-buttery popcorn, sizzles, tingles, and all sorts of unwanted feelings were what she felt sitting so close in the dark next to Clayton Morris.

It was almost too much being next to him in a dark theater once again for over two hours. It didn't matter that it was Will Smith and Jeff Goldblum on the screen in front of her and that aliens were blowing up buildings left and right. Not when Clayton's strong, muscular thigh just so happened to graze against hers when Will and Viv finally reunited with the helicopter whirring in the background and destruction all around them. Nope, just then she might as well have been watching the most romantic movie ever as she practically melted in her seat while just about jumping out of it and dropping her popcorn clear on the floor. Luckily Clayton had quick hands, and he caught the popcorn before it actually hit the ground, saving most of it and looking up at her with his wide, curious expression. "You okay?" he whispered.

"I'm fine," she said quickly with a nod. "I just got surprised for a second. You have more of those little hot dogs?" she added by way of deflection.

Clayton nodded. "Yeah, sure," then he looked at her sheepishly. "Sorry there is only one left, but you can have it. Do you want some Twizzlers?"

Liv just shook her head as she reached for the last pig in a blanket. "No, this is fine, thank you." She quickly stuffed her mouth so she'd no longer have to talk, and looked back at the screen. Suddenly over-stuffed and slightly embarrassed, should she have refused that last pig in the blanket? No, if she did it would show she was acting all girly and putting on date-like airs, which she so was not doing tonight. This was just them hanging out, nothing to be nervous about. Yeah, so why was it she was so thirsty she could barely swallow? Liv reached out for the soda and it was as if Clayton had anticipated her. There was his hand, outstretched with the soda already there in front of her face. She took it with a nod and a half smile. Taking a long gulp, Liv swallowed down hard and then put the soda back in the holder in front of them.

This is turning out to be a top-five disaster of an idea. Liv glanced over at Clayton with a quick side-eye. How was it that he was so darned calm? She took him in, while she chewed on a Twizzler. *Wait? Didn't she just refuse them? Gah! How was she now munching on one!* Talk about a turnabout? He was showing masterful control, whereas she was turning out to hardly have any. But why should she complain? He was only living up to his promise of taking her to the movies and attending as just friends. So why was she expecting more from him? Was it time to get truthful with herself and realize that she did want more from him?

It was ridiculous and she knew it. *Just focus on the movie.* She may get real with her feelings, but she also had to get real with what was practical and right in front of her, what she could and could not have. And she knew she could not have any sort of future with Clayton Morris. She reached into her bag of popcorn and was stunned to find his hand already there. Instantly she recoiled. "I thought you said you didn't like popcorn," she whispered.

"I said I didn't like it with all that butter. I like it like this just fine enough. Is it a problem?" he asked. "What? Don't you want to share with me?"

Liv practically groaned out loud over his question. Oh yeah, she wanted to share with him, all right. Fighting to clear her head, she reached forward for the soda. She practically drained it, making an undignified long slurp at the end. Just perfect, now they wouldn't have any more soda and there was still an hour left of the movie. She reached for her purse on the seat next to her and started to get up. But Clayton stopped, grabbing her wrist softly. "Where are you going?"

"I finished the soda, I'm going to get some more. I'll be right back."

He shook his head. "No, you let me do that. You don't have to go."

But she just started forward. "It's better that I go."

Liv took a step forward, her foot getting tangled up in Clayton's, and before she knew it she found herself pitching forward and twisting right into his lap. She landed completely inelegantly, her eyes wide with her mouth pitched in an O shape.

"You really know how to stick a landing, lady," Clayton said, his arm stable around her back while his thighs felt as strong as two oak logs against her backside. Liv attempted to wiggle in order to get up.

"I'd be careful how you do that. Too much wiggling and we may not be just friends by the end of this movie."

Liv looked at him. Taking in his open expression, marveling over the way his dark eyes glistened while the fight of the aliens reflected in them. He bit slightly at his bottom lip, and she could tell in that moment that he was struggling, just as much as she was. It gave her a perverse pleasure that she knew she didn't deserve, but was still happy to have. "Truth be told, I don't know if we were friends when the movie started."

He just nodded his agreement, making no move to let her go, and she made no move to get up from his lap, the feeling in that moment just too perfect to release, his gaze meeting hers, his lips so very near. Before Liv knew it, she was leaning forward and once again letting go.

Chapter 21

Who knew letting go could make Liv want to hold on so tight?

"You sure you want to do this?" Clayton asked. His voice deep, serious. He looked at her with that intense gaze, his eyes as dark as the lake on that moonlit night. Liv swallowed hard against the fear that threatened to bubble up to the surface and spill over.

She nodded at Clayton and grinned wide, and for that she was rewarded by his dazzling smile as he clasped her hand and squeezed it for reassurance. Liv kicked off her flip-flops then. "Okay, let's go for it, no more stalling."

Stilling her nerves, Liv ran in time with Clayton through the grass, enjoying the cool feel of it, and then the hard sensation of wood at the bottom of her feet, and as they got to the end of the dock and jumped off at the same time, Liv held her breath and closed her eyes, fighting a squeal for fear of alerting anyone to what they were doing.

The water was bracing with the shocking chill, but at the same time exhilarating. She came up sputtering and gasping for air, but Clayton was right there, his hand still holding hers tight as he wrapped his strong arm around her waist and gave her a proud smile. "That was fantastic!" he said. "You are fantastic."

In an instant, his lips were on hers, cool and wet, strong and enticing. Liv melted into his body—one with him and the water as he treaded and their bodies swirled around in a circle. In that moment the world, the past and present, came together in their own little pool of joy. Liv tried her best to just let go, to be and stay in the moment, but for all her trying she just couldn't.

How could this feel so right? Being with him again like this. The past threatened to bubble up and tumble with the present as the same joy she had back then melded with the happiness she was feeling now. It was all so similar, but did that mean it would of course end the same way? She knew it had to. That she had to keep herself grounded somehow, someway, in reality, in the here and now. It was the only guard she had for her heart and her future. She couldn't get caught up and end up on another twelve-year heartbreak treadmill where every man she met after Clayton would be hopelessly out of reach. She had to stay grounded, and she had to keep her heart protected now that she knew the truth. Moving past this and moving on was the only healthy thing for her to do if she ever had any chance of going back home and starting over in a new direction.

"Why are you doing this?" Clayton said to her. "Why are you already gone and you haven't even left me yet?"

Liv looked up at Clayton. How was it that he knew what she was thinking without her saying it out loud? "What are you talking about? I'm right here with you."

He pulled her in closer, and for a brief moment she

snuggled underneath his chin, enjoying the comfort of him.

"I know you're here," Clayton said. "But I also know you're not. You're guarding yourself, Livia. You're guarding yourself when you don't have to do that with me."

Liv pulled back and stared up at him. She shook her head. "I'm not guarding myself from you. I'm just . . ." She paused, looking for the right words in order to be truthful with him, but not hurt him in any way. "I'm just trying to protect myself. You know as well as I that this is only temporary. And though it's fun, meeting you here, frolicking in the water after midnight, acting like the kids we used to be, this is all only a dream. One of the best dreams ever, but still only a dream. My aunt's doing well, things at the shop seem to be going great, and she and Rena have implemented some wonderful changes. I think with her finally agreeing to hire a little extra part-time help, all will be fine and I can and should head back to New York. To my life there."

She felt Clayton stiffen, and a chill came over her that, despite the cool water, she didn't feel before. He looked her in the eyes. "You really don't have to go back, you know. You can stay here. You're looking for a new job. What about starting over here? I'm sure your aunt would love to have you. There is no reason for you to leave now."

Liv felt her brows pull together, and while part of her got a small thrill at the thought of possibly staying here and living on the lake with Clayton, a part of her couldn't help but be slightly angry and put out by his presumption that she would want to drop everything to stay. "How do you know there's no reason for me to leave? Despite not having a job, I do have a life in

New York. Friends, family. New York is my home and I love it. Like I said, this is lovely, but this is not real. Maybe we could have had something back when. But that ship has sailed. We have to both make do with the life courses we're on now."

"Who says we have to make do? Ships change directions as do people's lives. We can be in control of our own destiny from here on out."

"How can that be true?" Liv said. "How can we just be in charge of our own destinies when there are so many other factors? Like I said, we're not kids anymore and so much has happened in our lives. You have a kid. What about Hope? She's been through so much. How do you think she would feel about me coming into your life right now? She's barely over you and her mother breaking up, and she's going through so much at school, getting used to life here at Sugar Lake, she doesn't need that kind of turmoil."

He shook his head. "She'd think it was fine. She'd want me to be happy."

Liv looked him in the eye. "I didn't ask you what she would think, I asked how she would feel. There is a difference."

She watched as Clayton's expression went from determined to one far more somber, and she knew she hit on a stumbling block. Although his daughter should never be a stumbling block. Liv continued. "You know I'm right. Your daughter is the most important person in your life, as she should be. She should be your focus, and you should have no guilt or animosity about any relationship you enter into."

"I'm sure Hope will be fine. She'll be happy if I'm happy."

"Are you sure about that? This is all way too new, and I'm not willing to be the one to cause any more strain in your relationship with her or in her life. Our sneaking out here and having these wonderful stolen moments," she said, smiling, "this has been wonderful. More wonderful than I could ever have imagined. But it should be enough for both of us, and something I know I will cherish and never regret. When it comes to you, Clayton Morris, I don't want to have regrets anymore."

Liv watched as an internal struggle played across his features, and it pained her to see it. She knew exactly what she was going through, because she was feeling it too, and because of that she knew she had to end this heartache as quickly as possible, no matter how good being with him felt.

As Clayton walked with Hope from the ice-cream shop to the bakeshop he couldn't get out of his mind Livia's words from the other night. Maybe he should've disputed her more, somehow fought harder for her to stay. But in that moment, he couldn't come up with the right words. When Livia was in front of him, he was always inadequate when it came to the right words. She constantly left him tongue-tied and discombobulated. But how was it she didn't know how he felt about her? How crazy, over the top in love he was with her and how much he wanted her to stay and give what they were starting a chance grow.

He looked down at Hope as she was dipping into her double scoop of double chocolate ice cream and thought about what Livia had said. Was Hope even ready for the possibility of his taking on another relationship? It was true she was just starting to get over the fact that her mother was no longer in her life. Clayton mentally gave his head a shake. Come on,

time to get real. The girl would never be over her
mother abandoning her like she did. Celeste barely
called; the last time Hope had spoken to her had
been over a month ago, when Celeste called him, low
on funds having lost her wallet on some trek in an
Arizona desert. Like a fool, he'd wired her money, but
only after insisting she get on the phone and talk to
Hope, give her some reassurance that her mother still
cared about her.

Though he hated to admit it, maybe Livia was right.
Could it possibly be that the timing was just not right
for them and would never be right for them? He
should be putting his sole focus into his daughter and
into building her up as best he could. Giving her all
the love and strength she deserved. That should be
his main concern. And as Livia pointed out, he should
be grateful for the little time they had together to
enjoy this bit of closure. Letting out a breath and
more determined than ever, Clayton decided that was
what he would do. Enjoy whatever time he had left
with his Livia, since she probably would be gone soon.
He needed to accept his fate for what it was and continue to steer his ship in the best way he knew how.

As he and Hope entered Goode 'N Sweet there was
a flurry of activity, but Clayton's heart darn near exploded as Hope ran up to Miss Joyce and gave her a
big, one-armed hug, careful not to spill her ice cream.
She then turned and gave a huge and unexpected
grin to Livia, who was behind the counter. "Hi there,
Miss Olivia," Hope said. "It's good to see you again."

"It's good to see you again too, Hope. Are you enjoying your summer?" Liv asked.

Hope's eyes went skyward, and her grin went even
wider. "Am I? I couldn't be happier. I thought this

year would go on forever, but it's done now. I'm glad to have made it through and for the break."

Clayton looked at Hope proudly, then directed his comments to the ladies. "Not that she's taking that much of a break. I'm not ashamed to say that my super-smart daughter here won a top award in her summer engineering course."

"Well, all right now!" Miss Joyce said. "That's what I'm talking about. I love hearing about smart young women coming up in the world."

"Way to go, Hope!" Liv said. "That's how you do it! I see you're a force to be reckoned with. Your father was proud before, but look at him now strutting around like a peacock, as he rightfully should be. What will be do with him?"

Hope gave an exaggerated eye roll though she couldn't seem to hide her smile. "Dad, I told you it was no big deal."

"Maybe not to you, since you're so naturally smart, but to your old dad it sure is. Now let me be proud, young lady."

Hope grinned a little wider then and Livia gave him a smile and a nod that sent pleasure coursing through his body over how right the whole scene was. "Now, Miss Hope," she said. "How about you choose whatever you like as a celebration gift. I know you have ice cream there, but you can have it either now or for later, if you like. A girl should always have a little something sweet in reserve, is what I always say."

"Thank you. Do you have any peach cobbler? I was sampling the ice-cream shop's new pie flavors and they were okay, but honestly all they made me think of is how good a piece of your pie would taste."

Livia and Miss Joyce quickly turned to each other.

"Why, that man bun had better not have tried it," Aunt Joyce said.

"Now, calm down, Aunt Joyce. I'm sure he didn't. There are tons of ice-cream flavors in the world. He would not be the first to serve cake or pie flavors. And I'm sure some are bound to be similar to flavors we have," Livia said, trying to relax her aunt. Uh-oh. Looked like Hope rattled up a hornet's nest with that comment.

Miss Joyce practically simmered. "Similar! Well, I'll be seeing about that. You can be sure."

"Livia is right, Miss Joyce. Plenty of shops do that. And besides, how could anyone ever get even close to re-creating your masterful flavors," he said.

Miss Joyce seemed to soften a bit with his comments, but it wasn't much. She gave him a slight smile. "You're a sweet one, Clayton. But I don't know about that. My Livy here is coming on pretty well. You'd be surprised at how tasty her treats are."

He grinned and was not surprised to see Livia fighting a blush.

But Hope's eyes were wide. He could tell she didn't mean to upset Miss Joyce. Livia seemed to notice and gave Hope a reassuring smile. "Don't you worry. Now, what can I get you, Miss Future Engineer?"

Hope looked over at Miss Joyce cautiously. "Pick your treat, baby. Don't worry none over these grown folks' mess. You just enjoy yourself. This is your celebration."

Hope's lips turned up in a slight smile, and she once again started to peruse all the beautiful baked goods behind the counter. She finally settled on an individual pecan peach cobbler, and Livia nodded with approval. "Excellent choice. Those are fairly new, so I hope you like them. I tweaked my aunt's recipe a bit to make these mini ones. How about I box up a few for you. And you, your father, and grandmother can share them as a little celebration tonight?"

"Thank you so much, I'm sure we'll love them," Hope said. "If you don't mind, can you add one more for my uncle Caleb? Hopefully I can get him to come and celebrate with us too. I have money, I'll pay for his."

Livia shook her head. "You hold on to your money. Like I said, this is my treat and I'd be glad to add one for your uncle Caleb too."

Just then a warm breeze ran into the shop as the door opened, letting in the heated air and it was followed by a cool voice. "Care to add one more for that celebration tonight?"

Clayton froze as Hope turned around, her mouth opening in shock before it spread into a wide grin and she took off at a run. "Mama!"

Celeste.

"How did you know we were here?" Clayton didn't mean for his voice to come out as harsh as it did, but from the way Celeste's eyes immediately narrowed and the silence that filled the shop he knew it had.

She then looked down at Hope again and smiled. For a moment he thought she'd ignore his question as she hugged Hope, looking up at Clayton, her eyes and intentions unreadable. Celeste pulled back from Hope's embrace. "I stopped by the firehouse and they told me you two had headed this way."

Was he wrong or did she direct a glance at Liv then?

Hope hugged Celeste again, and something in Clayton twisted. "I missed you, Mama. Are you really back?"

"Where else would I be?" Celeste said, her eyes filling with tears. "I've missed you too, baby. I never want to be away from you so long again."

Clayton turned to Livia, catching the look of sad resignation as it came across her face.

Chapter 22

Founders' Day was turning out to be everything that Liv remembered: bright, sunny, full of cheer with happy kids running about, excited over the day's festivities and eager for the night's fireworks. The large field behind the United Church had been decked out with every sort of stall imaginable. There were pony rides and tons of carnival games, as well as some fun rides trucked in.

Though it was Sugar Lake's Founders' Day, folks came from as far as four towns over to participate in the festivities and celebrate with the local residents. The local businesses were mostly closed for the day or on skeleton crews, having shut down to set up stalls highlighting their wares, and thankfully everyone was doing brisk business. Goode 'N Sweet was practically sold out, and Aunt Joyce was overjoyed by the fact that the individual blackberry pockets and peach cobblers were the first to go.

But at the moment, they had the men of the family manning the pie booth—Cole and Clint, Warren and Wiley—while the women headed over to the real excitement, at the judging booth for the bake-off. Liv was trying her best to concentrate on the announcements of the winners, but her attention was caught by the beautiful family scene that was taking place in front of her.

Just up and over to the left, by the dunking booth, she could see Clayton as he paid his money to the carnival attendant and got three balls to take his turn at trying to knock down Coach Farrington, the Sugar Lake High School baseball coach. She watched him take a stance—a sure and steady pitching stance that reminded her of his teen days—but he pulled back and wound up missing on the first and then second try. She stared as Hope gave her father a pat on his back. Celeste—looking carefree and lovely, tall and slim, her hair long and straight as it hung past her shoulders, her eyes almond shaped and upturned at the end—gazed at Clayton with obvious admiration as she leaned in and kissed him easily on his cheek. She pulled back and gave Hope a smile as she took a bit of the girl's cotton candy and fed it to Clayton, causing Hope to laugh. He shook his head, and Liv watched him laugh too. This time he shrugged his shoulders and shook out his hands, and then he wound up before letting the ball go, hitting his target perfectly.

Hope jumped up and down, waving her cotton candy wildly while her father handed her a large stuffed bear. Liv closed her eyes and exhaled, committing the scene to memory, knowing—no, hoping—she would be able to pull it back up in her later moments of weakness.

"And finally, bringing home our top prize in blue ribbon, it's once again someone from Goode 'N Sweet—Olivia Gale with her berry swirl pie!"

Liv opened her eyes to Aunt Joyce shaking her and her mouth moving, but she wasn't quite able to make out the words. "I knew it would be you. Did I tell you? Didn't I tell you we'd sweep it all?" Aunt Joyce leaned in close to Liv, then whispered. "Just you look at that Lottie Douglas over there. Holding her participation ribbon. That'll teach her about going on and on to me about her dang fried chicken. She can take her chicken and most accomplished nephew. She can take them both and stuff it. Look at the real winners right over here."

Liv blinked and wondered how she got up on the stage in the first place. Had Aunt Joyce with her trick hip and all carried her up there? Oh well, she was there now, so she might as well go with it.

Liv smiled through clenched teeth and took the trophy, trying her best not to cast her eyes toward the dunk tank. Anywhere but the dunk tank. As they made their way back down and into the crowd eager to give their congratulations and compliments, it seemed that the dunk tank crew was coming toward Liv. She was surprised to see Clayton looking down at her, his expression in no way showing congratulations or even happiness. His eyes were hardened, and his tone suggested all business.

"Clayton, are you all right? What's going on?" Liv looked around, immediately thinking that perhaps something had happened with Hope. Then she looked to the side and saw that Hope and Celeste were just off by the ring toss game.

Clayton shook his head, "I'm fine. There's just a bit of a situation, and I need to borrow you for a moment."

Liv couldn't help but frown. What could he possibly need to borrow her for, and why in the middle of the Founders' Day celebration, and with his ex-wife and daughter so near. "I don't understand. What could you possibly have to say to me now? Today? Besides, it looks like you're quite busy, and Hope is waiting for you over there. I think you should go."

Clayton gave her an impatient glare. "Livia, it's not like that, and I wouldn't ask if it weren't important." He turned toward Aunt Joyce, and although she was busy accepting her accolades, Liv knew that she had half an ear on the conversation. "Miss Joyce, sorry, but I need to borrow Livia for a moment; I hope you don't mind. Congratulations. Not that I didn't know you all would sweep everything. You can expect me bright and early Monday morning to place my orders."

Aunt Joyce preened as she waved a hand. "Oh, don't you worry about that, Clayton, you know I always have something set aside for you. You kids be off now. I'll see you soon."

And with that, Clayton took Liv's hand and left her no choice but to follow him out of the Founders' Day celebration. Once they were away from the crowd she jerked her hand out from his. "What are you doing? This is causing a scene, you holding my hand, especially where people can see. Your daughter's right over there with your ex-wife no less. Really, Clayton, I don't think it creates a good picture for Hope."

Clayton turned to her. "Livia, my ex-wife is none of your concern. Heck, she's hardly even any of my concern, but this is not about her. I just need you to come on and follow me. There's been another incident at Goode 'N Sweet, and I didn't want to worry your aunt about it."

"Oh my goodness, not another fire? Please tell me it's all under control. I don't know what my aunt would do without that bakeshop," Liv said, bringing her hand to a suddenly out-of-control beating heart.

"Don't worry, there is no fire, and everything is contained and handled, but it looks like we've solved what's been going on. Let's head over there and see; you can advise me on how to handle things with your aunt. At least for now, let her have her moment."

It was later, the afternoon having turned to evening and Liv was disappointed, but at the same time she felt a bit of relief over seeing Deidre's husband, Paul from the ice-cream shop, being questioned by one of Sugar Lake's police officers. It was the same young officer who had stopped by when they had the Dumpster fire, and Drea kept giving him the cute-man-in-uniform side-eye, but then again that was par for the course when it came to Drea and cute men in uniforms.

But Liv needed to focus. Was this fire mystery finally now solved? She let out a cleansing breath.

"Relieved?"

She looked up at Clayton and nodded, then looked back over at Paul being questioned by the cop.

"I am," she said. Then she looked seriously at Clayton. "I'm also embarrassed to say I'm slightly relieved it turned out to be Paul. Though the greed of it all puts a bad taste in my mouth. The fact that he wanted the space to get rid of not only his ice-cream shop but ours too and replace both with a franchise type restaurant, that's just awful. Talk about thumbing a nose at the town and tradition."

"I can agree with you there. But money talks and easy money the loudest," Clayton said.

"True. But he did seem nice." Liv worried at her bottom lip a moment before looking back at Clayton.

"I hate to think of Deidre and what she and her daughter will go through once this gets out."

"Yes, that really is the saddest part. I don't know how much Deidre knew. That's something to speculate. But the fact remains that her daughter will be the one to suffer in the process."

She looked at Clayton seriously, taking in his somber expression. "It's always the worst when a child has to suffer for her parents' deeds." Liv let out a sigh. "I'm really ashamed to admit it, but for a minute I thought it may be someone else."

Clayton nodded. "Brent?"

Liv looked at him with shock. "You too?"

He shook his head. "Yeah, me too. But it wasn't him. Of that I'm sure. He and your aunt asked me to set up the cameras."

"Wow. I'm so glad to hear that. I'm glad that Aunt Joyce is healthy and has all her faculties and she can trust her family. I'm feeling like when I leave she's in the best hands."

"So you are leaving?" Clayton's voice was soft.

Liv stared at him long and hard then. Her voice came out low

"I always was."

Clayton nodded as his phone beeped when, at the same time, the first crack of Founders' Night fireworks erupted. They both looked up to the sky at the bursting red, blue, and green sparks. "We'd better get back. We've been gone a long time, and I'm sure folks are wondering what happened to us," he said.

Liv nodded back at him. "Yes, we'd better. Folks are probably getting curious."

Clayton let out a sigh. "Aren't they always?"

Chapter 23

Liv looked at the potential job offer once more before typing out her reply. She hit send and closed her laptop, letting out a sigh. She looked out the window once again, glancing toward Clayton's window.

"So, you've made your decision, huh?"

She turned and looked up at her sister as Drea entered her room. Liv nodded. "I have," she said. "And you've made yours. Are you certain about this?" she asked Drea.

Drea smiled as she sat down across from her. "I am sure, probably more sure than I have ever been about anything in a long time. Now is not the time for me to head back to New York. There really isn't anything for me there. For the first time in a long time, I'm feeling good about myself. Content. And I never thought that word could feel so good. I think I can make something of myself here, if not forever, at least for now. Aunt Joyce has agreed to let me expand on my idea of putting tables out back and creating more of a bistro dining area there. I think we can even expand on the Goode 'N Sweet idea and add some savory dishes.

Maybe a few savory pies and salads for the lunch crowd. With me and Rena helping out together, I'm sure we can figure it out." She looked worried, drawing her bottom lip between her teeth.

Liv reached and grabbed Drea's hand. "What is it, what's bothering you? Your ideas all sound wonderful to me."

Drea stared at her, her eyes shining brightly. "I don't know, do you think this'll be all right with Mom and Dad? I don't want them to feel like I'm abandoning them."

Liv shook her head and smiled. "I'm sure it will be fine with them. They've always wanted nothing more than the best for us, and for us to be happy. Sometimes I think to their detriment, which is why they put off their own happiness for so long. You should do this. If this is where you feel you should be and you feel you can grow, then go for it."

Drea smiled as she blinked away tears. "What about you?"

"What about me?" Liv asked. "I'm fine. I'm doing what I said I would do. Leaving near about when I said I would leave. My subletters just moved out, and I just received a great job offer that I absolutely can't refuse."

"Well, isn't that just like you. Little Miss Perfect always right on time."

Liv frowned. "Come on with that. It's been a minute since you called me that. Don't start. How can I refuse this? I can hardly believe they are offering me this type of package after only three video chats. Somebody upstairs must be looking out for me. It's more money than my last job, the perks are great, plus I'll be running my own department. Can't you be happy for me?"

Drea glanced out the window, her eyes going immediately to Clayton's window just as Liv's had moments before. "I am happy for you. I just want to be sure that *you* are truly happy for you. If that's what your heart is telling you to do, then you should do it. But don't go fooling me, Liv, or worse yourself, by putting on a mask and pretending it's your true face if it's not."

"Oh, come on with that now, Drea," Liv said. "I know what's real and what's not." She blinked. She would not look toward Caleb's window. She couldn't. "I always knew that for me Sugar Lake was just a dream."

Drea smiled then and let out a breath, taking her sister's hand. "Okay, big sis. If you say so. But you're wronger than wrong leaving me to handle Aunt Joyce on my own."

Liv laughed at the same time she tried her best to hold back a sob. "You're a big girl, and you're also a Gale woman. You'll handle her and anything else that comes your way just fine. Let me get some sleep. I want to get on the road bright and early in the morning to beat the traffic."

Drea got up and Liv rose too, giving her sister a hug, letting go so incredibly hard. "Oh, you'll get up just fine. You and I both turned into regular country gals. We get up with the roosters now."

As Liv sat in the brightly lit and sterile conference room she had to practically fight not to bolt out of there. For one, despite the cool air-conditioning, she was practically sweating through her tailored business suit. Though it wasn't yet officially fall, New York was already in that weird weather transition stage, of three seasons in a day where you could go from forty-five to seventy-five degrees and an umbrella must always be close at hand. Though she didn't take off her jacket for fear of everyone seeing what she was sure were now permanent pit stains on her silk blouse. Number two, her feet were being pinched to all get-out by the supposedly casual walking pumps that she was wearing to this get-acquainted interview. And for three, to top it all off she was sitting across from the company's Chief Operating Officer and the company's new chief sales director, who turned out to be the man that requested her for the head marketing position, none other than chief full of bull-crap artist himself, Damon freaking "where is my flat-screen TV" Harding.

Liv was more than done.

She had to give herself credit for looking over their proposal, pretending to consider their generous salary and quite lucrative benefits, and not telling them to completely shove it up their rears. There was no way she was putting herself in any situation where Damon Harding was a part of her day-to-day business. There was only so much she could take, and maybe in the past she thought she could take him, even as an ex, as part of her day-to-day for the right price. But it would seem that she'd come to realize that there was no price high enough for her to trade on her own peace of mind and happiness.

Liv looked at both men and gave them her best plastered smile, but even that didn't feel right, like too much effort and one they didn't deserve, so she dropped it and got down to business. "I thank you both for the offer, but looking over your company"—

she looked at Damon with her next comment—"and seeing your personnel structure, I have to regretfully decline." She closed the prospectus and pushed it back toward them. "I'm sorry, but I won't be taking the position here at GLM."

Without even waiting for their reply Liv got up and put out her hand to the COO to shake. "I'm very sorry, not to mention shocked, to hear that, Ms. Gale. You came highly recommended, and I thought this was a done deal." He looked over at Damon, who looked as if he could spit nails, he seemed so angry and embarrassed.

"I'm sorry to disappoint you. It would seem you were given promises under false pretenses."

Liv put out her hand for Damon to shake, but in his anger he just looked at her, so she pulled her hand back with a half smile, went for her handbag, and started toward the elevator bank.

"You're making a huge mistake, you know that, right?" Damon's voice hit her ears just as the elevator doors opened.

She looked at him and shook her head. "Am I?" she asked. "Funny, it doesn't feel that way," she said as she stepped into the elevator. "As a matter of fact, it feels like one of the best decisions I've made in a very long time." Then as the elevator doors began to close, she shouted, "And don't forget you still owe me a TV!" Liv burst out laughing when she saw the embarrassment bloom over Damon's face as the receptionist started to laugh behind him.

As Liv made it back to her apartment, her dinner just picked up from the new salad bar that opened two blocks down, where the fresh veggies looked freshly thawed, she couldn't get past the quiet as she closed and double locked the door behind herself. It was too quiet. Quiet despite the city sounds outside her window and amplified, she guessed, by the fact that she still was down a TV.

The quiet brought down the high she was feeling over turning down the job with Damon, and once again the same old thread of sadness she'd been engulfed with ever since she'd driven away from Sugar Lake started to weave its way throughout her being. It also reminded her of the chill she couldn't seem to shake. She shivered and was annoyed. She had no reason to be cold. At the moment it was a seasonable seventy degrees and the air was clear and crisp now that she was out and away from the hateful glare of Damon Harding. No blazing heat or high humidity and no blasted ants or even bees. Heck, she should be doing a happy dance. Not doing this odd thing of going from sweating to shivering all the while moping like a sad salad barfly.

Liv looked over at her living room wall, tempted to give it a bang. But come on, really? Even the reggae-playing neighbors decided now was the time to go radio silent? It was a little too much.

Thinking of her exit from Sugar Lake with the long hug and a good-bye from Aunt Joyce, there were no tears, at least not until she got into the car. Aunt Joyce told her she wouldn't accept that. So they both held on, tears only glistening and holding tight to the tips of their lashes. She'd made Liv promise to come back as soon as she could. To keep baking and bring back some good recipes she could add to the menu when she did return.

But when would she return? Would it be next year or the year after that or even a year after that? When would she be able to go to Sugar Lake again, to see Clayton and not fall, ridiculously, madly, and terribly in love with him? Something she had no right doing with the state of his life. She knew she couldn't. And she wouldn't, not after seeing so much joy on his daughter's face over having her mother back. It didn't matter what Clayton had said. What mattered was that child's happiness. She had to leave and give them that fair chance.

And there you go trying to control everybody again.

Drea's words in Liv's mind stopped her short as she went to pull the takeout dinner out of the bag. She almost told her sister out loud to hush up, but that would seal the deal and she would have officially tipped over into the crazy category. But was Drea right, was she trying to control a situation that she had no right to? She looked around her empty apartment and at her salad bar takeaway. It all seemed so pointless and so not what she wanted to eat or where she wanted to be.

She thought about her ride away from Sugar Lake. The fact that she drove off at four-thirty that morning without any good-bye to Clayton, not able to find the words and not trusting herself to be strong enough to refuse him if he just so happened to tempt her once more.

Liv stilled while opening her plastic fork–knife pack. If she couldn't refuse him, did that mean she was refusing what she really wanted for herself?

It was then that anger and recognition hit her all at once. If she didn't trust herself to be able to refuse Clayton if he were to ask her to stay, then what was she doing here now?

Why was it so easy to say no to that job, her supposed dream job, even if it was Damon offering it? What job would she be able to say yes to here?

In her heart of hearts, the job she really wanted she'd already had for the past six weeks back in Sugar Lake. She shook her head then. Darn it, for all her supposed flightiness, her sister saw it before she did. She really was the happiest when she was baking. When she was creating something new and different with her hands, and more so, like Aunt Joyce, she was overjoyed when her creations were giving joy to others. Restructuring, no matter how well she did it, never did that. And it never would compare.

As for the rest—the kisses, the bursting of her heart when she was in Clayton's arms—all that part, that part was the cherry on top of it all, and that was a part she couldn't control.

So take control of what you can.

"Dang it. Do you have to talk so much?" Okay, now she really was going crazy and she *was* talking out loud to her sister's voice. She needed to do something about this. She needed to do something period.

Liv ditched the salad and headed for her kitchen, the urge to bake almost overwhelming. She rummaged through her pantry looking for ingredients to make something, anything. She found evaporated milk, flour, sugar, and vanilla extract. There were some canned peaches and peanut butter from she didn't remember when. She didn't know what she was going to make, but it didn't really matter. She could mix all this into something. She had eggs and butter. She'd make it work. It didn't have to be perfect, it just had to come out good enough to get her through the night. Liv went back to the cupboard to see what else she could find, then paused. What was she looking for? And why was she looking for it here?

She turned then and pulled her trash can over to

the counter. In frustration and with a bit of resignation, she swept all the contents in. There would be no baking tonight. Not for her in this apartment anymore. The pantry stunk, and she didn't even have decent honey.

Liv smiled to herself, her decision made. She could still have a happy life even if she wasn't in control of every step along the way.

Couldn't she?

Suddenly the over-a-cliff feel of it made her heart race.

Just then there was a knock on her door, jolting Liv out of her scattered musings. Who could be there without having been buzzed from downstairs? Caution nipped at Liv, but she assumed it must be one of her neighbors with a question or some such thing. Maybe Mrs. Taylor inquiring about her return. Still she looked through her peephole and gasped when she saw Clayton Morris's image looking back at her, though quite distorted and slightly nervous.

Her heart thumped hard and erratic, feeling as if it were tripping over itself, and she had to silently tell her hands not to shake as she flipped back the locks on her door and opened it. Maybe he was a mirage. It could very well be she'd finally tipped and completely tilted off her emotional and mental axis.

"Hey there, Livia."

This was no mirage. Mirages didn't speak. She cautiously leaned forward. And mirages didn't smell like woods, heat, and honey, and she sure as heck knew her hallway never had that particular aroma. No, this was him. Clayton Morris was here, standing in her New York hallway, looking wrinkled and weary in shorts and a tee, with about a good day's growth of scruff scattered across his cheeks. She also couldn't